CHRISTOPHER

Safe Haven: Is This the End of Everything?

Christopher Artinian

CHRISTOPHER ARTINIAN

Copyright © 2020 Christopher Artinian

All rights reserved.

ISBN: 9798612811244

CHRISTOPHER ARTINIAN

DEDICATION

To all the fallen heroes.

CHRISTOPHER ARTINIAN

ACKNOWLEDGEMENTS

To the amazing woman I get to share this journey with, Tina. None of this would be possible without you. I can never say thank you enough.

As always, a huge thank you to the gang across in the fan club on Facebook. You guys never let me down, and I am so honoured that you continue this rollercoaster ride with me.

A great big thank you to my pal, Christian Bentulan. I love his artwork, and he is such a great guy to work with. Also many thanks to my editor, Ken – a great editor and a lovely chap to boot.

And last but by no means least, a very big thank you to you for purchasing this book.

CHRISTOPHER ARTINIAN

PROLOGUE

THEN

"And the Lord said unto me, Noah, it was not by accident that your parents named you thus. Like my son will rise again, you are he reborn. You are the seed of Methuselah, son of Enoch and as you saved all life on Earth before, so shall you, again, for I am sending a second great flood." He paused, looking beyond the stage lights to the huge gathering in the darkened hall. Not a sound rose from the auditorium; it was almost as if everyone was holding their breath.

"Then what happened? Tell us! Please tell us!" a voice finally cried.

Noah grasped the lectern and continued, his rich Texas drawl blanketing the audience in reassuring honesty and warmth. "Well, I tell you what, where I grew up if you went downstairs one morning and said that God had visited you in the night and told you that you were actually the seed of Methuselah, your next trip would be to the funny farm in a white van and a snug little jacket with straps around it." The audience all laughed. "Yes, sir. That was not something

I was going to say out loud, but here I was, fifteen years old in my bedroom and I was hearing this voice. Now, my family were all good Christians, yes they were. We were front row centre every Sunday morning in church. My mom was the guiding force behind every bake sale, every church event. My pop, well friends, he was just about the best man I've ever known. He would help everyone and anyone because he took it as his duty to always, always do the Christian thing. But if I'd have told them about this conversation, well, let's just say that leap of faith might have been a little too far, and I knew it." He paused again, took a drink of water, and dabbed his forehead with a dazzling white handkerchief before returning it to his pocket.

"Praise the Lord," a woman shouted out from the back of the large hall.

"Yes indeed, ma'am, praise the Lord. So, there I was, having this conversation, and I suddenly had the most horrible, terrifying thought. I remembered back to my readings," he said, holding up a dog-eared copy of the King James Bible. "God had made a covenant with Noah. He had decreed that *neither shall all flesh be cut off any more by the waters of a flood; neither shall there be a flood to destroy the earth.* And on remembering that, I started to wonder if it was our Lord almighty that I was talking to or if it was some trick that Satan himself was trying to ensnare me with."

"Satan, be gone!" shouted a voice.

"Fret not, my friends. I challenged the voice that spoke to me. I said, 'Lord, if that is you why do you break thine own promise?'" He paused and looked into the darkness once more. "He replied not with a serpent's tongue but with the voice of a child. He said, 'Noah, what I breathed unto you was this; I said, *I will not again curse the ground any more for man's sake,* and by that vow I still stand.' Well, friends, round about now, I was just more confused than ever, I tell you."

A small ripple of laughter fluttered around the room. "Tell us! Tell us!" shouted a man near the back of the crowd.

"I said, 'Lord! Forgive me for I do not understand. You have said to me you are going to unleash another flood on the earth yet stand by your covenant still. How can this be so?' Well, friends, that's when I knew that it was our Lord that I was talking to. He said, 'Noah, the flood that is coming is of a different kind. It will not harm the earth, the plants of the earth or the beasts of the earth other than Man. Man has become too sinful, too corrupt once again and it is you, Noah, you who I charge with finding the chosen ones so that Man can start again. The flood I am sending will wash the earth clean of Mankind so that you can build civilisation anew, in my son's image, not just in shape but in deed.'"

"Surely!" a woman at the front called out.

"And so it was told!" shouted another voice.

"Yes, friends. The time is coming." He looked to the side of the stage. "C'mon, sweetheart, come out here and join me."

Raucous cheering and applause began as a former beauty queen in her late thirties with flowing black curly hair and a smile as wide as her face swaggered onto the stage in the highest of heels and the tightest of dresses. She stopped next to Noah, leaned into the microphone and said, "Why, thank y'all."

"Now, most of you surely know that this is my beautiful wife, Angeline, or Angel as she's better known. She is the one who convinced me that I needed not just to speak my message but shout it out loud. She is the one who said to me, no, told me that I had to start the Noah Jackson Ministry."

"Yes!" came a roar from the crowd and everyone in the auditorium began clapping and cheering. It was several minutes before the sound died down enough for Noah to continue talking.

"I said to her, 'Angel, Angel darlin', the message I need to spread is too big. We don't have two dimes to rub together.' Back then, I was just working in my pop's shoe store. Folks, I knew I had a calling, and I knew I had to do something about it but I didn't know what until God delivered this beautiful woman to me. She said, 'Noah, I have faith in you. Speak what you know to be true, and others will have faith too.'"

"Speak it!" shouted a woman from the front row.

"Yes, sir!" shouted another.

"Well, not for the first time and not for the last, she was right. Ten years later, in conjunction with my good friends at Emerson's Bank, JKC Petroleum, Hero Cola and of course IFG Shipping and Holdings we are launching *The Ark*, a luxury cruise ship capable of accommodating five thousand blessed vacationers. My friends, I have never been so excited in my life, and I know pride is a sin, and please forgive me, but right now, I am so proud of what we have all accomplished together." A huge screen lit up behind Noah revealing a newly built cruise liner in a vast warehouse building in a dockyard. "Now, my wife wants to say a few words."

There was more rapturous applause as Angel stepped up to the microphone. When the clapping finally quieted down, she smiled widely and said, "Hi y'all," only for the applause and cheering to start once again. "Well, you're just all so sweet. Thank you. Thank you." She raised her hands to calm the crowd down. "I wanted to tell you about the vision my husband had for *The Ark*. Now yes, it's true, there is a flood coming. We don't know when, but as sure as I'm standing here in front of you right now, it's coming. And what do you know?" she said, turning around to look at the screen. "We've only gone and got ourselves an ark built to save the chosen ones." There were more deafening applause and cheers, and Angel turned back towards the crowd. "Now, it would be a sin to let such a beautiful boat as this—"

"Ship, honey. It's a ship," Noah interrupted.

"Well, s'cuse me darlin', a beautiful ship as this,"

she said, smiling, "to just sit in the dock. I got that right? It is a dock, ain't it?"

The audience laughed and applauded. "Yes, sweetheart, that's right," Noah said, laughing too.

She turned back to the audience and looked around the crowd. All eyes were on her. "Well, let me tell you folks, right here, right now, that *The Ark* is going to be doing God's own work. Our cruises are going to go all over the world to historical religious sites and sites of worship, but at the same time, we're going to be working with some of the world's biggest charities to deliver aid. Can you just imagine that? You ever feel guilty about taking a vacation, knowing that there's so much suffering in the world? I know I have. But now you can take a vacation, you can go to chapel every day, you can even hand-deliver food to some of those starving babies in Africa if y'all want to."

The huge hall erupted once more, and Noah and Angel shared a loving look. When the noise showed no signs of abating, Noah put his hands up. "Folks … folks … she's not done yet."

The clapping came to a stop and Angel unleashed her killer smile once again. "In addition, there are state-of-the-art recording and broadcasting facilities on board, so not only will we be doing good and spreading the word from the Noah Jackson Ministry all over the world, but we'll still be beaming back live on the Noah Jackson ministries channel so y'all can see just how much your donations are helping those in need. And I know what some of you are saying, I know some of you are saying, 'But if this flood's coming, what's the point of saving those in need? What's the point of helping others?' Well, I tell you, folks, when my husband told me about his conversation with our Lord, I said the same thing, and this is what he said." Angel backed away from the microphone, and Noah stepped up to it.

The image of the giant luxury cruise liner disappeared, and a close-up of Noah Jackson's face filled the entire screen. "I said to her, 'Angel, darlin', *Thou shalt love the Lord thy God with all thy heart, and with all thy soul, and with all thy mind. This is the first and great commandment. And the second is like unto it, Thou shalt love thy neighbour as thyself.* Those are Jesus's own words, and I know God has spoken to me and told me his plan, but he has not told me when. He has not told me who the chosen shall be, so, now more than ever, it is essential that we do his work and spread his teachings, so that we may be considered worth saving.'"

Angel took a tight hold of Noah's hand, turned towards the crowd and said, "Amen!"

"Amen," came the hysterical response from the audience as cheers and applause erupted once more. The couple looked at one another, leaned in and kissed; then the massive screen behind reverted back to the cruise ship. Noah and Angel peered into the crowd and cast the odd wave before eventually walking off the stage, hand in hand. The giant screen continued to show the ship, but website addresses and donation hotlines for the Noah Jackson Ministry began to scroll down as well.

They nodded and smiled and shook the occasional hand as they walked back to their dressing room. They passed their two burly security guards, Doug and Viktor, and closed the door behind them.

"What the fuck was that?" Noah hissed, tearing off his silver tie. "It was like I was talking to an empty fucking hall. You were meant to get Levine to Coach them, I mean, Jesus H Christ, that's what we fucking pay him for. I could barely hear the one who said, 'Satan be gone.' It was like I was talking to my fucking self."

"Just one minute, you sack o' shit," Angel replied, pulling her high-heels off, throwing them into one corner of the room and unzipping her dress. "You told me after the last time that you were going to speak to Levine. You were going to tell him just what you wanted so a debacle like Nashville didn't happen again." The warm, rich and friendly southern accents now disappeared as the pair shot barbs at one another.

"Goddammit, woman, I said nothing of the sort, I said—"

Angel grabbed hold of the thick mop of distinguished greying brown hair on top of her husband's head and pulled it to the side. "I've had just about enough of your shit, Noel!"

"Let go of my goddamn hair, Angeline," he said, grasping her arm tightly in his left hand.

"You want something doing from now on then get one of your whores to do it," she said, yanking her hand away with a fifteen-hundred-dollar toupee sprouting through her fingers.

"Aargghh. You fucking cu—"

She thrust the wig into his open mouth and punched him in the face. Noah went toppling over the couch and landed heavily on the floor. There was a knock on the door. "Mr Jackson?"

The bodyguards had been with them nine of the ten years since the ministry had begun. They were in the inner circle. They were both well-paid security professionals having served time in law enforcement before going to work for themselves.

"It's alright. We're alright," Angel said, standing over her pathetic looking husband whose teeth had clamped around his tongue as he had fallen. He desperately tried to fish the now bloodied hairpiece from his lips as his legs still dangled over the frame of the upturned couch. "I told you, you never call me that word."

He jumped to his feet. "And I told you that you never call me Noel. All it needs is for one slip—one slip in public, Angeline, and this whole little house of cards comes toppling down."

"Seriously, hun? You think I'll fluff my lines as the dotin' wife?" she said, slipping back into her warm Texas drawl. "Well, I tell you, sugar, there's only one of us who will ever topple this house o' cards, and it's the lyin', stinkin', thievin', adulteratin' sack o' monkey shit that's standin' in front of me now."

"You dumb piece of white trash. You might want to pick up a book once in a while. It's adulterous, and it's not like you don't have a goddamn queue at your bedroom door. I've seen shorter lines at Disney World." He gathered himself and slowly stood up, walking over to the mirror. He retrieved the handkerchief from his pocket and wiped away the blood from his lips and chin. "At least I don't have to worry about any embarrassments. Least I chose me a barren whore." He looked towards her through the mirror and her shocked and horrified expression made him grin.

"You're a bastard. If people knew who you really were—"

"If people knew who I really was, we'd all be in prison. Now, be a good girl and go get my glue," he said, replacing the wig on his head and trying to manoeuvre it into the right position.

Tears began to run down Angel's cheeks. She ignored her husband's request and walked over to the dressing table where an open bottle of Southern Comfort called her. She poured a glass and took two thirsty gulps. "I want a divorce."

The cruel smile left Noah's face, and he walked across to her, taking the glass out of her hand, taking a drink himself and then refilling it. "Now, I know you don't mean that."

Angel took another drink. "I do mean it, with all my heart."

"You want me to say it? You want me to say I can't do this without you? You want me to tell you that if it wasn't for you I'd still be Noel Brown, a footwear salesman at my dad's shoe shop? You want me to tell you that then I will. But listen up, 'cause this is the last time. We're in the big leagues now. This marriage of ours has been a sham for years, all part of the illusion, but Jesus, Angel, we're just about to launch a luxury cruise liner. We've gone from big-top sermons with snake handlers and faith healers to stadiums with corporate and celebrity endorsements. We're at the top of the game, but there's more to have, more to take if we're willing to do what's needed."

Angel took another drink. "We're going to go to Hell for what we're doing."

Noah smiled. "Trust me, Angel, the Lord has spoken to me, and Hell will visit every child of the land 'cept the chosen ones."

She looked at him long and hard then suddenly laughed. "I hate you," she said tenderly.

"Oh darlin'," he replied softly. "I hate you too, with all my heart."

1

NOW

A gentle breeze swept through the trees keeping all the insects at bay for the time being. It had been another unseasonably warm autumn afternoon, a perfect day for foraging, but now darkness had fallen.

"We'd better think about heading back," Wren said, shining her torch in Sammy's direction.

"Okay."

"You don't sound very keen."

Sammy looked at her friend and sighed. "I miss Emma."

Wren started to say something then stopped herself. "How's Mike?"

Sammy picked up her full backpack and placed it on her shoulders. "Sad."

"Maybe you and me could go foraging on the shore tomorrow. I'll drag Wolf's lazy arse out of bed, too, and we can have ourselves a picnic on the beach. How does that sound? Maybe Jake would like to come."

"I'd like that. Jake prefers to spend all his time with

John though. They go everywhere together. Everything's changed since Emma left."

Wren slid her own backpack on and put a comforting hand on the younger girl's shoulder. "Fine! We'll have another girl's day out," she said, shining the torch ahead to light up their way, even though she knew these woods better than virtually anyone.

The two of them began to head out of the trees. "Wren."

"Yeah."

"Why do you spend so much time with me?"

"Don't you like me spending time with you?"

"Yes. I like it a lot. But there are some girls your own age in the village."

Wren smiled. "I never really got on with girls my own age. I like spending time with you. You remind me of me."

"Since the crops started coming in, people aren't interested in foraging anymore."

"I know. But that's better for us. We have the woods and the shoreline to ourselves," Wren said.

"Did your sister like foraging?"

Wren let out a little laugh. "Oh, good grief, no. My sister liked makeup, and nail paint, and designer clothes and boys."

"Doesn't sound like you had a lot in common."

"We didn't. Not in the time before all this started. But then…"

"Then what?"

"Then we became closer than ever."

"I'm sorry," Sammy said, weaving her hand into Wren's.

The older girl looked down at Sammy, and the two carried on walking in silence until they finally reached the tree line and stepped out into the tall grass. "That's beautiful," Wren said, looking towards the enormous full moon rising over the bay.

"Look!" Sammy almost screamed, pointing to the bay. The blue-white light made the water look magical, and as if straight out of a fairytale, a pod of dolphins moved across the water like a well-rehearsed ballet troop.

"Shall we go down to get a better look?"

"Can we?"

"Why not? It's not like there's anything good on telly." Sammy giggled, and the pair of them began to run. They ran over the verge and across the road, onto the greener grass on the other side and down the embankment. They slowed as they reached the jagged rocks and Wren shone the torch into every crevice to make sure they could find a firm footing. Then they both started to run again as soon as they hit the soft sand of the cove. Wren flicked her trainers off, and Sammy followed suit. They both stood there on the still-warm sand as the water lapped around their feet. It was a picture-postcard view, a flashback to a time when all was right with the world. They held hands again, two orphaned girls who had lost their sisters and now adopted each other.

As the fins and tails emerged then disappeared beneath the almost black surface time after time, the girls pointed and laughed and giggled. They had front row seats to nature's great carnival, and whatever was wrong with their lives was forgotten for the briefest chiselled out moment of joy.

Wren and Sammy remained there until long after the dolphins had disappeared from view. The air was still warm, and the refreshing saltwater felt good on their bare skin.

Eventually, they both resigned themselves to the fact that the beautiful creatures would not reappear and they released each other's hands. They were about to walk back up the beach when Sammy stopped sharply. "What's that?" she asked, pointing to a silhouette seemingly bobbing in the shallow water of the cove.

Wren couldn't see it for a moment, but then her

eyes focused on the black thing drifting towards them in the water. The darkness did not help their determination as to what the object was, but as the calm waves carried it closer to shore, Wren slipped off her jeans and her backpack, handed Sammy the torch, and ran towards it. At first, giant splashes erupted behind her, but then, as the water got deeper, the splashes became waves and running became wading.

The water level was just below her chest when Wren finally reached the object, only to realise it was a body. She turned it over, and the white glow across the bay provided her with enough illumination to see who it was.

"John?" she half said, half whispered. But as the figure's eyes flicked open and Wren suddenly noticed the fresh neck wound, a terrifying realisation struck her. This was not Beth's rosy-cheeked little brother anymore.

*

The night Emma had left Safe Haven she had no idea where she would end up. She was racked with sadness, guilt and anger. She had lovingly wrapped Sarah's body and placed it in the back of the car then just started driving. It was only when she saw signs for the Kyle of Lochalsh that a dusty memory from the time before gave her an idea.

Michelle, Emma's one-time girlfriend, had organised a week for them in a luxurious log cabin a few miles out of Kyle. She had booked it eight months before they were due to go, a kind of apology for Michelle spending far more time working than with Emma. They had a full itinerary mapped out of places to visit and things they wanted to do. That holiday was their focus, their happy-planning time together where they could forget all the petty annoyances of everyday life.

Even though Emma had never been there, she knew the route well. She'd remembered that route in great detail, avoiding cliffs and bridges wherever possible, they were among Michelle's many phobias. Thanks to the apocalypse, the vacation never took place, but as Emma left

Safe Haven behind her and her head finally cleared, she knew that was exactly where she should head.

A part of her was resigned to the possibility that the holiday property's rightful owners may well have beaten her to it. It had been early morning when Emma had finally arrived, and to her delight, the cabin was empty. Since then, she had set up a life for herself. She fished in the nearby river and foraged in the woods. Occasionally she would head out to scavenge, she'd keep whatever she needed and take the rest to Kyle of Lochalsh to trade.

It had surprised her to find that there was a thriving community there, much like Safe Haven but more concentrated. They were friendly and accommodating and happy to barter. It had surprised her even more to discover another lost soul, an empty shell looking for nothing more than physical comfort and someone else to mourn with. Tabitha, or Tabby as she was better known, was beautiful. Another time, another place and things may have been very different, but for now they were just two people who held on to each other when the pain was too much. Two people to get drunk together and hate the world.

"I was wondering," Tabby said as she chopped the wild garlic they had collected from the end of the garden.

"What?" Emma replied.

"Do you think I could move in here with you?"

Emma smiled. "You're kind of moved in now."

"I mean properly. I mean leaving Kyle and coming out here, so it's just you and me."

Emma looked out of the patio doors, beyond the decking and over the top of the trees towards the moonlit ocean a couple of miles in the distance. The silhouettes of several boats dotted the horizon, but that was nothing new. Kyle traded with a few settlements from further down the coastline, and as fuel supplies diminished, more and more people took to using boats, particularly sailboats, to travel. "I don't know," she said, turning around. "Pickfords removals might be a bit hard to get hold of."

Tabby stopped chopping and smiled. "There's not much. A few knick-knacks, that's all."

Emma walked across to the counter where Tabby was preparing the food and placed a gentle hand over hers. "I'd like that."

Tabby's face lit up with a broad grin that made her eyes sparkle in the light of the lanterns and candles. They had not sparkled much since she had lost her two children. "Thank you. It's just this is the only place where I ever feel even slightly normal now."

"I know what you mean; things have been a lot more manageable since I met you."

"Who knows, one day we might stop feeling like this and be able to move on."

Emma returned her companion's hypnotic gaze and placed a hand on her light brown cheek. Tabby leaned into it before pulling it away and kissing it. "Thank you."

"Don't thank me. We help each other. That's what we—"

A startling noise sliced through Emma's words before she had a chance to finish her thought. The two women looked at each other fearfully.

"What the hell is that?" Tabby asked, clenching her fist tighter around the knife.

"Gunfire … lots of it." The pair of them rushed outside to hear the crack of even more rifles.

"It sounds like it's coming from Kyle," Tabby said. "What should we do?" The two women continued to listen over the next few minutes, but the sound gradually came to a stop. The uneasy feeling stayed with them as they returned indoors.

"Whatever it was, it's over now. We'll find out tomorrow when we go in for your stuff."

"I suppose," Tabby said, returning to cutting the wild garlic, only now the smile had gone from her face.

Emma slid the patio door closed and looked in the direction of Kyle. She could not see it for the massive forest that stood between her house and the small town, but it did not stop her looking. She remained there for another minute before walking across to the range and throwing in another log. Despite the warmth of the day, a sudden chill had gripped her, and she knew it wasn't going to disappear in a hurry.

*

Mike and Lucy were sitting on the bench, each with an arm around the other's shoulder. They were taking in the full beauty of the bay as the giant moon gradually made its ascent. The black water rippled gently in the bay below, and the serene beauty allowed them to escape their thoughts for a few moments. Minutes before, they had watched a pod of dolphins pass by. It was not an uncommon sight on this stretch of water. Dolphins, porpoises, seals, even whales and the odd shark were all regular visitors. That did not mean seeing them was any less enchanting, any less exciting.

They had been in the kitchen when the fins appeared out of the water. Lucy was the first to spot the pod, and they rushed outside to watch them. Now, even though the dolphins had disappeared from view, the two of them remained there, perfectly content. Lucy's head leaned into Mike, and he kissed the top of it gently.

"I should really go and pick up Jake and John," Mike said.

"You're such a killjoy. They'll be having the time of their lives. What kid wouldn't want to pitch a tent next to the beach on a night like tonight?"

"They said they wanted to camp out, and they've been camping out all day. No way am I letting them stay there overnight."

"What do you think's going to happen? You think they're going to get drunk and invite some rowdy teenage girls back?"

"I just want to know where Jake is."

"You know where he is."

"You know what I mean," Mike replied.

"Control freak," Lucy said, smiling.

"I'm the first to admit it." He kept his arm around her. "Maybe I can wait a few more minutes." He leaned in and kissed her head again.

The silhouette of a tall ship drifted on the waves further south in the bay. Some smaller vessels surrounded it, and although a little out of the ordinary, it was not something they hadn't seen before. Sea travel without the use of fuel was becoming more and more common, and the outlying islands now made regular trade missions to Safe Haven. Each time, their flotillas became more numerous and grander. They had seen one tall ship before, it had been even bigger than the one they saw now but that didn't take away from the grandeur of this vessel as they both admired it.

"Looks like we've got visitors," Lucy said.

"Probably across to trade from Rum or Mull," Mike replied matter-of-factly. "They're getting some impressive fleets together these islanders. We might have to get Raj and Talikha to get us one."

Lucy smiled. "And who would we get to sail them? You're fancying yourself as a ship's captain are you?"

"I could totally do that. Shiver me timbers," he said in his best pirate voice, and Lucy started giggling.

"Oh yeah, you've got me convinced. It's like sitting next to Blackbeard. Seriously, though, Raj and Talikha have been amazing. Anything I've wanted for the infirmary they've managed to find for me on their trips across to the islands."

"Yeah. I don't think in all the time I've known him he's ever let me down. I've let him down plenty, but he's always been there for me."

The two of them sat in silence for a while, contemplating how far they'd come in the last few months, then they lost themselves in the view once more. Lucy nestled her head further into Mike then ran a hand down his arm playfully.

"Y'know, it seems a terrible waste," Lucy said.

"What does?" Mike asked.

"Both of us have got the evening together for the first time in a long time, and we've got the house to ourselves."

Mike smiled. "Yeah, but Wren will probably be bringing Sammy back soon."

"What's wrong, Mikey? Losing your sense of danger?" she said, lifting her head from his shoulder to look at him. Even in this light, he could see that she had mischief in her eyes and that smile on her face that could make him do anything.

Mike moved in to kiss her, and as their lips met, he slid his warm hand underneath her T-shirt and round her back. "Let's go upstairs," he said, breaking the kiss.

"Now that's the Mike I know and love."

The few months since Emma left had been hard for both of them. Mike blamed himself for everything, and it had been tough for Lucy to keep him on this side of sanity. After the events of Loch Uig where he had admitted seeing hallucinations of Fry and even talking to him, she tried to help, tried to coax him back to a stable psychological state any way she could. It had been hard, and he had been prone to dark mood swings, but in the last few weeks, there had been signs that he was returning to his old self.

He took her hand and began to lead her into the house when both of them stopped dead as a scream made the blood in their veins freeze.

Without pause, they both started sprinting in the direction of the sound.?

2

For a few seconds, Wren stared at the creature, unable to believe what she was seeing. It had been months since she had seen a RAM, a live one anyway. After the trip to Loch Uig, she had not ventured out much, preferring instead to stay in and around Safe Haven. Now she was staring death in the face, literally, and what's more, it was someone she knew. The frozen bewilderment did not last long as a gargling growl emanated from the back of the monster's throat, issuing a spray of seawater with it.

Her heart began to pound rapidly, and as the beast reached for her, she let go of its body, and it rolled face down into the black water once more. Wren turned and headed towards the beach as fast as she could. The creature eventually found its footing and stood up. It was unsteady at first, like a newborn foal, and then it began to follow.

"Run!" Wren shouted to Sammy, who was still standing at the shoreline, pointing the torch towards her friend, not fully understanding what was going on.

Now the creature's throat had been cleared of seawater, its growls were more audible, and as it waded towards the sand, Sammy grasped what was happening and let out a scream that filled the entire cove.

"Aaaggghhh!" She wanted to turn and run more

than anything, but she couldn't leave her friend. Wren was wading through the chest-high water as quickly as she could. When she was on shore, they would both escape together but not until.

Wren turned back briefly to see her pursuer was still a little unsteady but clearly had no intention of giving up the chase. "Sammy, I told you to ruuu—"

"Aaaggghhh!" Sammy let out another terrified scream as Wren disappeared under the surface. "Wren! Wren!"

Wren's head reappeared. "I'm alright," she said, spluttering and coughing. "Run, Sammy. Please!"

Sammy remained there with tears running down her face. Her left foot took a step back; then she stopped. *No.* She looked around and grabbed two fist-sized pebbles. The young girl bravely ran into the water a few paces and, aiming the torch as well as she could, hurled one of the small rocks at the advancing creature. The missile sailed by, missing the figure by half a metre. The second one struck it square in the chest. It paused for only a second, but every second counted now. Sammy ran back to shore and pulled more pebbles from the sand, filling her pockets before returning to the water. Not much farther and Wren would be running rather than wading, and they could escape.

Sammy launched another pebble, then another, and another. The fourth was the game-changer, almost a perfect oval and weighing about as much as the average coffee mug; the rock spun through the air. There was a loud crack as it made contact with the beast's face. Even in this light, Sammy could see a small explosion of tissue a split second before the pebble fell into the water. The creature stopped for one, two, three, four, five—before starting to wade again. The young girl tore her eyes away from the beast as loud plops caught her attention.

The seawater splashed behind Wren as knees, shins and finally feet appeared out of the water. Sammy turned back towards the monster from the deep to see that it had now changed course and was heading directly towards her. She threw another pebble at it, but just before it left her hand, the young girl wavered, and the shot missed its target. Her eyes had been drawn to something else ... several things.

"Wren! Wren!" she screamed.

Wren, who had finally reached the sand, turned and for a second did not comprehend what she was seeing, but then she realised. "Oh Shiiit!" The heads of six more creatures had popped out of the water and were making their way towards them. "Sammy, run! Run, now!" Wren sprinted to her backpack and came to a skidding stop on her knees, the sand mounding up around her. She reached in, pulling out one of her pistol crossbows and a few bolts, then ran back to the shoreline where Sammy was still standing. "Sammy, I said run," Wren said, grabbing the torch, taking aim and firing. The bolt disappeared over the creature's shoulder, despite it being less than ten metres away. Wren silently chastised herself. She had fallen out of practice, fooled by the safety and calm of Safe Haven.

She pulled the self-cocking lever, loaded another bolt and fired again. This time, the small arrow disappeared into the creature's head, and the John monster plunged forward, face down in the water. Her bull's-eye shot did nothing to deter the other beasts though. There was a time when her sister, Robyn, was by her side and she would not have thought twice about putting up a fight, but she could not risk it. She turned, grabbing Sammy's hand, and they both began to run up the beach.

"Sammy!" It was Mike's voice.

"Mike! Mike!" Sammy screamed back.

A few seconds later Mike and Lucy appeared on top of a giant rock overlooking the bay before scrambling down to the sand. "RAMs, Mike. They're RAMs!" Wren cried as he reached them. *This couldn't happen in Safe Haven ... but it was happening.*

Mike looked beyond Wren and Sammy towards the

dark, shimmering water. There were six silhouettes in varying depths, trudging towards the shore. "We can't let them get out of here. We can't have another outbreak in Safe Haven," he said, turning towards Lucy.

"Mike, there's something else," Wren said, still trying to get her breath back.

"What?"

"The one I killed. It was John."

It was the first Sammy had known about this, and she immediately began to cry. "But he was with—" Lucy started and stopped herself just as quickly. They all knew who John was with, and as these hellish shadows birthed from the sea like the devil's own spawn, there was only one question consuming them. *Which one is Jake?*

*

Supper had been a quiet affair. Emma and Tabby had picked at their food, neither having a great appetite since hearing the shots earlier. They had emptied their plates onto the compost pile and headed back inside to read a little before bed. Both of them were starting to drift when another noise carved a fresh horror through the evening.

"What's that?" Tabby asked, her eyes widening to the size of ping-pong balls.

"It sounds … it sounds like a crash alarm," Emma replied, more than a little perplexed.

"A what?"

"I once went on a school trip to an airport. We got to visit the airport fire service, and they hit the emergency siren they used for when a plane was in trouble. That's just what it sounds like."

"Err … okay, and the nearest airport would be?"

"Not anywhere near here."

"So, what the hell is it?"

"I don't know, Tabby, but it sounds like it's coming from Kyle," Emma replied, picking up one of the lanterns and heading into the bedroom.

Tabby ran after her with the other. "What are you

doing?"

"Look, nobody sounds an alarm if everything's okay. If they're in trouble, I might be able to help them," she said, grabbing her rucksack from the top of the wardrobe. She reached up again and brought down her shotgun.

"And the gunfire earlier on ... what about that? We could be heading into all sorts of shit. This is a bad idea."

"There are a lot of decent people, a lot of families there. I can't ignore a cry for help," Emma replied, heading back out and taking the keys from the small dish in the kitchen.

Tabby slipped her boots on. "Okay, but I'm going on record to say that this is a really bad idea."

"Duly noted."

The sound of the siren was even more bone-chilling as they stepped out into the evening air. Suddenly, their noses began to twitch too. The pair of them stood for a moment, looking in the direction of Kyle, then they noticed a glow warm the sky about a mile south of the small town's outskirts.

"What the hell is that?" Tabby asked.

"It looks like a fire."

"But it's nowhere near town. What could be burning there? And tell me I'm wrong, but it sounds like that's where the siren's coming from. I don't understand."

"I don't either, Tabby, but I'm going to find out what the hell's going on."

*

Raj and Talikha left the librarians' house with Humphrey by their side, happily wagging his tail. On a trade mission to one of the Inner Hebridean islands, they had bartered some of Safe Haven's produce for a vast collection of *National Geographic* magazines. Ruth, Richard and David had been ecstatic, and they had insisted on returning the favour by inviting Raj and Talikha to dinner. Although spending an evening with the librarians was not really their idea of a good time, the couple were far too polite to turn down the invitation, and as it turned out, they had more fun than they expected. However, they were happy to be out in the fresh air once more, heading towards the pier.

A low-pitched growl started in the back of Humphrey's throat, and the Golden Lab froze, glaring into the darkness. The smiles immediately disappeared from Raj and Talikha's faces. The blue stillness beyond was full of shadows.

"What is it, boy?" Talikha asked, nervously.

"Probably a fox or a badger," Raj replied.

Humphrey's growls intensified, and Talikha's hand tightened around Raj's. "I don't think—Aaarrrggghhh!" The pounding feet, the demonic growl, the sprinting silhouette with outstretched arms appearing from out of nowhere sent a pang of fear through Talikha like no other she had ever felt. Raj shook his hand free from hers, ready to do whatever he had to in order to defend his wife and his dog, but as the fevered growls of the beast cut through the dying echoes of Talikha's scream, it was Humphrey who made the first move.

The monster pounced, flying through the air like some giant bat, heading straight towards the figure that had let out the terrified yell. Talikha remained glued to the spot, unable to tear her eyes from the lunging shadow.

Humphrey sprang, his powerful leg muscles launching him like an acrobat being fired from a cannon. He clamped his jaws around the flying beast's arm and twisted his head, knocking the creature off course. The pair crashed onto the ground, both rolling, before immediately gathering themselves once more.

Raj pushed Talikha. "The pub! Get help now!"

Talikha did not pause. She understood the danger of indecision better than most, and she began to sprint in the direction of the Haven Arms. Music was playing as it did most nights and a few well-placed lanterns lit the outside and the inside creating a welcoming beacon for all those who needed the sanctuary that Jenny's pub provided. Talikha leapt over the wall and ran through the small wooded area, the blood rushing within her, blocking out the fear and worry for the twenty or thirty seconds it would take her to reach the pub's doors.

The creature sprang to its feet, ignoring its canine assailant, it lunged towards Raj. Humphrey pounced again, and the two went cascading to the ground once more. Now the beast struck out at the dog attempting to loosen the Labrador's vice-like grip. Raj had no weapons, and in the shadows, he could see nothing on the ground that could be used as a truncheon or bludgeon, but as his best friend was now at risk from the ghoulish monster, he began to kick and stamp like a mindless football hooligan.

The beast, now being attacked from two sides, lashed out more wildly. Raj suddenly felt fingers wrap tightly around his trouser leg. He knew only too well that if the nails of the monster penetrated the material and scratched his skin, Talikha would become a widow. He brought up his right foot high then thrust it down. Nose cartilage crumbled beneath his foot. There was a loud thud as the creature's head crashed against the tarmac. Momentarily stunned, the beast stopped struggling, but Raj knew better than to leave a job half done. He raised his foot again and brought it down even harder. Then again and again. There was a loud crack as the RAM's skull smashed open. The grasp around Raj's leg immediately loosened and for a second the Hindu vet thought that the horrific ordeal was over, but then he heard more pounding feet and growls tearing towards him through the darkness and knew that the nightmare had only just begun.

*

Mike grabbed a rock, marginally bigger than the average softball.

"What the hell's that for?" Lucy asked.

"If these things escape into the night, half the bloody coastline could be infected by morning," Mike replied.

"So what, you're going to kill them with a rock?" Lucy asked.

"If you can shine my torch at those things, I should be able to pick them off with my crossbow long before they get to the sand," Wren shouted.

"Get Sammy back home, get a gun and come back down here. We'll be fine, trust me," Mike said, grateful for the darkness so he couldn't see Lucy's eyes. He ran across to join Wren, and Lucy took Sammy by the hand, reluctantly doing as Mike asked.

Mike took the torch and cast the beam towards the nearest RAM as it made a beeline towards them. Wren loaded the crossbow, aimed and fired. At the same time, the creature stumbled, disappearing into the shimmering black blanket of sea.

"Did I get it? I didn't see, did I get it?" Wren asked as she loaded another bolt into the bow.

"I don't know; I didn't see either."

"I don't see it. I didn't see the bolt go in. I had it dead in my sights."

"Well, there's no sign of it. You must have done," Mike said, panning the torch around to the next silhouette.

Wren fired again, and this time the bolt clearly disappeared into the beast's forehead, and the creature collapsed forward into the water. Mike shifted the light beam once more as Wren cocked the loading lever. She pulled the trigger again, instantly stopping another advancing RAM. She took down two more in a matter of seconds, they were winning. This would all be over soon.

Mike shifted the torch to the next creature just as a volley of gunfire sounded in the distance. Wren looked at him, and he stared back in the diffused glow of the flashlight. "What the fuck is going on?" he asked.

"I don't know, Mike, but I've got a really bad feeling in my gut."

*

The wheels of Emma's car squealed as they left the long track from the cabin and hit the tarmac, it was another few hundred metres before they reached the A87, but then Emma threw whatever caution remained to the wind and put her foot down.

The tyres screeched again as they took bend after bend and she could feel Tabby tensing in the passenger seat beside her. "It's okay, I've taken this road a thousand times, I know every—" She jammed on the brakes, and the vehicle began to careen across the tarmac.

"Aaaggghhh!" Tabby screamed while Emma frantically turned the wheel in the direction of the spin, desperate not to flip the car.

The convoy of vehicles that were speeding towards them managed to stop just in time. Emma released her grip on the wheel. She could feel a thin layer of perspiration on her forehead as well as a few beads of sweat running down her back. The car had stopped at a diagonal, its front end inches away from the crash barrier that was the only obstacle between them and a sheer drop.

Figures began to emerge from the vehicles that had been coming towards them. They could not make out any details, other than some of them were most definitely armed. The familiar shape of SA80s cast long, frightening shadows as the half a dozen men and women walked into the full beams of the headlights.

"Shit," Emma said under her breath.

"What do you mean shit? Get us out of here!"

"They'll have blown us to pieces before I even get turned around."

"Emma?" shouted a voice. "Is that you?"

Emma and Tabby looked towards one another before Emma tentatively opened the door. "Who is it?" she called, slowly climbing out.

"It's Ryan and April."

Emma let out a breath of relief and headed towards them. The siren was still blaring in the distance. "What the hell's happening? We heard firing."

"Infected. Lots of them. They were on us before we knew what was going on," Ryan said.

"Infected, from where?"

"We think … the sea," April said, barely believing the words that were coming out of her mouth.

"What?" Tabby asked, joining them.

"We think the infected came from the sea."

"But how? And what's with the siren?" Emma asked.

"This wasn't an accident or some kind of freak occurrence," Ryan said.

"I don't understand any of this. What are you saying?" Emma demanded.

"Emma, most of the town has been wiped out. This was an attack. Kyle of Lochalsh is no more. It's gone."

3

Shaw and Hughes always carried their sidearms; once soldiers, always soldiers. As soon as Talikha had barged through the doors of the Haven Arms and announced that there was at least one infected in the village, they grabbed the nearest lanterns and ran to the door.

Shaw flung Jenny the keys to the arms store in the village hall. "Make sure everyone who knows how to use a gun has one," he ordered before disappearing into the night.

There was a mad flurry of activity. The village had been at battle stations numerous times before and the good humour and cheer in the pub vanished in an instant as everything became about protecting Safe Haven. One of their own was in trouble; that was all that mattered.

Talikha, now armed with a poker from the fireplace, beat a fast path back to where she had left her husband as Hughes and Shaw followed. Both had been in the pub to have a quiet pint before calling it a night, but neither's senses had been dulled.

They arrived on the scene to see one of the creatures already down, and Humphrey sat bolt upright, glaring into the darkness, growling. Both men placed the powerful lanterns on the floor and moved back in order to gain whatever small advantage they could from the lights. It was a few seconds before the first RAM emerged from the shadows. Shaw took aim, firing his Browning 13 and taking the beast down with a single shot. Another monster appeared, and before Hughes got a chance to fire, Shaw took the second beast down too. Another creature leapt out from the night and this time Hughes beat his friend to it, making a well-aimed headshot.

The monster's body skidded across the tarmac to a halt. A fourth and fifth creature were dispatched in a similar manner then no more appeared. The five living, breathing warm bodies peered into the blackness, waiting, listening. Raj had hold of Humphrey's collar, making sure the dog did not go off on his own to hunt down any further monsters.

A few more seconds passed, and Shaw and Hughes began to breathe a little more easily. "Where the fuck did they come from?" Hughes demanded, holstering his Glock 17.

Shaw was about to answer when more shots sounded at the far end of the village then more somewhere further up the coastline. The two soldiers looked towards one another in the light of the lanterns. Shaw reached for the radio that was clipped to his belt and hit the talk button. "Jen, are you there? Over."

"Yes, I'm nearly done."

"Jen, listen to me. Sound the siren. Sound the siren now."

*

"Shit!" Mike growled as the creature that had stumbled earlier reappeared in the shallows. With each stride the beast took its pace increased. "Hurry up, Wren, for Christ's sake."

"I am hurrying," Wren said, pulling the self-cocking lever on the crossbow, loading and firing. The increase in the approaching monster's speed and its greater agility in the shallow water was something Wren could not account for in her shot. As the beast became more animated, the bolt only managed to cut a divot out of the side of its head before glancing off into the water.

Realising there would not be enough time to reload before the creature was on top of them Mike dropped the torch and charged out towards it. The rock he had picked up earlier was still held firmly in his hand, and as he leapt through the air towards the growling silhouette, there was a movement of light behind him. Wren had picked up the torch and was shining the beam directly towards them. The monster lunged as Mike landed. The water splashed high, almost creating a half cocoon around them. Mike smashed the rock against the beast's head.

The creature paused momentarily, stunned by the blow. It brought its arms up again, reaching through the cool air towards its prey, but Mike brought the rock down again, harder, and this time he felt the sharp edge penetrate bone. The RAM was beyond dazed now, but Mike was not going to take any risks. He struck a third then a fourth time, over and over again until the creature dropped face down into the water. Suddenly, Mike was surrounded by darkness once more, and out of the corner of his eye, he saw the torchlight move across the water to the final beast.

There was a momentary pause then a small explosion as a bolt entered its head before it too crumpled into the water. Mike slowly looked around, making sure there was no more movement, and then trudged the few feet back to the sand.

When he had managed to get his breath back, he placed a hand on Wren's shoulder. "Are you okay?"

"There was no need for you to do that. I had time to reload."

"You can't take risks with these things."

"Duh! Really? Having lived by myself out there for months, I never would have known that.

"Good job you were here to rescue me, Mike," she replied, grabbing her jeans and putting them back on.

Wren's feisty streak always managed to put a smile

on Mike's face. "I'll trust you to make the shot next time."

"Yeah, Mike Fletcher trusting someone. I'll mark that day in my diary."

"You keep a diary?"

She finished putting on her jeans and trainers then picked the crossbow up and held it in front of his face in the torchlight. "Do I look like the kind of girl who keeps a diary?"

Mike smiled again, but then the smile disappeared just as quickly. "Jake wasn't among those things. What exactly happened here?"

More shots sounded in the distance, and both of them started to run across the sand. "John had only just turned," Wren said as they continued to move.

"How do you know?"

"The blood was still flowing a little. I've seen enough of those things up close to know a long-termer from a newbie. I think they must have come around from the other cove. They were probably drawn by Sammy's scream. They appeared fast, I know that."

Mike stopped running. "The next cove," he said almost to himself. The whole coastline was made of up rocky inlets and small beaches, an army could remain hidden unless someone happened upon them, but the fact that those half-dozen beasts had ventured towards the screams suggested that if there was anyone left in the cove, they were either hiding or dead … dead dead, not undead.

"What are you doing?" Wren said, stopping too.

Mike handed her the torch. "Get back to the house, tell Lucy where I am." Without giving Wren a chance to respond, he turned and started sprinting in the opposite direction.

He had already started to scramble up the rocky incline at the far end of the small beach when Wren turned back to her original direction of travel, shaking her head. She began to climb too, casting one glance back towards the sea and the bodies washing onto the shore. She had no idea what was going on or where these things had come from, and all she wanted now was to go home and see her grandad, let somebody else deal with what was going on. As the mournful scream of the air raid siren started to make the very air around her bristle and vibrate, she realised that whatever was going on in Safe Haven was much bigger than she could imagine and the chances of her seeing her bed any time soon were diminishing more by the minute.

*

Emma had led the convoy back to the cabin. There were six vehicles plus her own; thirty people, just a fraction of the Kyle population. They all crowded into the large kitchen diner, gathering around the lantern-lit table. The siren was sounding in the distance, and as they shot glances into the night, the inferno was still clearly blazing.

"Where were you heading?" Emma asked.

"Somewhere ... anywhere but there. We'd made that place our home. We thought maybe we could live out some kind of normal life there," Ryan replied.

April started to sob again. "I suppose ... I suppose that's it now. We have to head back out on the road on the off-chance we might find somewhere."

Tabby glanced towards Emma. "Well, look," Emma said, "for tonight, make yourselves as comfortable as you can here. We'll pick up the pieces tomorrow morning."

"There aren't any pieces to pick up," one of the other refugees said.

"Emma's right. Let's find a place to kip down tonight and look at things fresh tomorrow," Ryan said, and people gradually broke away from the crowd. Tabby did her best to furnish them with blankets and any bedding she could. She settled a family in one of the bedrooms and let the others find their own spaces. For tonight, the place would be a commune.

Emma, Ryan and April continued to stand around the table a little longer. "I'll go and find us a place," April said, nodding gratefully towards Emma. When she was out of earshot, Ryan flopped down on one of the chairs.

"I don't know what I'm going to do," he said, brushing his hands over his stubbly face.

"You got nearly thirty people out. If you'd done nothing, they wouldn't be here now," Emma said, crossing to the cupboard beneath the sink and opening it up. She pulled out a pair of binoculars, opened the patio door and stepped out.

A few seconds later, she heard the screech of wood against tile as Ryan pulled his chair out and walked into the garden to join her. "What are you doing?" he asked.

"Did you notice those sailboats in the bay? They seemed to arrive just before sunset."

"Can't say I did. I don't really have a good view from where I live ... lived."

Emma spun the focus wheel on the binoculars and then concentrated, peering into the distance. "Whoever they are, I'm pretty certain they've got something to do with this." As she looked now, more boats had joined them, and a procession of smaller vessels was heading towards the shore. She handed the binoculars to Ryan.

"Why do you think they're doing this?"

"Obvious isn't it? It's actually quite clever, in a pretty insidious way."

"You've lost me," Ryan said, handing the binoculars back to Emma.

She could just make out the contours of his face in the moonlight. *How could someone so naive have lasted for so long?* "They cause an outbreak, turn the population of the town into flesh-crazed monsters, then lure them away with a loud siren and a fire while they head in and ransack the town. The pirates of the apocalypse."

"You sound like you admire them."

"I don't admire them. I hope they all fucking die, but whoever came up with this idea had a brain, and they knew that a couple of sailboats out in the bay wouldn't seem out of place, so they either had inside knowledge or they've been watching us."

"How can people do this?"

An image sprang into Emma's head. She was back in Loch Uig, and Webb was standing over her with a pair of secateurs in his hand. An unholy grin decorated his face, and his eyes were lit with excitement. "Trust me; you'd be amazed at what people can do."

"I'm going to find April. Thank you for this, Emma."

"Don't mention it." He went back inside, but a moment later, she felt another presence by her side. "Before you say it, I'm sorry. I couldn't just turn them out into the night."

"I wasn't going to say that," Tabby replied.

"Oh. What were you going to say?"

"I was going to ask what are we going to do now?"

"I know exactly what we're going to do."

"What?"

"We're going to head to Safe Haven."

4

It was difficult to ignore the air raid siren, in fact, it was impossible, but for the time being Mike only had one concern and that was finding Jake. He stumbled and clawed his way up the craggy rocks, over the scrub grass, and down the other side into the next cove. The sand reflected the moon's beams, a blanket of white punctuated only by the odd pebble here and there. He took a wrong turn on the rocks and, rather than finding a safe route down, he chose to leap the last few feet. Soft dry sand buried his trainers up to the ankles, but he soon shook it loose as he sprinted onto the beach, swooping down to pick up a sharp, jagged stone, just in case.

"Jake! Jake!" he shouted, the echoes bouncing off the surrounding cliff faces and out to sea. "Jake, where are you?" Mike stood in the middle of the beach, twirling around, searching for movement, listening for any sound beyond that of the siren that might give him a clue.

Then he saw it. Halfway up a rock face, behind a salt-burned growth of shrubs, there was movement, a flicker of white against the darkness. "Mike?" called the quavering voice, only just audible.

"Jake?" He ran across and started to climb up

towards the youngster. The smooth black surface was almost vertical, and as he felt out the mounds and crevices that allowed him to scale it, he wondered how his younger brother had managed, but then fear was a great catalyst when it came to conquering inhibitions.

"They got John," Jake sobbed as Mike reached him.

"I know, Jakey, I know." There was a small plateau behind the shrub, and Mike placed his right foot on it for support. "I need you to climb onto my back and wrap your arms around my neck. Do you think you can do that?"

Jake sniffed loudly and then left the small nook behind the bush and climbed onto Mike's back. "I heard a scream. It sounded like Sammy," he said through his tears.

"Don't worry, Sammy's fine. What happened?" Mike asked, still shouting to be heard over the siren.

"We saw the dolphins and John went into the water to get closer to them. I told him it was dangerous, but he wouldn't listen. I was calling him from the shore; then those things appeared from around the rocks. They started coming towards me, and I ran, but then I looked back and they were all heading to John and then—" His tears took over.

"It's okay, Jakey. It's okay. You did the right thing." They reached the sand and Mike lowered his little brother onto the soft surface. "Come on, let's get you back home." He took his little brother's hand, and they started to jog across the beach. All the time the air raid siren was singing a desperate aria into the air.

*

"Jen, how's it going there? Over," Shaw asked.

Jenny hit the talk button on the radio. "Nearly done," she shouted over the sound of the siren.

"Do me a favour. Get the second generator going and get all the lights on."

Jenny looked confused. "Did you say get all the lights on?"

"Yes. We'll be there soon. Over and out."

The radio went dead, and Jenny just looked at it for a moment. Torch beams were flashing around the interior of the village hall as people took weapons from the cache. The panic in the air was palpable.

"What the hell's going on?" Barnes asked as he and Beth burst in through the double doors. The two of them were already armed and had been just up the road at George's when the siren had first sounded.

"Infected," Jenny replied. "Shaw wants me to power up the generator and get all the lights going."

"The lights?" Barnes asked, just as perplexed as Jenny had been.

"That's what he said."

Barnes took the radio from Jenny as she and Beth ran out to start the second generator. "Shaw, this is Barney. Did Jenny understand right? You want all the lights on? With the siren going too, we're just inviting the RAMs to attack. Over."

"That's the point; we're falling back to your position now. These things are all over the place. We need to draw them in. Listen, I'm glad you're there. Get some lanterns in the grounds then get the people with weapons onto the roof. Over."

"Understood. Over and out."

*

"I really don't like the idea of Sammy and Jake being left alone," Lucy said as she put her foot down harder on the accelerator.

"Look, it's not ideal, but they're in the attic and the ladder's up. Sammy's not just any kid, she'll stay up there until we're back," Mike replied.

Two vehicles sped past them in the other direction, and Wren turned rapidly in her seat. "That was Grandad," she said.

"He'll be heading to the mangonels," Mike replied. "I think that was Richard and David behind him."

"Why though? These are RAMs we're facing, not

raiders."

"It's a smart move by Shaw. Get everybody on a battle footing."

Mike looked across towards Lucy. He could see in the glow of the dashboard lights that tears were running down her face. He reached across and took her hand. "It's okay, we'll get through this, whatever it is."

"Tell that to John. Tell that to Beth when she finds out that her little brother's dead."

Mike pulled his hand away. When he saw John, the only selfish thought that had run through his head was, *Where is Jake?* Did being a good brother make him a bad person? "I'm sorry. I hadn't even thought."

More cars sped by in the opposite direction, but soon they saw the glow of the community hall, although that was not their destination. Lucy sped through the small village and finally brought the car to a skidding stop outside the infirmary, the four static caravans that constituted Safe Haven's medical facility. Stone chips sprayed up clattering against the outside of the vehicle. A few seconds later, another car came to an equally abrupt halt at the side of them; it was one of Lucy's nurses.

They all exited the vehicles and ran inside. A look of relief swept over the face of the young nurse on duty as they entered Ward One. She and the lone patient had been listening to the radio transmissions. "They say there are infected. They say they're going to put up a stand at the village hall," she blurted.

Everything suddenly made sense to Mike. That's why all the lights were on there. The creatures would naturally be drawn to the sound of the air raid siren, and the lights would beckon them further the second they were in sight. Mike picked up the handset. "Shaw, it's Mike. We've got no guards here. What's going on?"

"Mike, you tell me. It's fucking mayhem. You're meant to have four militia reporting there, are you saying none of them have shown up?"

"That's what I'm saying."

"Okay. Stay there, kill the lights. If you run into problems, let me know, but I think we're going to have our hands full here for a while."

Mike put the radio back in the cradle just as more vehicles arrived. It was the rest of the nursing staff, but still there was no sign of any guards. When they were all inside, Lucy took charge. "Okay, we need to be quick about this. We have to get the patients from the other wards across here and get all the lights turned off. It's a lot easier to defend one caravan than four, so let's get to it."

No sooner had she spoken than the nurses and trainees dispersed. Mike, Lucy and Wren walked out into the middle of the court. The air raid siren was still in full vigour, and the three of them stood back to back. Despite Wren only being sixteen years old, she had proven herself to be a more than capable fighter, and she had both her pistol crossbows drawn and ready. Mike had his shotgun in one hand and a machete in the other, while Lucy stood there with her Glock 17. One by one, the lights of the static caravans went out as the patients and staff exited.

"How come you keep all the wards open with so few patients?" Wren asked, always inquisitive.

"We need to keep them aired and heated. I don't know if you've noticed, but the damp air causes a lot of mould. I like to keep at least one patient in each ward. Keeps the building in shape for when we need it."

"Makes sense."

"Seriously. We're under attack from a horde of zombie flesh-eaters, and that's what was on your mind?" Mike said.

"Just wondering, that's all."

They fell silent again as bursts of gunfire started to sound from the direction of the village hall. "And so it begins," Lucy said under her breath.

"There's something in the trees," Wren said, and Mike and Lucy both turned to see which direction she was looking in. They saw bushes and branches move and raised their weapons ready. Humphrey came bounding out, followed by Raj and Talikha, and the three of them instantly lowered their aim once more. They quickly greeted each other before all of them piled into Ward One.

"Who are we still waiting for?" Lucy asked.

"Nobody," a nurse replied, "we're all here."

"Then why are the lights still on in Ward Four?"

"Oh," the nurse replied guiltily.

"I'll go and turn them off," Mike said, flicking the light switch in their own ward then heading towards the door. Lucy grabbed his arm before he could open it.

"Too late," she said.

They all gazed through the window at the figures that had been taking a shortcut through the woods towards the deafening sound of the siren. Five of them were now assembled around the brightly lit static caravan. They mounted the three steps and began to throw themselves at the door.

"Nice work," Mike said, turning towards the nurse.

"I'm sorry," she said, her brow creasing.

"Don't worry sweetie, it's easy enough to do," Lucy replied.

"It's not right that there's a dog in a hospital ward," said a grouchy old female patient.

"What did you say?" Mike asked, walking across to her bed.

"I said it's not right that there's a dog in a hospital ward."

"Mike, leave it," Lucy said.

"Our town's under attack and your big concern is that there's a dog in the ward."

"It's not right, it's unhygienic!" she protested again.

"Listen to me, you old bag; I'll put you out there before that dog, do you understand? So, there's the door, and if you don't fancy that option, you just stay there and keep your fucking mouth shut. That dog has more of a right to be in Safe Haven than anyone."

"Well, I've never been spoken to like that in my life."

"All I can say is you've been fucking lucky. Trust me, I'm not that pleasant to be around at the best of times, and this isn't the best of fucking times. So keep your fucking mouth shut!"

"Mike!" Lucy said more firmly.

The old woman just sat there in her bed with her mouth wide open, and Mike walked back across to the window. There was even more gunfire coming from the direction of the village hall now.

"Sounds like a shooting gallery over there," Mike said as he continued to look across to Ward Four.

"What should we do?" Wren asked.

"We wait," Mike replied.

"Wait? Why?"

"All those things will be heading towards the siren unless something more interesting crops up along the way. All we need is another half dozen to appear out of the woods while we're trying to clear them and we'll be in a whole heap of trouble. We'll give it another five minutes, and then we'll go out there."

Almost as soon as Mike had finished speaking, three more beasts appeared from the wooded area next to the lit caravan, and he looked towards Wren. "Okay, point taken," she said.

*

Lanterns littered the car park of the village hall, the doors were locked so there was no entry point for the creatures, and twenty men and women stood on top of the roof, carefully taking aim at each approaching RAM. Beth walked across to stand by Shaw. "You spoke to Mike?"

"Yeah," Shaw said, aiming his rifle and making another headshot. "Why?"

"John was with Jake. I just wanted to make sure he was okay."

"Beth, if anything had happened to Jake, Mike would be round here tearing these things apart with his bare hands."

"Fair point," she said, bringing up her scope and taking down another creature as it charged towards the building.

*

Mike, Lucy and Wren stepped outside, the noise of the air raid siren disguising any sound that they made as they got into position at the bottom of the steps. Lucy nodded, and the lights flickered on in the static caravan. George had rigged the lighting circuit to run on car batteries, so even when the generators weren't running, there was always illumination.

For a moment, the creatures continued hammering at the door of Ward Four, oblivious to the fact that supper was preparing to serve itself outside of the first static caravan.

"Mike, what are you doing?" Lucy half whispered, half shouted as he started walking towards the creatures.

The beasts were still throwing themselves at the door when Mike pulled the fore-end of the shotgun, raised the weapon to his shoulder and fired. In the shadowy light, the explosion of blood and tissue looked black against the white entrance door. For a few seconds, the crack of the shotgun could be heard over the sound of the air raid siren, but the reverberations around the courtyard ended again just as quickly as the remaining seven creatures turned towards Mike. The beast with half a head collapsed, and the rest charged.

Mike cocked the weapon again and fired a second time, then a third, bringing down two more charging beasts. The pump-action shotgun was Mike's go-to firearm. He did not possess the patience or the skill to learn how to use a rifle or handgun properly, but the spread from a shotgun blast almost guaranteed that he would hit something if he was close enough and pointing it in the right direction. He fired three more times in quick succession, blowing off the arm of one creature and blinding but not killing another. A third flew backwards, disappearing into the darkness, and Mike dropped the shotgun to the ground, reaching back with both hands and withdrawing the crisscrossed blades of the machetes from his rucksack.

He felt a presence on either side of him, and the familiar report of Lucy's Glock 17 followed by the blurring glint of a metal bolt launching from one of Wren's pistol crossbows announced their arrival to the battle. Mike tensed, ready to strike as soon as any of the creatures were in distance, but it was over before it had even begun.

He stood there with Wren and Lucy by his side. All three of them looked towards the already rotten corpses lying still in front of them. "What now?" asked Wren as Mike retrieved his shotgun from the ground.

"Now we head back inside and wait for further instructions from Shaw," Lucy said.

The siren continued to howl, but the gunfire was gradually becoming more sporadic. "You made that look easy," one of the nurses said as the three of them walked back in.

"Oh yeah," Lucy replied, "it was a real walk in the park. Can I see you for a second?" she said, turning to Mike.

"Sounds ominous," he replied with a smile, but even though he could not see Lucy's face, he could sense she wasn't smiling. She grabbed him by the wrist, picked up a lantern and the two of them walked through the dark interior of the static caravan, down the short corridor and into the bathroom. Lucy clicked the small lamp on. "Look, before you say anything, we were going to have to attract their attention somehow, and I thought getting a shot off first would give us the adv—"

"I'm not worried about that. Listen to me. Did you notice anything strange about those RAMs?"

"What, other than them being reanimated corpses? You mean there's something stranger than that?"

"Don't be a wiseass."

"Sorry." He thought for a moment then answered her. "No, no, I didn't."

"I didn't recognise a single one of them, and judging by the smell and state of decomposition, some of those things had been dead a long time."

In the throes of battle, he had not even thought about who the creatures had once been, only that they needed to be killed once and for all. "So... I don't understand; where did they come from?"

"That's the question we need to be asking, and I bet when we head to the village hall, we're going to see the same thing over there."

"Shit!"

"Yeah."

The pair sat down on the edge of the bath, the siren and gunfire just white noise to them now. "So, what are you thinking?"

Lucy leaned forward. "Okay, so there are only two routes into Safe Haven by road, the North Ridge and the East Ridge. Provided neither of those has been hijacked there's only one other possibility."

"Those fucking boats!" Mike said, jumping to his feet.

"Exactly!"

They burst out of the bathroom, and Lucy immediately turned the lantern off. Mike almost ran to the radio and plucked it from the cradle. "George! Richard! David! Anyone at the Barricade! It's Mike. Over."

The Barricade was what they called the elevated site where the mangonels stood. It had been key in securing victory the night the madman, Fry, had waged war against the town. Now, if Lucy's suspicions were correct, they were at war again. The radio crackled. "Mike, it's George. Go ahead. Over."

"There was a tall ship offshore earlier on with some smaller boats around it. Are they still there? Over."

"You noticed them as well, did you? When the air raid siren started, they headed out to sea. Over."

Mike paused before pressing the talk button again. "Any sign of anyone on the roads? Over."

"Everything's quiet here, Mike. I think all the action's in town. Over."

"Okay. Thanks, George. Over and out." He waited a few seconds then brought the radio up to his mouth again. "North Ridge, East Ridge, are you seeing anything on the roads? Over."

"All quiet on the eastern front. Over."

"This is North Ridge. Nothing to report here. Over."

"Okay. Keep your eyes peeled. Over and out." Mike was about to place the radio back in the cradle, but it crackled to life once more.

"Mike, it's Shaw. Over."

"Shaw. Mike. Go ahead. Over."

"What was all that about? Over."

"We'll tell you when we see you. Over."

"We're mopping up here. I'm going to organise roving patrols in the Land Rovers through the night, and I'll sort out a full sweep tomorrow morning, but I think we're almost done. When I cut the siren, that'll be the all-clear. I'll see you then. Over and out."

A few minutes later, the warbling siren fell silent and as soon as the last vibrations had dissipated Lucy flicked the lights back on in the static caravan and turned to the nurses. "Get everyone back to their respective wards," she said and started walking towards the hallway.

"Where are you going?" Mike asked, chasing after her.

"I need to get some sedatives."

"What for?"

"Because we're about to tell Beth that her little brother is dead."

5

Mike had volunteered to be in one of the Land Rovers for the first shift of patrols. By the time Jules had reached the Barricade from dropping off supplies at the North Ridge, the pandemonium had ended, but always keen to do her bit, she volunteered too. The mood was sombre in the car as they travelled up the coastline, pulling into every small cove along the way. The temperature had dropped dramatically and it was a bad time to discover the heater had developed an intermittent fault. Mike stared out of the window, scouring the shadows for any out of place shapes as Jules drove.

"So what do we do next?" Jules asked.

"Well, I'm guessing there'll be a council meeting, and you'll all decide," Mike replied distantly.

"What do you think we should do?" Mike turned in his seat to look at her. No words came out of his mouth, but even in the darkness, Jules knew what he was thinking. "Okay, stupid question."

"Actually, it's not," he said, returning his gaze to the shores and inlets below.

"Okay, you've got my attention, what do you mean?"

Mike turned back towards her. "It's not like we can just jump into a car and head after them, is it?"

"Well, maybe not, but we've got boats, Raj and Talikha are—"

"And which way do we go? They could have gone anywhere."

Jules turned back to the road. "So, what do we do?"

"I don't know, Jules. All I know is that we were attacked tonight and one of my best friends lost her little brother."

"How did she take it?"

"You didn't really just ask me that."

"I mean will she be okay?"

"Luce gave her sedatives and Barney took her straight home. Beth's been through more than most here. She's tough, but I don't think I've ever seen her so crushed. This place is meant to be safe. We've taken such precautions, but we never seriously considered an attack coming from the sea."

"I suppose we're going to have to put some measures in place so it can't happen again," Jules said.

"How? This is a long stretch of coastline. It's easy to put barricades up on the roads, but how the hell do we plan for an attack from the sea that could arrive anywhere along the coast at any time? Maybe Shaw and Hughes have some ideas."

"What are you saying?"

"I'm saying I don't have the answers."

"Jesus, I wish I had a witness here 'cause nobody would fuckin' believe me if I said to them those words came from your mouth."

As dire as the situation was, a smile cracked on Mike's face. "Funny cow, aren't you?"

"Less of the cow, you cheeky little shite."

"I meant it as a term of endearment."

"Yeah, well, when we stop the car, I'll give you a kick in the bollocks and I'll mean that as a term of endearment too."

Mike sniggered. "I don't know, Jules, we seem to have put up an awful lot of fights to protect this place. Maybe it will never be the fortress I hoped it would."

They drove in silence for a little while then Jules reached across and took Mike's hand. "Listen to me, no joking. I've been where you are now. I've been in a place where everybody has looked to me for answers and I haven't had any to give. I know what it's like for someone to die and for you to feel responsible even though it wasn't your fault. It's a shitty feeling. You and Lucy know me as well as anyone, you know I don't bullshit, so when I tell you none of this is on you, I mean it." She squeezed his hand tightly before letting go.

"Thanks, Jules. That means a lot."

"Yeah well, nobody could have seen this coming. We'll do what we always do. We'll rebuild, and we'll learn from our mistakes."

"There are only so many times people are going to do that before wondering whether they're better off somewhere else."

"There you go again, taking responsibility for things that are outside of your control. What others do is up to them; you cannot control it; you cannot take responsibility for it. All you can do is react when it happens."

"That's ... actually scarily coherent thinking for you."

"You are such a gobby twat. I'm trying—"

"I'm kidding."

"Yeah well. You're not wrong; those weren't my words. They're the words George said to me."

"This place could do worse than have him in charge."

"No, I think the current system works well. The council makes the important decisions then you go off on one, completely ignore them and do what you want. It's balanced perfectly."

"Hey. If memory serves, I did that for you."

Jules smiled. "And it worked out so well."

"We saved a lot of people from that psychopath, Webb."

The smile left Jules's face. "I can't even imagine what they went through."

"You don't need to."

"We can't ever be sure there aren't people even more twisted out there."

"Err, aren't you meant to be giving me a pep talk?"

"Pep talk's over. My point is tonight was a bad night. There'll be plenty more. Suck it up and carry on doing what you're doing. This place needs you."

"Bossy, aren't you?"

"Fuck you."

"And you swear a lot."

"I swear an appropriate amount depending on the company I'm in and you, you mouthy, arrogant little twat-faced bollock head can fuck right off because in my life nobody has been a bigger pain in my tits. You actually get off lightly. If I swore as much as you deserved, my sentences would just be nothing but a long line of fuckin' fucks separated by the odd punctuation mark with a prick thrown in here and a wanker thrown in there for good measure. So fuckin' shut your fuckin' gob, piss dick."

"You do realise all this hostility is just your way of coping with the suffocating sexual longing you have for me, don't you?"

"Jesus Christ! Hold on to Lucy with all you've got 'cause I swear there isn't another woman on the planet who would suffer you for more than five minutes without placing a pillow over your fucking face while you were sleeping."

There was a pause; then they both burst out laughing. "Thanks, Jules, I needed that."

"Me too." She brought the car to a stop at the

Barricade. The moon was high over the bay, and the water shimmered and glinted in its beams. "We'd better head back. I'm pretty certain any stragglers would have been drawn to the siren."

"Yeah. It's going to be a long day tomorrow." Mike looked at his watch. "Well, today." He picked up the handset. "Shaw, this is Mike. Over."

"Go ahead. Over."

"We've reached the Barricade—nothing to report. We're heading back now. Over."

"Yeah. We haven't seen a thing either. I've posted three lookouts up and down the coast to keep their eyes on the water, and I've called a council meeting first thing tomorrow. Head back to the hall and your replacements will be waiting. Over and out."

Jules turned the Land Rover around, and they started back to the village. She had made this journey a thousand times before, and she could do it blindfolded. Despite the narrow and winding cliff top track, they made good time, and the adrenaline that had been surging through both of them started to dissipate. She took the final bend before the descent into the village and jammed on the brakes, stalling the car.

A naked woman was standing in the middle of the road with her back to them. Jules looked at Mike, and he looked back at her before they returned their attention to the figure in the headlights' beams.

"This fuckin' night just gets weirder and weirder."

*

Emma had remained on the patio despite everyone else turning in for the night several hours back. She had viewed the silhouettes of the boats through the binoculars. A number of the smaller ones had been taxiing back and forth between two tall ships. She had once been down in Portsmouth visiting Michelle and seen ships like those during a display. Dozens of them with enormous masts had wowed tourists with their grandeur.

At first, the vessels had seemed to be from a bygone age, but when she and Michelle had stepped on board for a guided tour, it was clear that was not the case. They were equipped with all mod cons to make the crew as comfortable as possible. As Emma looked out to these grand black silhouettes floating on the dark mirror of water she was convinced that the two sailboats she now looked at were from that display, or, if not, definitely from the same boatyard.

"Aren't you coming to bed? It's really late," Tabby said as she came up behind Emma.

"Not really in the mood for sleeping."

"At least don't freeze to death," she replied, placing a thick coat around Emma's shoulders.

The crash alarm had finally gone quiet about an hour before and now the night was virtually silent, but the glow of the fire out of town remained as a stark reminder of what had happened. "What time is it?"

"What?"

"What time is it?"

Tabby looked at her watch. "Three thirty. Why?"

"We should set off soon."

"This early? What's wrong with waiting for daylight?"

"A feeling."

"What feeling?"

"I've been watching them all night. This was really well planned. I'm guessing they've done this a lot and I'm guessing they'll continue to do it. All the bows are pointing north, so it's reasonable to assume that's where they're heading next. The sooner we get to Safe Haven to warn them the better."

"Are you sure you're ready for this? Are you sure you're ready to see your brother again?"

"Whatever problems I have with Mike don't matter right now. Sammy and Jake are in Safe Haven. I have friends I love who I have to warn. I can't allow what happened here to happen there."

"Will we come back here when we've warned them?" Tabby asked.

"Come back to what? There are hundreds of infected just a few miles away. When the embers of that fire burn black, they'll start spreading out to look for food. What we had here has gone."

"So where will we go?"

"One thing at a time, Tabby. One thing at a time."

*

Jules and Mike remained in their seats for a moment, just looking at the naked woman as she continued towards town. She seemed oblivious to the fact that the headlights were pointing directly at her rear.

"Err... I know it was a warm day, but—"

"It's Beth," Mike said, opening the car door.

"Careful," Jules said, "she could be sleepwalking. You've got to be really careful."

"Beth ... Beth!" Mike called softly after her, but she continued to head towards the village. Mike and Jules looked at one another before running to catch up with their friend.

Jules was about to say something to her when she stopped. Beth was speaking. It was hard to hear at first, but as they got closer the whispered words made the already chilly night air positively Baltic. "This is the end of everything. This is the end of everything. This is the end of everything."

"Beth. Beth, sweetheart," Jules said as she and Mike walked along by her side, farther away from the parked Land Rover and drifting into the darkness beyond the edge of the headlights' beams.

Beth's eyes were wide open, and Jules almost recoiled as the cold of her friend's naked skin took her by surprise. She placed a gentle hand on Beth's back to try to get her attention without startling her. "This is the end of everything. This is the end of everything. This is the end of everything."

Mike waved a hand up and down in front of Beth's face. Her body looked blue in the moon's glow, and not all of that was due to the light cast. They were nearly a mile from Beth's house and the temperature was still dropping.

"Beth ... Beth," Mike said this time, but she just kept on walking and whispering. "What do we do?" He looked over towards Jules.

"Believe it or not, this isn't a situation I've ever dealt with before. I mean when I did my management training at the Home and Garden Depot, I must have missed the fuckin' module on waking up naked sleepwalkers who keep repeating apocalyptic prophecies over and over."

Mike got in front of Beth and started walking backwards, all the time waving his hands in front of her face in the hope that the movement would somehow break her trance. "Beth. Come on, we need to get you home. Annie needs you more than ever."

"This is the end of everything. This is the end of everything."

"Okay. I don't mind telling you this is creeping me the fuck out," Jules said.

"Beth! Beth! Please stop," Mike said as Beth glared right through him towards the road beyond. He looked again towards Jules and finally placed his hands on Beth's shoulders. "Fuck! She's going to get hyperthermia." He stopped dead, and Beth walked straight into him.

Despite the human barrier, she tried to continue walking, all the time repeating the same stark warning. "This is the end of everything. This is the end of everything. This is the end of everything."

Mike took hold of her face. "Beth! Beth!" He grabbed her by the upper arms and began to shake her. "Beth! Beth!"

Finally, Beth did stop walking. She stopped whispering too, but Mike and Jules would have paid anything to hear whispering again as a deafening nasal scream erupted from within her, making the air raid siren from earlier on seem positively melodic.

"Great fuckin' job, Mike. What bit of be careful was confusing?"

"Beth! Beth!" he shouted, desperately trying to shake her awake.

Then the screaming stopped as quickly as it had started. Beth just stood there with her arms by her side, looking.

"Thank Christ," Jules said. "Beth. Beth, darlin', we're going to get you back home."

Mike whipped off his jacket and placed it around Beth's naked shoulders before putting an arm around her and guiding her back to the car. Jules opened the back door, and Mike carefully lifted Beth in, closing the door firmly behind her.

"We need to get her to Luce. You sit in the back, I'll drive."

Jules climbed into the back seat, and the tyres screeched as Mike did an abrupt three-point turn. "It's okay. We don't need to worry anymore," Beth said after they'd been travelling for just under a minute.

"Worry? Worry about what?" Jules asked.

"I saw my mum and dad and Peter. They told me."

A shiver ran down Mike's spine. "They told you what, Beth?"

"That we'll all be together again soon." She caught Mike's eyes in the rearview mirror, and even in the subdued light he could see the smile on her face. "All of us."

6

The cavalcade of vehicles headed north on the A890. It was slow going. The winter months had left the roads in a poor state of repair and with no council to fill in potholes, it was easy to break a spring or get a puncture if concentration lapsed for even a few seconds.

"You haven't said a word since we set off," Tabby said, looking across at Emma.

"Not really feeling chatty."

"You never said how you left it with your brother."

"I left him a note."

"Saying?"

"Some pretty unpleasant stuff."

"Like what?"

Emma turned to look at Tabby in the glow of the dashboard display. "It's complicated."

"Okay." Tabby looked a little hurt.

"I'm sorry. I don't really want to talk about it. I promise I'll tell you everything one day, but this is enough of a hurdle for me to get over without having to relive painful memories too."

Dawn was not far away, and Emma knew that soon she would be face-to-face with Mike again and she'd have to confront those memories head-on, but just for the last little part of the journey was it too much to ask that she could get lost in her own thoughts?

*

"I've given her a stronger sedative, but that's pretty much all I can do. She's sleeping again now," Lucy said as she returned to the kitchen.

Barnes, Mike and Jules were all sitting around the table with mugs of tea. "Thank God you two found her. She could have stepped off a cliff, anything could have happened," Barnes said.

"How's Annie?" Jules asked.

"She cried herself to sleep. I can handle that. Beth, though, when we left you, she stopped crying, and she just went quiet. I thought it was the sedatives working on her, but then she started whispering... It was like fifty conversations were going on in her head at the same time. It was really freaky," replied Barnes.

"Look, for the time being just let her rest. She needs to sleep. Her brain needs to process what's going on. Stay with her. Keep her warm and make sure she doesn't go walkabout again."

"Okay. Thanks again. I'm not going to leave her side. I can't believe I did before."

"Hey, yesterday wasn't easy for any of us. Don't blame yourself," Lucy replied.

Jules looked at her watch. "Well, I need to get back and get some shuteye before the council meeting. It's nearly six o'clock, I might be able to get a couple of hours at least," Jules said, standing up.

"I think we could all use some sl—" Lucy's words were interrupted as the radio handset sitting on the kitchen counter crackled to life.

"Shaw, this is East Ridge. We've got multiple vehicles approaching. Over."

Everyone around the table looked towards the handset. A fresh air of panic swept over them. There was a pause but finally the radio hissed. "This is Shaw. How many vehicles? What type of vehicles? How fast are they travelling? Over."

"Hang on. They've come to a stop. It looks like two people are getting out." There was a long pause while everyone waited with bated breath. "One of them's holding a torch, hang on, I think they're using Morse code. Over."

"What are they saying? Over," demanded Shaw.

"Oh my God, Shaw, it's Emma."

*

The convoy set off again, slowly. Emma's heart began to thump frantically as she started to recognise familiar natural landmarks. Instinctively she reached out for Tabby's hand. This was one of those moments when she needed comfort, when she needed that other body so she didn't feel completely alone.

"Are you okay?" Tabby asked.

"Not by a long shot."

"Well, they've not opened fire. That must be a good sign, right?"

Emma laughed. "That wasn't my number one concern." They carried on travelling for a few more minutes and then Emma pulled her hand away. "I should probably have asked you this before, but do you have a problem with heights?"

"I can't say I'm a fan. Why?"

"'Cause this road … climbs a little, and when I say a little, I mean a lot."

"Oh, God. Is this that thing you were telling me about? That passage? What was it called?"

"Yeah, Deadman's Pass. Now, you might want to stop asking questions, hold on to something tight, and close your eyes."

*

Tears began to run down Emma's face as she pulled up outside the village hall and saw Sammy and Jake standing there. Of all the guilt she felt, it was leaving them that had given her the most internal conflict. They were just innocent bystanders, but she knew that if she had not walked away that night, something bad… worse would have happened, and there would have been no road back.

Now, as she applied the handbrake and the sun began to cast its first rays, she could feel the joy and excitement that her little brother and sister shared. She opened the car door and fell to her knees as both siblings ran towards her. It had been a long night, Emma had not slept one wink, but embracing Sammy and Jake for just a moment gave her more energy than ten hours' slumber.

"We've missed you so much," Sammy blurted.

"I missed you too," she replied, kissing first one then the other over and over. When the embrace finally ended, Emma climbed to her feet. Shaw, Hughes, Jules, Ruth, Raj and Talikha were all there to greet her with warm hugs and kind words. Lucy hung back from the crowd. She was the one who had brought Sammy and Jake. Mike had chosen not to come.

Eventually, when everyone was all hugged out, Lucy stepped forward and gave Emma a tight embrace. She did not speak. Neither knew what to say, Mike's absence spoke volumes.

"We're absolutely delighted to see you again, Em, but what is this?" Shaw said, gesturing to the vehicles and the emerging figures.

She broke her embrace with Lucy. "I came here to warn you. We were attacked … from the sea. The last I saw of the boats, they were heading north, in your direction."

"You're a little late," Shaw replied.

"What? How?"

"We got hit last night."

"When?"

"Just after dark."

"That's impossible."

"What do you mean?"

"That was when we got hit."

Shaw and Hughes looked at one another with raised eyebrows. "That's ... concerning," Shaw said.

"I see you haven't lost your ability to massively understate the severity of a situation."

"What can I tell you? It's a gift."

"Look, we're obviously going to have to talk about this, but right now my friends could do with food and somewhere to rest. They only got a couple of hours' sleep last night before heading up here."

"Okay. First things first," Lucy said, taking over. "Everybody heads across to the infirmary for a physical exam before they unpack as much as a pair of socks."

Emma nodded and turned to explain the procedure to the assembled crowd. Everyone climbed back into their vehicles and followed Hughes, who jumped into one of the Land Rovers and escorted them. Tabby lingered for a while, but Emma told her to go ahead while she and Lucy followed on foot. Sammy and Jake had given Emma another cuddle before being guided away by Ruth to start the preparations for breakfast at the village hall.

"So, Mike didn't want to see me?"

"Can you blame him?"

"No. Not really... And you?"

"I understand why you went, Emma. I don't like the way you did it. Mike's been carrying a lot of guilt around for a long time. He was already fragile, but when you disappeared ... when you left him that letter, he was beyond devastated."

They walked for a little while before Emma responded. "If I had it to do again, I'd do it differently."

"Look, I'm happy you're back. I'm really happy. You're like a sister to me. I love you, and I've been worried about you all this time, but I don't know how to fix you and Mike, and he's my priority."

"I understand."

"I don't think you do. He virtually shut down. He'd only just started to come around, and then all this happened," she said, waving her arms around. "We lost John last night."

A stark look swept over Emma's face. "What?"

"We lost John. He turned. Jake was with him."

Emma immediately looked back in the direction Sammy and Jake had disappeared. "But he's okay?"

"Mike found him halfway up a cliff face, he'd seen everything. Sammy and Wren were attacked by those things, but they managed to escape too. Mike and Jules found Beth wandering naked down the road in the middle of the night talking to herself, and now you show up."

"Thanks."

"I didn't mean it like that. All I mean is that he was just getting his head together and then everything turns upside down again. You might need to cut him some slack."

"I didn't come back to reopen old wounds, I just came back because I needed to warn you."

Lucy regarded Emma for several seconds. "Where do we go from here?"

"I don't know. I hadn't really thought past that."

"Well, let's get you checked over and then we can take it from there."

*

Jenny sat down beside Mike at the bar. "I suppose it's too early for a drink," she said, smiling.

"Funny, I was just thinking the same thing." Shaw had been across to give the two of them a quick brief before disappearing once again to make preparations for the council meeting.

"You do realise that you're going to have to go see her at some point."

"I know. I'm just psyching myself up."

Jenny reached across and placed her hand over Mike's. "Look, love, I don't pretend to know all the details or all the ins and outs of what went on between you two, but she was hurting. She was hurting, and she lashed out at the person closest to her then disappeared. When you lose someone you love, I mean really love, it can easily send you over the edge. I've seen it a thousand times before. Lucy told me what was in the letter."

Mike looked up at her sharply; then his look warmed. Jenny was family, she was like the aunt he could always confide in and who would always help, no wonder Lucy shared with her. "And?"

"And it was a crappy thing for you to have to deal with, but she wrote it because she was angry and she had to blame someone. When you see her, don't look for the girl who left that night, look for the girl who's here now."

Mike felt a weight on his thigh and looked down to see Meg, Jenny's dog, looking up at him with her calming, warm eyes. He could not help but smile and gently stroke her head. "I'm guessing that's her way of saying, 'Listen to Mum, she knows what she's talking about.'"

Jenny smiled. "She's got a wise head on her shoulders has my Meg."

"Thanks, Jen. It always helps talking to you."

"That's what I'm here for. We help each other."

The pair hugged tightly. "Well, I'd better go make an appearance."

"Just remember what I said."

Mike left the pub by the back door and walked through the wooded area to the campsite where the infirmary was situated. If he found Lucy, he would find Emma. One of the nurses was crossing from Ward Two to Ward Four.

"Lisa!" Mike called.

She was carrying a heavy box and Mike ran across to take it from her. She carried on walking and he walked alongside her. "Thanks, I can't remember the last time we had so many people to check."

"Have you seen Lucy?"

"I think I heard one of the girls say she was in Ward One."

The pair of them walked up the steps to the

entrance of Ward Four, and Lisa turned around. "I'll take the box now."

"No, it's fine, I'll take it in for you," he said, opening the outer door and pushing the inner one.

"Mike—"

There was a short, sharp scream, and Mike wasn't sure if it came from him or the naked woman he was now looking at, but he immediately turned around and handed the box to Lisa. "Sorry!"

"I tried to tell you. This is where we're doing the female exams."

"Yeah, I kind of figured that one out. Ward One, you say?" He barged out of the door, grateful to feel the fresh air against his red cheeks. This time, after climbing up the steps and heading through the outer entrance, he tapped lightly on the inner door and waited until it was answered.

Talikha opened it and smiled her usual polite smile. "Hello, Mike."

"Hi, Talikha. Where's my sister?"

"She and Lucy are in the examination room."

"Thanks," Mike said, walking through what used to be a mobile home's living room but was now a hospital ward, albeit with just the one occupant in for the time being. He nodded politely at the single patient and continued through to the short corridor leading to the private rooms. He knocked.

"Just a minute," called Lucy before opening the door. "Hi."

"Hi," Mike said before looking beyond her to Emma, who was buttoning up her jeans.

Lucy beckoned Mike through. "I'll leave you two alone," she said, brushing past him and closing the door behind her.

Emma fastened her top button then just stood looking at Mike, who stood looking back at her.

"Hi, Mike."

"Hi, Em." That was the exchange for a whole

minute while they continued to stand there, taking each other in. "Weather's been nice lately," he said with a smirk.

A smile broke onto Emma's face. "Yeah. Great for the garden."

"Any holidays planned?"

"Was thinking about going to Crete if I could get a reasonable flight." They both shared a snigger before their faces turned more serious. "I thought about coming back a thousand times."

"What stopped you?"

Emma sighed. "You." There was no humour in her voice or on her face.

"Oh. Right. Well, as long as we've sorted that out then."

"Look, this is hard. That night, when I left ... it was the right thing and the wrong thing. I needed to escape."

"From me?"

"Yes. From you. From this place. From myself. I just needed to get out of here. Sarah wasn't just my partner, Mike, she was my future. I didn't see a way forward without her. I couldn't see a way forward here. A big part of me blamed you, but I soon realised that if anyone was to blame, it was me, and then later I stopped blaming myself too. It was the right thing to do to go to Loch Uig, and even if I'd been here, I couldn't have stopped what happened. It was a shitty series of events, but ultimately the only one to blame was the bastard who pulled the trigger."

"So ... where does this leave us?"

"Us?"

"You and me. I mean are you coming back?"

Emma brushed her hands over her face. "God, Mike, I mean you heard what happened?"

"Yeah."

"And this is what you're worried about?"

"Look, Em, I haven't been ... right since you left. I've not been able to focus on anything. You're the person I've always been closest to and to wake up and just not have you there anymore, to wake up and read that letter it sent me into a bit of a spiral."

"I did say I'd always love you."

"Yeah, but you also said you didn't want to be around me, I made you feel guilty, while ever you were around me you'd never find peace, and that if I came looking for you, you'd probably shoot me."

"Jesus! What did you do, memorise the bloody thing?"

"Some things are harder to forget than others."

"Look, I know better than to make decisions in the heat of the moment now. Let's just take this a day at a time. Fair enough?"

Mike stared at his sister. "Fair enough."

Emma stood up. "So … you going to give me a hug or what?"

Mike walked across and wrapped his arms around her. The pair clutched each other tight, and after a while, Emma tried to pull back, but Mike still held on. She suddenly felt a tear from his cheek against her temple. "I was so scared I'd never see you again," he said in a broken voice.

Forgetting her thoughts of breaking their hug, she held him even tighter and placed her left hand on the back of his head, occasionally stroking his hair like a mother trying to comfort a child. "I'm sorry. I'm sorry for what I did." She couldn't help it. She was so sure she would remain strong but Emma burst into tears too. "I'm sorry, I'm sorry, I'm sorry." Her words turned into rasps as the weight of the last few months came crashing down on her.

"I love you, Em."

"I love you, but please stop crying; otherwise I won't be able to stop, and it will totally ruin my image when I go back out there and the people from Kyle see me."

Mike pulled back, his eyes bloodshot and streaming, but now there was the start of a smile on his face. "You've got an image?"

"Yeah! Everybody thinks I'm this badass, so I can't go out there looking all girlie holding on to my brother's arm, crying like a little kid."

"Sorry. I didn't realise I was cramping your style so much."

"It's okay. I'll let it go this once." She hugged him again and kissed his cheek. "Lucy said you'd had some problems." She started wiping away her tears.

Mike snorted. "Yeah, that's one way of putting it."

"She said that you went to dark places."

"It was more like the darkness came to me, and to be honest, I don't think it's finished with me just yet."

7

Noah walked the long corridor to the Jackson suite. There were lots of luxury suites on *The Ark*. When it was operating as a high-end cruise ship, most would set the average couple back about ten thousand dollars per night, but the Jackson suite made a few of them look like budget hotel rooms.

He opened the outer doors and entered the foyer. Despite the well-built interior, despite the thick oak panelling along the walls of the hallway and the even thicker oak door leading into the opulent lounge, Noah could still hear his wife screaming.

"Don't stop! Don't stop! Don't stop!"

The false smile that had adorned his face all day had vanished the moment he had begun his trek back to the palatial suite that was now his home. The flood had come as he had prophesied and as he had prophesied, it was not like the first. In reality, it had been a plague more than a flood, but *The Ark* had done what *The Ark* was meant to. It had saved the chosen ones. "Chosen" was probably a little bit of a stretch, but, nonetheless, the magnificent ship had been full to capacity the day after the news of the dead returning to life had broken; that was apocalypse capacity not vacationing capacity.

For the best part of ten years, *The Ark* and its sister vessels had been the most profitable cruise liners on the high seas. Some of the devout spent their life savings to go on an oceanic pilgrimage. Others, less interested in the religious aspects of the cruise and more interested in the deluxe surroundings, were choppered in and out to spend a few days here and a few days there. They had permanent cabins and suites, both wealthy private patrons and corporate bodies wanting to use the ship's more private enclaves to discuss deals that no one would want to discuss with the possibility of a parabolic microphone being pointed at them from a parked car or a playground. The corporations that had helped fund the building of the mammoth ships all received preferential treatment, with CEOs and senior board members able to use the facilities as and when they pleased.

The whole operation was ingenious. When Angel with her femme fatale smile and a business degree from Brown had knocked on doors to put forward a proposition, so many had come close to laughing; they agreed to the meetings nonetheless just so they could spend half an hour drooling over her from the other side of the boardroom table. It was only when they had their lawyers and accountants go over the proposals in depth that they understood what a goldmine the whole venture was. Genius was too small a word, and as charismatic and engaging as Noah Jackson was, it was clear that the brain of the operation was Angel.

Noah Jackson Ministries was a registered charity, and creative accountancy and some of the best lawyers in the country ran rings around the IRS, as Noah Jackson Ministries climbed into bed with a few of the largest and most sinister corporate entities on the planet. The fact that several of the activities that the good Christian vacationers could partake in were to do with delivering aid to *those poor starvin' folks in Africa and whatnot* meant that the lines between charity and commercial enterprise became blurred beyond recognition.

The whole concept was a smoke and mirrors magic trick that left every federal auditor scratching their heads and every TV evangelist weeping because they were several years too late to pull off the greatest legal heist of all time.

The Ark had done all that and more, but the one earnest purpose of the seafaring division of Noah Jackson Ministries had been to provide sanctuary for the uber-wealthy and their various entourages if the shit went down, regardless of what said shit may actually entail. Before D-Day, or Z-Day as some called it, there had been worldwide cyber-attacks causing financial chaos, worsening relations between the West and the Middle-East. The trade war with China had looked like it was going to escalate into something far more dangerous, and tensions between India and Pakistan were at an all-time high. Of course, if anything kicked off in a major way there, their neighbours would soon get involved, and then we'd really be off to the races.

So plans were put into place to mobilise whichever Jackson Ministries vessel was in port at the time of the pending apocalypse as an escape vessel. That term proved too simplistic though. It was far more than an escape vessel. As well as the vast food storage area that already existed, two decks were filled with tinned and dried food products as well as MREs in case things got really desperate. There were fuel tankers at various positions in the Atlantic just waiting; that was all they were doing year in year out. When the fuel was within a few months of its best-by date they would head to shore, unload and reload before going back out. The ship could hold up to five thousand people, but just less than two thousand, including catering staff and crew, were on board as it set sail.

The Ark was equipped with biohazard suits, Geiger counters, and stores of drugs to combat radiation sickness. There was a full deck of more basic accommodation where private security personnel could be housed to make sure that the ticket-buying patrons were still protected to the utmost in a post-apocalyptic world. There was even an armoury, which was fully equipped by Stenna/Holson, one of the world's biggest arms manufacturers and, coincidentally, a division of IFG Shipping and Holdings.

The day of the outbreak, some of the biggest names in the corporate world chartered flights to Texas. As chance would have it, it was *The Ark* rather than one of her sister ships that was sitting in the port of Texas City just waiting to take them to safety. The cost of a ticket on the USS Apocalypse? $17.4 million per man, woman and child, with an additional $12 million for each member of staff who took a space in the lower, less luxurious quarters; all this was payable before boarding, with a third of it up front as a non-refundable deposit at the time of booking.

Noah remembered that first day as if it were yesterday. He remembered how he had felt like the king of the world. He had watched the figures stack up on the computer screen, his eyes disbelieving. He didn't realise at the time, though, that it would all be worthless. He had expected some level of normality to resume after the outbreak had been contained, after the governments of the world had broken out their emergency plans and dealt with the disaster. But, alas, it was not to be.

They had picked up the broadcasts that the UK had remained unaffected shortly after they had set sail. They had got as close as they could, but the Royal Navy had made it very clear they were not welcome, so they travelled the Atlantic looking for safe harbour and finding none. A few months after the UK and Ireland stopped broadcasting, they began to make their way back to Europe.

All this time they had hoped to find somewhere to land, somewhere to start afresh, but all they had found was their food supplies, their medicines, their ... everything depleting more each day. Now, though, there was a slim hope ... no ... hope wasn't the right word. There was no hope for Noah. He realised soon after *The Ark* had set sail that he was nothing more than a puppet. He would have ended his life some time back, but, as ironic as it sounded, he had found some sort of religion.

He had prayed for forgiveness for what he had done, he had prayed a lot, and as much as he wanted to die, he could not bring himself to take his own life for fear that it would offend God. As he thought about it, it sounded ridiculous, but there it was nonetheless. Out of all the shit he had done, all the scams he had pulled, all the adultery, the strong-arming, the blackmailing, the cocaine, the prostitutes, male and female, the *relief* packages sent to African villages that had actually been arms shipments … out of all that he had done and was still doing, it was the taking of his own life that he was afraid would offend God.

"Err, Mr Jackson, I think Mrs Jackson is busy, sir," Doug said.

"Yes! Yes! Yes!" Angel continued to scream from inside the room.

Noah let out a sad laugh. "Either that or she's auditioning for a remake of *When Harry Met Sally*."

Both guards couldn't help but laugh too. "I'm sorry, sir," Doug said.

"What are you sorry about?" Noah replied. "You two are the only people who have had my back all these years. You're the only two who've never let me down. You've got nothing to be sorry about."

"Sir, are you okay?" Viktor asked with only a hint of the Russian accent he had when he first set foot in the United States.

"The world's come to an end. I'm stuck on a ship with the most over-privileged and insidious human beings who have ever walked this planet, and my wife's in there screwing the hired help. Why wouldn't I be okay?" he replied with a grim smile and opened the door.

The door to the bedroom was closed, which reinforced just how loud Angel's excited screams were. "Yes! Yes! Yes!"

Noah banged on the door three times. "Angel, you and your friend finish up in there, we need to talk." The noise immediately died down, and Noah walked across to the drinks cabinet. He pulled out a bottle of Jack Daniels Number 27 Gold. He unscrewed the top then poured a single, double, triple, quadruple before taking another glass and pouring a shorter measure for his wife.

He turned as the bedroom door opened and two young Hispanic men who he was almost sure had served him dinner the previous evening scurried out. Angel came strolling out a moment later. She wore just panties and a white shirt, open at the top. She smiled bitterly. Once she would have been mortified to have been caught in the act, but now she did not care.

"Your timing always was impeccable," she said, slithering over to where he was standing and picking up the glass. "This better be good."

"Troy thinks he's found it."

Angel's dead eyes suddenly sparkled with excitement. "What makes him think that?" she asked, taking a thirsty gulp.

"For a start, they repelled the attack."

"What? How?"

"Troy said they delivered the packages, the same way they always do, then, next thing they know, an old-fashioned air raid siren started screaming."

"That's it? You interrupted my ... entertainment for that?"

"He said that they scoped the place out beforehand. It's a long stretch of coastline, just one road, mainly cliffs down to the water, lots of cove and inlets. Hills, cliffs and woods to the back. Looks easily defendable, hence the fact they defended it."

Angel let out a sigh before sinking into the comfort of a well-cushioned armchair. She took another drink. "Still a lot of supposition on Troy's part. The place could be a stink hole."

SAFE HAVEN: IS THIS THE END OF EVERYTHING?

Noah took a drink from his glass. "Could be, but at least those people think it's a stink hole worth defending."

"Isn't the weather up here notoriously bad?"

"My daddy used to say there was no such thing as bad weather, just bad clothing," Noah replied with half a smile.

"Your daddy was an idiot, but this thing has been running on fumes for the longest time, and if we don't find somewhere soon, we're going to have all sorts of trouble on our hands. Troy has just about sucked dry every tank of HFO and MGO from here to Timbuktu."

"Well, listen to my sweet little Texan bluebonnet getting all nautical on me."

"Get Troy here, I wanna speak to him."

"Don't you think you should put something on first?"

"Don't worry, darlin', I'll make sure I'm wearing my best smile."

8

Shaw sat at the head of the tables and smiled as Emma took a seat beside Lucy. "Just like old times," he said.

Emma looked towards the space where Sarah used to sit. "Not quite."

"No. You're right. I'm sorry. It's good to have you back though."

"I agreed to sit in on this meeting because I thought I might be able to help. I don't know if this is going to be a long-term thing or not."

"Fair enough. We're just happy to have you here now. So, I hope nobody minds, but I've asked George to pop in to see us too," Shaw said, looking around at the faces. This group had made all the major decisions concerning Safe Haven over the last few months. They had steered the settlement from its shaky beginnings after the attack by Fry and his men to the thriving community they were today. They thought they had planned for everything, but they had never expected this ... seafaring marauders.

George walked into the village hall and nodded politely at all assembled. He placed a holdall on the floor then sat down in the vacant chair that Sarah had once occupied. "Morning," he said a little nervously. George was never one to be the centre of attention, and he coloured a little as he looked around the pushed together tables. Raj, Jenny, Lucy, Emma, Hughes, Jules, Ruth and Shaw were all friends, more than friends, but he still felt uncomfortable as they all watched him take his seat.

"Morning, George. Thank you for joining us. I've asked you here this morning—"

"You're wanting to expand our navy," George said with a thin smile on his face.

"You can read me like a book."

"Actually, it's something I've been thinking about ever since last night."

"And?"

"Well," he said, reaching into his inside pocket and pulling out a tin of tobacco and a pipe. "Anybody mind?" he asked, looking around the table.

"How the fuck do you still have tobacco for that thing after all this time?" Jules said as George took a pinch of brown flakes out of the tin and pressed it into the chamber.

"Shaw, Hughes, Mike … whenever any of them go out on scavenging missions, if they happen across any, they're always good enough to bring some back for me."

"They never fuckin' bring anything back for me."

"It's baffling, isn't it? And you're always such delight to be around too."

"Fuck you, old man." Everyone around the table laughed and suddenly George felt a little less self-conscious.

"Anyway, as I was saying, in the short term, given that our greatest threat is more than likely to come from the water now, rather than the land, we can take two of the mangonels from the Dead Man's Pass approach, leaving just one in place there. If you think you can scramble up a couple more fishing boats, we could get them fitted on board and have them positioned equal distances apart up and down the coast. That's in the short term."

"Not really much of a defence, but go on, what are

your longer-term ideas?" Shaw asked.

George reached into the holdall and picked out a thick, tall, antiquated, hard-backed book. He stood up and walked over to where Shaw and Hughes were sitting, placing it on the table in front of them. Several pages were bookmarked, and George immediately flipped to the page he wanted. The right-hand side was filled with tiny writing, but the left page had a diagram. "Here we go."

"A trebuchet?" Shaw said.

"No. A dozen trebuchets, and these," George replied, flicking to another bookmarked page. He flattened it out, revealing a title in big black lettering that said, "Siege Crossbows." "I've thought about it and materials aren't an issue. I could use Richard and David to help me with finalising the design and a few able bodies to help put these things together."

Shaw looked at the crossbows then flipped back to the trebuchets. "You really think you could manufacture these in bulk?"

"Bulk might be a bit of a stretch, but a dozen of each isn't out of the realms of possibility."

"That's a lot of work, George," Jules said.

George took a long suck on his pipe and released another plume of smoke into the air. "It is, but if you let me handpick my team, I can get it done. After all, this is Safe Haven. We don't want to get sued for false advertising, do we?"

The joke received polite smiles, but then Jules leaned across and took hold of George's hand. "I need you to promise me that you're not taking on too much."

George clamped the mouthpiece of the pipe between his teeth and placed his other hand over hers. "I promise you, poppet, I'll be fine. Between you and Wren, I know I can't get away with much, so I'll make sure I don't overdo anything."

"Where is Wren?"

"She went into the woods with Wolf."

"Is she okay? I mean after yesterday. That must have been a hell of a shock."

"Wren has always been special. She's always been self-reliant. More than anything, she was angry with herself."

"Angry! Why?"

"She'd got out of practice with her crossbows."

"Seriously?"

"She said that if she'd been any slower, it could have meant her and Sammy's life. So, first thing this morning, she took Wolf and disappeared with her rucksack."

"She's quite a girl."

"You have no idea."

"So, when do you think you could start work on these?" Shaw asked.

"Are you saying I can have who I want?"

"You can have who you want and what you want. This is our number one priority."

"In which case, right now," he said, picking the book up. "I'll go find Richard and David, and we'll get started."

*

Troy made most women swoon but not Angel. With her, it was the other way around. She knew he would do whatever she asked. They had struck up a relationship soon after *The Ark* had left port on its final cruise. He worked as the head of security for an oil tycoon and his wife. He was so highly regarded and trusted that rather than being given one of the lower deck rooms where most employees resided, he was gifted a suite.

He was South African by birth and had been in the military for a short time then went to work for one of the world's biggest arms manufacturers before finally becoming Lyle Brannigan's personal protector. He knew and guarded all the tycoon's biggest secrets. He headed the team that protected Brannigan's family, and his chiselled chin, wide shoulders, suntanned skin and thick head of black hair with distinguished grey flecks running through it had women's hearts racing. He had become one of Angel's playthings for a while, but then she had tired of him despite the fact he had fallen for her in a big way.

He had regaled her with stories of his life and achievements. He told her about how he had scaled Everest, Kayaked down Banana Falls, and spent six months leading a fleet of tall ships around Europe in one of the biggest exhibitions of its kind. He had led a remarkable life, or so he tried to make her believe. But Angel had been told lots of tall tales by men who had tried to win her favour. Rarely had she believed them, but when it turned out that she had an opportunity to put one of Troy's claims to the test and it rang true, she developed a new respect for the man.

Now Troy led a fleet of six tall ships for Angel. When fuel began to dwindle to dangerously low levels, it looked like all hope was lost on board *The Ark*. When they happened across an exhibition fleet in Plymouth, Angel decided to test Troy's metal. He had become her right-hand man, training crews to sail and do whatever tasks were required to make sure life aboard the luxury cruise ship stayed as comfortable as possible for the millionaire and billionaire inhabitants. Brannigan was happy to release him from his services as he was one of a growing number of people who arrived at the conclusion that Troy might be the one man who could save them all.

Angel reached the loading dock to find the door already open and the gangway in position.

"Will this take long? I hate being down here. It's so grimy."

"Do I need to remind you it was you who wanted the meeting and, trust me, you wouldn't want this meeting on board *The Ark*," Troy replied.

"You don't need to remind me of anything, sugar, let's just get this over with."

Troy waited by the exit and chivalrously let Angel

step onto the makeshift bridge first. She gripped the two handrails with all her strength and tried not to look down as the waves lapped a few metres below. When she reached the other side, two burly crewmen took hold of her hands. She recognised them as former crewmen on board *The Ark*, and they both nodded respectfully as they helped her onto the deck.

The movement of the water was much more noticeable on board the *Manticore,* and it took Angel a few moments to stop the queasiness in her stomach.

"Let's head below then, shall we?"

"If we must," Angel replied. Even when something distasteful was her idea, she always protested and had a face like she was sucking on a sourball. It helped maintain the image that she was just an innocent and all the bad stuff, the dirty and dark deeds were on someone else.

"We'll go to my cabin first, for a quick chat," Troy said as they went below deck.

"A chat, Troy. That is all we are going for, mind." They entered, and Troy locked the door behind them. Angel sat down at a writing desk while her host poured them two drinks. "Nice little place you got yourself here," she said as he handed her a glass.

Troy looked around the cabin. "It serves its purpose. How are you, Angel?"

"Sugar, how I am depends very much on what you're going to tell me."

A momentary sadness swept over Troy's face. He had hoped for a little warmth … a little something from Angel, but it was clear that he was nothing but a hired hand. He produced a map and flattened it out on the desk. "There," he said, pointing to a village.

"Lonbaig? Well, that looks tiny."

"It's not just the village." He pointed to two more points on the map. "Here and here are the only routes in or out. The village is the hub, but it's the whole coastline. I had spotters across there before our attacks. They told me they'd seen all sorts of planting operations and building going on. They're developing it, growing it. Whoever lives here knows the geographical significance of the place."

"Spotters?"

"Who do you think I am? Do you honestly think I would just launch an attack without finding out what I was attacking first?"

"Well tell me, Troy, how did that work out for you this time?"

"They were more resourceful than we expected, that's all."

Angel's eyes narrowed a little as she looked at her host. "And houses? There are enough houses?"

"Plenty for what we need," Troy replied. "This is it. This is our one chance to finally have a base, settle down." He finished his drink and poured another. "You want a refill?"

"No. I want you to stop wasting my time and tell me how this is the answer to all of our prayers."

He downed his second drink, and this time the sound of the glass slamming onto the desk made Angel jump a little. A smile unlike any she had seen before crept onto Troy's face. "I don't believe for a second you haven't thought about this up until now, but I know you, Angel." He filled his glass again. "I know you better than you think. You're clever. You want me to say this as if it's my idea, but it's been your idea all along."

"I don't think I care for your tone."

"I don't think I care what you care." He took another sip from his glass and let out a long breath. "*The Ark* is a floating tomb. Most people on there don't have any skills that will help in this new world. Hell, I've been on hunting trips with a lot of them and the animals had to be drugged for them to make a kill. They might be big men and women around the board room table, but out there they're like newborns. Without me and my kind to protect them, they won't last a week."

"What are you saying?"

Troy shot to his feet, picked up his glass and flung it across the room. It smashed against the wooden wall and the remaining thick amber fluid drizzled down the oak panelling. "No more games, Angel, you know goddamn well what I'm saying."

"Calm yourself, Troy, I won't be spoken to like—"

Troy yanked her from her chair and pinned her to the door. She let out a stifled scream, and his face neared hers. She could smell his whisky-soaked breath and realised that he'd probably been drinking before she had arrived as well. How many times had this happened to her before she became the darling of the religious right? She had left that life behind; she had left those men behind. She brought her knee up hard and connected with Troy's testicles. As he started to double over, she pushed forcefully with both hands, and he fell backwards, banging hard against the floor. She turned and had the door half open when Troy shouted, "We were always your escape route."

She paused, opened the door a little wider then closed it again. "I don't know what you mean," she said weakly, pressing her forehead against the thick wood.

"Oh, don't play the innocent southern belle with me, sweetheart. That's not the you I fell in love with."

Angel's mouth dropped open a little in surprise. She always knew Troy had feelings for her, but love? She turned around to look at him as he struggled to get to his feet. "I—"

"You want me to say it? Fine, I'll say it. Since the second we set sail from Texas and you realised that this was the end of times you've been looking for an out. You thought that filling your life with hedonistic pleasure, screwing every man with a nice smile would be enough, but you soon realised that you were on the ship of the damned, surrounded by people you despised. Oh sure, you could relate to the workers, the grease monkeys, the bodyguards, the lower echelons of *The Ark*'s society, because that's where you came from. But the ones who expect to continue living the life of luxury, the ones who expect things to be different for them, even when the world outside has gone to hell, you hate them as much as I do."

"They're not all like that," she protested weakly.

"Yes, they are. And the cracks are already beginning to show. That palace has been on the waves for nearly three years now. It's nothing short of a miracle that you've kept it going so long, but I know how the supplies are dwindling, how the special reserves have run dry. I know there's a thin veneer of tranquillity, but underneath panic is setting in. Me and my fleet have brought you food and supplies. We've kept *The Ark* chugging along for months now, but you and I both knew that the second we found somewhere to escape to we were going to abandon ship and the plans didn't include your husband or his overprivileged friends. Oh, don't get me wrong, I understand why you wanted him keeping in the loop; we needed to throw some bones to them so the mutiny didn't begin until our plan was in motion. But—"

"That's—"

"True. Every last word of it." A smile broke through Angel's steely gaze realising there was little point in keeping the pretence up any longer.

"So this is the place?" she asked weakly.

"This is the place."

"Then sober up, Troy. We've got work to do."

9

It was late afternoon when Wren and Wolf began their journey home. Wren had done the only thing she knew how to do when things went bad. She had tried to hone her skills, to train, to better herself so if she was ever faced with a situation like the previous day again she would be prepared.

It was at times like this that she missed her sister the most. They had always been there to support each other when this frightening new world had become too much. She loved her grandad, but he did not understand her as Robyn did … had.

Wolf happily walked by Wren's side, always vigilant, always protective. Barring yesterday, there had been little to fear in Safe Haven since her arrival but now... She looked at her German Shepherd and smiled appreciatively. "You'd have taken them down, wouldn't you, boy?"

Wolf cocked his head to glance up at her then returned his eyes to the treescape ahead. Wren knew these woods as well as anyone, and it was not long before the tall pines became a little less dense and finally broke, giving way to a view of the shimmering sea.

Today had been unusual. Today, she had not

returned with bags full of mushrooms or wild garlic or hazelnuts or any of the delights she and Sammy often brought back. Today had been about familiarising herself with her crossbows again. Once she started the target practice, she soon fell back into the swing of things.

The two of them made their way to the road and followed it towards home. A motor suddenly interrupted the calm. "Need a ride?" Mike asked, pulling up beside them.

"I'm sure that line used to work for you in Yorkshire, but not here I'm afraid."

Mike broke into a smile. "That's pretty quick for you. Have you been practising that one?"

"Of course. I spend my life thinking of funny things to say just to impress you. It gives me a purpose."

"I thought something would have to. So, do you want a lift or not?"

"No thanks. I'm enjoying the walk."

Mike nodded. It was another warm day, and there were few places in Britain more picturesque. "Are you okay?"

"Yeah. It's just a nice day, and I'd prefer to—"

"No. I mean after last night."

"I'm as okay as someone can be after something like that."

"If ever you want to talk, I'm here."

"Talk to you? You want to be my therapist?"

"I haven't met a therapist yet who I haven't wanted to punch. No, I was thinking more as a friend."

"So, you want to be my friend?"

"Well, I figured you should have at least one. Y'know, other than Wolf."

"And I should pick the psycho with a short fuse and a penchant for beating the crap out of people who piss him off? You think I'm that hard up?"

Mike laughed again. "Well, the offer's there if you change your mind."

He was about to release the handbrake when Wren blurted, "How are Beth and Annie?"

"Not great."

"Who'd do something like that?"

Mike turned off the engine and climbed out of the car, walking around to the passenger side and leaning against the bonnet. "I thought after everything you'd been through you'd be beyond this."

"Beyond what?"

Mike crouched down and began to stroke Wolf. "Beyond being surprised by what levels people can sink to."

"I…" She broke off and turned away, doing her best not to cry.

Mike stood up and eased her back round towards him. "What is it?"

"It was a close thing last night. Sammy and me, we could have been finished."

"But you weren't."

"Yeah, but it was a close thing, and…"

"And what?"

"It's hard, Mike. Even for a community like ours. As well organised as we are, as well prepared as we are, it's hard."

"I know."

"No, you don't. My sister being out there, facing all of this, it scares the hell out of me. There's part of me that knows she can deal with anything and there's another part that…"

Mike gently wiped the tears from Wren's face with his thumbs. "Listen to me. You and I are very similar in lots of ways, Wren."

"If you're trying to make me feel better, that's not a great way to start."

Mike laughed, and Wren smiled despite her tears. "We don't accept defeat. We always fight and carry on fighting even when most people think it's a lost cause. We both understand the reality of what it's like out there, but you and I will never give up, no matter what the odds. I'm guessing Robyn will be the same, and that's why you should never give up on her. Yes, there are a lot of shitty people out there. It's dangerous, it's scary, and it's tough, but provided you keep going, there's always a way, there's always hope." Wren sniffed and wiped her nose on her sleeve. "Nice. Which finishing school did you go to again?"

Wren sniffed and stuck her middle finger up. "The Edinburgh College of Screw You!"

"You've been hanging around with Jules, haven't you?"

They both smiled. "Thank you, Mike."

"For what?"

"When I talk about my sister to most people, I can tell they're just humouring me. They don't believe she could still be out there after all this time, but when I talk to you, I don't feel that way."

"Wren, if your sister is half the person you are, then she's still out there somewhere."

"Y'know, as far as psychos go, you're by far my favourite."

"Wow, that might be the nicest thing you've ever said to me."

"Don't get used to it; I'm having a weak moment."

Mike stepped forward and hugged her tightly. At first, she went rigid; then she reciprocated, placing both her arms around him. "Sometimes, when people say things are impossible, it's because they don't have the guts to face what needs to be done to make them possible. You do and Robyn will too." He released his grip and got back into the car.

Wren remained standing there, watching the vehicle disappear out of sight. Her palms were sweaty and her heart was thumping fast in her chest. Eventually, she broke her gaze from the road and looked down at Wolf. "Stop looking at me like that." The German Shepherd just tilted his head and made a high-pitched whine. "Don't play innocent; I know what you were thinking. I don't like him that way." Wolf tilted his head the other way and whined again. "Oh, shut up."

*

Angel watched Noah get ready in front of the dressing room mirror. She felt little but sickness and revulsion for him now and wondered if, had this apocalypse never happened, she would have run out on him. She had just come out of the shower and lay on the bed, naked, a large bath sheet beneath her to make sure she did not get the duvet wet. She still had a great body, and most men would not have been able to resist the temptation, but Noah was not most men. He saw past the outward good looks of Angel. He saw her for what she truly was.

"Why do you still bother with all this?" she asked, meeting his eyes in the mirror.

He was halfway through knotting his tie, and he stopped suddenly. "If I had now until the end of time, I could not make you understand."

"Oh really? Try me."

He swivelled around on his chair and looked at her. "You and I have done an awful lot of bad things in our time, honeybunch. Things that have probably carved us a nice little cradle in hell next to the devil himself."

"Oh my! Well, aren't you just becomin' like a poet in your old age?" she said with a mocking smile on her face.

He smiled too, bitter and condescending. "I'm becoming ... have become a lot of things. I've become wiser. I know when to give up on lost causes too." He turned back around to the mirror.

"So go on, shug. Impart this wisdom on your wife. After all, that's what marriages are all about ... sharing."

He picked up the Bible from his dressing table. "Decades ago, this used to mean something to me, but the more I preached from it, the less it meant until it became nothing but a meal ticket. More than a meal ticket, it became a massive enterprise. We expanded and franchised and became incorporated up the wazoo. We got phone lines and websites and feet on the ground doing nothing but collecting donations in return for eternal salvation. And did I believe that's what those people would get? Hell no. I came to believe in nothing but making more and more money. This," he said, waving the Bible up and down like a bird flapping its wings, "was just a means to an end."

"Oh, and let me guess, now you've found Jesus," she said, giggling to herself.

He turned back around, looked in the mirror, and stared into his own dead eyes. "That's right, Angel, laugh it up."

"So, every night you go out there and give your evening sermon to smaller and smaller audiences, only now you've found God. Do you honestly think these captains of industry and their families see this as anything other than what it is? You know why people booked the apocalypse package on this ship, and it was nothing to do with finding eternal salvation. Oh sure, you've got a few believers, but each day that goes by, each dish that's scrubbed from the menu, you get less and less people showing up until it's just going to be you preaching to an empty auditorium. These people are just about as far away from any sense of what that book is about as the devil himself."

Noah put the Bible back down and finished knotting his tie. "As I said, you wouldn't understand." He turned in his seat to look at her. "There are some good people on this ship. I know I'm not among them, but now, finally, I think I can help them. I think I can help them find peace and help them find the salvation they need, and if I can do that, then maybe my life won't have been such a waste after all. Maybe I can at least do something good before I nestle down in that special place in Hell that's been reserved for you 'n' me."

Angel burst out laughing. It was not mocking laughter; it was general hilarity, which hurt Noah even more. Her augmented breasts jiggled up and down as her stomach heaved. "Oh my, that is just priceless."

Noah remembered back to the time he had first seen her in his father's shoe shop. He had been stunned mute by her beauty, but now all he felt was disgust. He knew that the heart that beat beneath those warm, supple breasts was colder than one of Neptune's moons. "I'm happy I can bring you amusement." He stood up, put on his jacket, picked up the Bible and went to the door. "I'll see you at dinner," he said, walking out of the room. He could still hear her laughter as he walked down the corridor.

Angel continued laughing for a full minute after Noah had left. She remained there on the bed for a while, as naked as the day she was born, and then suddenly jumped to her feet. She had another meeting with Troy, this one would not be like any other, and it was best that it came before dinner than after.

Angel never just threw on clothes. Everything she wore was purposeful, considered, calculated. She put on a pair of tight-fit Vivienne Westwood jeans and placed a gold chain around her neck. The pebble-sized locket dangled just above the shadow that denoted the beginning of her ample cleavage. She walked across to her wardrobe and selected a white Reiss blouse, put it on and then made sure that enough buttons were open so that people's eyes would be drawn to the sparkling locket. It was a carefully crafted ensemble, just classy enough to remain on the right side of sexy without looking trampy. She smiled in the mirror, a well-practised smile, the one that wowed moguls and statesmen alike. She spent a few more minutes toying with the idea of wearing a pair of heels but in the end opted for a pair of six-hundred-dollar Prada pumps.

Finally, she was all set, and she went to the door, turning to look at the room before heading out. How many more nights would she need to spend here?

Angel made her way down to the loading bay. It was a lot quieter than it had been earlier on in the day. This time Troy was not waiting for her when she arrived, but, instead, one of his burly crewmen greeted her.

"Ma'am," he said, nodding his head.

"Why hello, and who might you be?"

The man was in his late twenties, well-built, well-tanned as if he had spent most of his life outdoors. "I'm Jacobs. The captain asked me to escort you to his cabin."

"The captain? Well, we'd better not keep the captain waiting now, darlin', had we?" she said, looking Jacobs up and down.

The younger man flushed red. "Err, no ma'am. If you'd follow me, please."

"Oh, I'd just about follow you anywhere, sweetheart." Jacobs laughed nervously and led Angel across the short gangway.

He took her below deck and knocked three times on the door to Troy's cabin. "Come in," came the response.

Jacobs opened the door and ushered Angel through with his hand. "Why, thank you, darlin'," she said, stepping inside.

The door closed again behind her. Troy was pouring whisky into three waiting glasses. "I'm sure you've met Beatrice before," he said.

Angel looked at the young woman perched on the chair she had occupied earlier in the day. "Mrs Jackson? I didn't realise you were ... joining us." The young woman turned bright red with embarrassment.

"Oh, don't you worry your pretty head, sugar. I'm just here for a quick meet with Troy, and then I'll leave you two to your evening." She looked down at the floor. "Well, I know things are hard, but have things got so bad that we have to have plastic sheeting instead of carpet?"

The young woman laughed politely. "Troy was just telling me how the cabin was going to get a new coat of varnish tomorrow and he didn't want it dripping."

"Uh-huh, well, I'm sure Troy just thinks of everything, doesn't he?"

"Here we go, ladies," he said, handing the two women glasses with a thick dark purple liquid in them.

"Now what in heaven's name is this?" Angel asked, locking eyes with Troy.

"Well, now. This is my own special recipe blackberry whisky sour."

Angel did not relinquish her stare. She looked beyond Troy's brown eyes, beyond his false smile and deep into his soul. She brought the glass up to her lips and paused, sniffing at its contents. Finally, she took a drink. "Well now, isn't that just the most divine thing that's ever been put in a glass? Where's yours, hun?"

A smile threatened to appear on Troy's face as he finally broke eye contact with Angel and walked back to pick his drink up. "I prefer my whisky straight up," he said, grabbing his glass and taking a drink.

The two of them turned towards Beatrice, who was just watching the thick purple liquid as it swilled slowly around the glass. "What's wrong, sugar?" Angel asked.

"Err, I'm not really much of a drinker. My daddy doesn't really approve of ladies drinking."

"Well, hasn't your daddy heard o' something called women's rights? What's good for the goose is good for the gander, sweetheart, and let me tell you, I've seen your daddy fall down drunk plenty. Maybe he's just worried you'll like it too much and he'll have to share."

Beatrice laughed. She had a nice laugh, a sweet laugh. She was twenty-two years old, very precocious, very innocent, very easily led, and as she pictured her father falling down drunk, she raised her glass. "What's good for the goose," she said and took three big gulps before wiping her mouth with the back of her hand. It took a second for her taste buds to catch up, and her eyes widened. "Goodness gracious."

"Ain't that something?" Angel asked.

"It most certainly is that," Beatrice replied, taking another big gulp. She rolled her tongue around her mouth and smacked her lips together. "It's got kind of a coppery aftertaste."

"Here," said Troy, throwing a glance towards Angel, "let me put a little more syrup in that for you." He walked across and tipped the blackberry syrup bottle, making the drink turn an even deeper purple.

Beatrice took another drink. "Mm, that's better. Sweet." She continued to look at the drink like a child who had just discovered a magic potion.

Angel's brow creased, and she looked towards Troy who just shrugged his shoulders. "So darlin', how do you feel after your first grown-up drink?"

"Feels warm going down. I can feel it. It feels … nice."

"Yeah, that's how it's meant to feel."

Beatrice took another drink and smiled. "It feels as though—" Suddenly she couldn't talk any more. She looked at the glass in her hand, but now it seemed as though it were a million miles away, almost as if her hand didn't belong to her anymore. Troy said something, then Angel said something, but they seemed to be speaking another language. Beatrice watched as the glass was plucked from her fingers by Troy's big sun-browned hand. *Where was he going with her drink?* Then that warm feeling, it wasn't as warm anymore. In fact, it was downright cold ... freezing. The iciness started deep inside somewhere, she couldn't quite pinpoint it. *Was this what it was like to get drunk?* She thought she liked it at first, but now she was pretty sure she didn't. She didn't like it at all. With the cold came fear, fear the likes of which she had never known before. It was as if something was in her body with her, something dark, something evil. Every second it was getting stronger, this feeling that something didn't belong, this feeling of being invaded, violated. *What was happening to her?* She was losing herself, to what she did not know, but she was definitely disappearing like the sun behind a cloud. No, like the moon. The frigid, desolate, lonely moon up in the sky. That was it. She was like the moon being cloaked in an eternal biting blackness. She felt a single tear run down her cheek, she felt it kiss the corner of her mouth as it rolled onto her chin. Then Beatrice didn't feel anything ... ever again.

"So how long is this meant to take?" asked Angel, completely unaware of what was going on inside Beatrice.

"Shh!" Troy said, holding a finger up and staring towards the young woman sitting on the bed.

Beatrice ... what was Beatrice, remained there, like a sculpture. The colour had drained from her skin in little more than the blink of an eye, and the iciness that had enveloped her now hung in the room like freezing fog. A shiver went down Angel's spine as she looked towards the young woman half fascinated, half horrified. Troy reached for the long-bladed hunting knife from his belt and stood in readiness.

The pale figure on the bed coughed once, twice, and each time blood spluttered from its mouth then it closed its eyes. It remained there a moment longer, and when it opened them, they were no longer human eyes. Shattered ebony pupils danced on the surface of milky grey orbs as the creature first turned its head towards Troy then Angel. Spoilt for choice, uninhibited by the weapon in Troy's hand, the Beatrice thing pounced.

Angel screamed. It was the first time she had ever been up close and personal with one of these things. The prospect of Troy failing and leaving her alone in the cabin with what was, in essence, a true monster scared her half to death, but it was a groundless fear. Troy had dealt with his fair share of monsters. He brought the knife up in a blur, and the creature fell like a goose shot from the sky. The body landed on the plastic-covered floor with a heavy thump, and it was all over.

Troy wiped the blade off and returned it to the sheath on his belt. Blood had splattered over his hand, and he quickly washed it in the sink, over and over, to make sure there was not a single trace left.

Angel just stood, looking down in horror at the dead creature then up towards Troy. "I thought you said they didn't bleed."

"No. I said they hardly bleed. When they're freshly turned they bleed a lot more than ones that have been turned for a while." He finished cleaning his hands, stepped over what had been Beatrice and walked over to where Angel was standing.

She looked at him, finished the rest of her drink and handed the empty glass over. "Want another?"

"What do you think?"

"Why did you kill her? Why didn't you use her like the others?"

"You think we gather them one by one? We lure a bunch of them into a cage and trap them there until we need them. Gathering them one by one is a surefire way to get your ass bitten." He handed the glass back to her. This time the drink was amber, no blackberry.

Angel gulped it down. "Well, at least we know it works."

"And then some. So, it's roughly a minute from ingestion to BOOM!"

"How much did you use?"

He reached under a serviette and pulled out a syringe with red fluid in it. "Not much."

"If their blood is coagulated, how can you get it in a syringe?"

"He opened his wardrobe and brought out a blender. Smoothie anyone?"

"I think I'm going to be sick."

"Well, if you are, do it now, while the plastic's still down."

"Ugh!" Angel held her stomach. "What do we say to Mr Urqhart when he asks where his daughter is?"

"It's not really a big deal, is it? We're notching about two suicides a week at the moment. Poor Beatrice just couldn't take it anymore."

"How the hell did you get her down here in the first place?"

"She's been sweet on me for some time. I asked her if she'd like to come on a tour of the ship and she couldn't get down here fast enough."

"What happens to her now?"

"Now she becomes fish food," he said with a grin.

"What are you so happy about?"

"Why, your accent darlin'," he replied, mimicking her. "Now that you're good and scared, it's all gone and disappeared."

"Fuck you, Troy." She gave him a glare then mellowed a little. "So, where do we go from here?"

"Well, I'm heading there with a few of my people. We're going to be poor refugees. If these suckers are still taking in strangers after all this time, I'm going to take advantage of that. Get a feel for the place, figure out the best way to do this," he said, pointing to Beatrice.

"You mean like tainting a water supply or something?"

"No. We don't want to be poisoning the things we'll need when the place is ours, but if we study them for a few days, we'll figure out exactly what we have to do."

"Okay, but I'm going with you."

"What's the matter, Angel? Don't you trust me?"

"Not for a second."

10

"Help!" Lucy gasped as she woke from another nightmare. She had been having them for a few days, ever since John had passed. She waited for a moment before reaching out to feel Mike's warmth. Her hand found nothing but cold bedclothes. She reached for her torch and switched it on. Mike's side of the bed was empty, and Lucy began to get an uneasy feeling. A few months before, Mike had suffered some kind of breakdown. He had begun to hallucinate. One night, Lucy had gone downstairs to find him in conversation with Fry. She had not admitted witnessing it until long after the event, but now she was worried she was going to find the same thing happening again.

She made her way down the stairs quietly. A sinking feeling consumed her as she approached the living room. She stood in the doorway for a moment and saw Mike sitting in the same chair he had that night she had found him. Only this time, he was not talking; he was silently looking out of the patio doors over the bay.

"Don't worry, I'm alone, Fry had an appointment," he said.

"Funny boy. Couldn't you sleep?"

"No."

"What's on your mind?" Lucy asked, walking into the room and sitting in the other armchair.

"I was thinking about John and how quickly everything can just turn upside down."

"Life's always been like that, Mike. That's why you need to make the most of every minute."

"Yep, that's pretty much what I was thinking," he said, picking up a glass and taking a drink.

"What you got?" He handed it over to her and she sniffed the contents before taking a drink. "Jesus. It's like paint stripper."

"Haven Arms vodka."

"I think I've just gone blind in one eye," Lucy replied, taking another drink and handing the glass back to him.

"You get used to it." The two of them sat in comfortable silence for a moment.

"Well, as long as you're okay, I'll head back to—"

"There is something else."

"What? What is it?"

"When we went to Loch Uig, do you remember our conversation in the woods?"

Lucy took back the glass and took another drink. "We had lots of conversations."

"There was one in particular."

"Look, Mike, there was a good chance we weren't going to come out of that alive, and I was never going to hold you to something—"

"So you do remember."

"Getting a marriage proposal isn't something you really forget, no matter how it happens."

"I suppose not."

"But as I said, Mike, it's—"

"I couldn't go through with it," he blurted.

"You don't have to explain."

"No, I do. I couldn't go through with it, not without Em here. I couldn't go through with it knowing that I'd driven her away, not sure if she had started a new life somewhere or whether she was in a gutter at the side of the road. I just couldn't."

"Let's change the subject, there's no need to apologise, I understand."

"No, you don't," he said, standing up and walking across to where Lucy was sitting. He crouched down in front of her. "I couldn't go through with it then, but since she came back, it's been on my mind, constantly. I want us to get married." For a moment, Lucy couldn't breathe. She sat there in shock just looking at Mike in the moonlight. Her eyes were as wide as saucers as she did everything she could not to cry. Mike got down on one knee and pulled something out of his dressing gown pocket. He slid it onto the fourth finger of Lucy's left hand. "It wasn't really much of a proposal last time, but Luce, will you marry me?"

Now Lucy could not hold back anymore, and the tears began to flood from her eyes. She looked down at her finger to see it was real, a gold ring with a large sapphire, black in the moon's rays, set between two diamonds. It was beautiful. She shuffled forward, threw her arms around Mike and squeezed. As the side of her face pressed tightly against his, he could feel her warm tears against his skin. "Yes, yes, yes, yes," she whispered then squeezed even tighter.

It was several minutes before she managed to bring herself under control. "Are you okay?" Mike asked.

"I'm way better than okay."

"Luce, I'm sorry I waited so long to do this. I'm sorry you haven't had the easiest ride with me, but I promise I'll make it up to you."

She wiped the glistening streaks from her eyes and cheeks with the heel of her palm. "You don't need to make anything up to me. I wouldn't have stuck around if I didn't want to."

"I love you."

"I love you too."

Lucy stretched her fingers and angled her hand towards the moonlight. "It's beautiful. It fits perfectly."

"I thought it would, but just in case, I've got the same ring in about five different sizes."

"How long have you had this?"

"A while … months. I got them when we were on a scavenger mission. One of the houses we hit in Garve was owned by a jeweller and there was all sorts of stuff. These were all I was interested in though. Like I said, Luce, I just needed Em to be here. It wouldn't feel right doing it without her."

"We can't announce this yet," Lucy said, the smile disappearing from her face for the first time in minutes.

"I know. But it can be our secret. Well, ours and Jenny's."

"Jenny knows?"

"Jenny was the one who helped me with the ring. She told me what I needed to look for."

"When was this?"

"Actually, it was before Loch Uig."

Lucy giggled. "Okay, any more surprises?"

"Err, no."

"So, we'll wait for a few days. It wouldn't be right announcing this after Beth's just lost her brother. But then I want to shout it from the rooftops."

"Jen said she'd throw us an engagement party, but—"

"But nothing. We're having an engagement party."

"You're going to be one of these high-maintenance women, aren't you?"

"Damn straight," Lucy replied, taking another long drink and handing the glass back to Mike.

Mike climbed to his feet and went to sit in the other armchair. "I'll ask Bruiser to be my best man."

Lucy stood up. "We can sort out all the finer details

later. Right now, we need to get to bed."

"I'm going to stay up a little longer," Mike replied.

"Too bad."

"Why?"

"Remember what happened when you gave me *Charlotte's Web*?"

Mike remembered back to that night in Candleton when they had made love into the early hours of the morning. "Erm, not really a night I'm going to forget."

"Well, that was for a book. Just think how grateful I'd be for a sapphire ring," she said, brushing his shoulder seductively as she walked across to the doorway.

"Y'know what, now you come to mention it, I think I will call it a night." He almost jumped to his feet and followed her up the stairs.

*

"You look tired, Lucy. You have a bad night?" Jenny said with a smirk.

The village hall was already half full as the traditional communal breakfast was served. Safe Haven had never turned away refugees. Some had spent just a few days before moving on elsewhere, others had wanted to settle down and build a life, but all were welcome. "Oh, aren't you the funny one. Does Ruth know?"

"You should know me better by now. Mike asked me to keep it quiet, so I haven't told a soul."

"Thanks, Jen. We're going to sit on it for a few days. Doesn't really feel right with what just happened."

"I understand," Jenny said, looking at Lucy's left hand. "Where's the ring?"

Lucy quickly pulled a gold chain from underneath her T-shirt. There was the locket that contained the photo of her daughter, Charlotte, and jingling against it was the ring. As Ruth approached, Lucy hid it once again beneath the shirt. Ruth placed two trays down on the table; on them were three plates with toast and one pot of tea with three cups. "Honestly, that woman is a miracle worker," Ruth said, handing out the cups and plates.

"Who, Mary?" Lucy asked.

"Yes. Another ten came in yesterday, but there's always enough food. Nobody ever goes hungry."

"Another ten? How come I didn't see them?"

"Came in late last night," Jenny said. "Don't worry, they got checked. Shaw escorted them to the infirmary himself. One of them was your lot."

"My lot?" Lucy asked.

"American."

"Whereabouts were they from?"

"America."

"Uh-huh. But whereabouts in America?"

"I don't know," Jenny replied, spreading jam on her toast, "does it matter?"

"I suppose not."

The three friends tucked into their breakfast and talked about everything from the new defence plans to Mary Stolt's culinary skills. It was only as their meal was coming to an end that Jenny noticed Lucy had gone quiet.

"What is it?"

"That woman."

"What woman?" Jenny asked, turning around.

"God, Jen. Don't just stare at her."

"Sorry."

"That woman over there, in the far right corner, was she one of the ones who came in yesterday?"

Jenny surreptitiously turned and glanced towards the couple Lucy was looking at. The woman and the man seemed to be taking stock of their surroundings, eyeing up everyone and everything. "Yes, that's them, why?"

"She looks familiar."

"You know her?"

"I'm not sure. I can't quite put my finger on it."

"Well, I can tell you one thing for sure, she was worth a few bob in the olden days."

"How do you figure?"

"Darling, you don't get to that age with boobs like that. Look at them. Jesus, Jake could park his bike between those things without making them so much as wobble. They don't come cheap."

Lucy and Ruth burst out laughing. "You have such a way with words."

"Wish I'd have got mine done while I still had the chance."

"Hi," Mike said, seemingly appearing from out of nowhere.

"Hi, sweetie," Lucy replied.

"You girls having a nice chat?"

"We're talking about Jenny's boobs."

"Err ... okay."

"What do you think, Mike?" she said, grabbing hold of them through her jumper and jiggling them up and down. "Do you think there's enough to grab on to? Or should I have had them done when I had the chance?"

Mike just stood there like a rabbit caught in the beam of a car's headlights. "I ... err ... they're fine. They're fine."

"Just fine?"

Mike coloured bright red. "They're nice."

"Just nice? What's wrong with them?"

"Nothing. Nothing's wrong. They're perfect."

"Perfect? You think Jenny's boobs are perfect?" Lucy said.

"Jesus Christ. I just came over here to say hi. Can we please stop talking about Jenny's boobs?"

"Jenny's perfect boobs?" Lucy said.

"Fuck off, all of you," Mike said, turning around and marching out. He heard the table erupt into raucous laughter behind him as he trailed out of the hall. He walked through the car park and made his way along the road to the dock, which was a flurry of activity.

Shaw, Hughes and Raj were in deep conversation with Ryan and April. "Hi Mike, I was just thinking about you," Shaw said.

"That's never good."

"You've met Mike?" Shaw asked.

"You're Emma's brother?" April said.

"That's right."

"She's something else."

"Tell me about it."

"We're planning a little outing," Shaw said.

"Oh yeah, to where?" Mike replied.

"Kyle of Lochalsh."

"Kyle of Lochalsh? You mean the place where a few days ago these people barely escaped with their lives? The place that was attacked by marauders? The place that was overrun with flesh-eating zombies? That place?"

"Yeah, that's the one."

"Sounds great. When do we set off?"

"Ooh, sarcasm, that always helps," Shaw said.

"I just don't understand why you'd want to head down there, knowing what the situation is," Mike replied.

"Well, technically, we're only heading to the harbour to start with. Ryan and April said there are a few fishing boats there that could be of use to us. They're fuelled and ready for action."

"That's assuming they haven't been taken or drained of fuel, which is a big assumption considering."

"There is something else," Shaw said, looking towards Ryan.

"What's that?" Mike asked.

"The settlement's weapons and ammo cache. It's stored at the bank. If there is any possibility we can get to it that could really be useful."

"What you got? A couple of BB guns and some ball-bearings?" Mike asked, dismissively.

"Twenty army issue SA80s, five Glock 17s, a high-explosive hand grenade and two red phosphorous grenades, plus a whole lot of ammo. We got taken by surprise the other night, we couldn't get to it before the area was teeming with infected," Ryan said.

"Okay … you don't think the raiders will have taken everything."

"The safe, it's an old-fashioned combination type. Unless they've got a skilled safecracker among them or some explosives to take the door off, they're not getting in. But think about it, why would you be interested in the contents of a bank now? Chances are they didn't even go in."

"We're just going to head down for a look-see. We're not going to take any risks, but it's definitely worth a trip, don't you think?" Shaw said.

"Haven't you got to oversee things here?"

"Yeah."

"And I'm guessing Barney's staying with Beth."

"You guess right."

"So, who have you got?"

"Well, right now, there's Hughes, Raj, Talikha, April and Ryan."

"Isn't Kyle miles away?"

"By road it's a real trek," Ryan said. "By sea it's not that far at all."

"We're just heading down there for a look. If it seems too dangerous, then we don't go near it. If it seems okay, we get what we want and head straight back," said Hughes.

"It's not like you to turn down a trip like this," Shaw said, smiling.

"Look, I'm all for us heading out if there's some tangible benefit for the community, but these marauders, they know what they're doing. That place will be threadbare by the time we get there. Anything of value will be gone, and—"

"In which case, we head straight back. There won't even be any need to step off the b—" Shaw was interrupted by the screech of tyres, and all heads turned as a Ford Fiesta came to a sudden stop.

Barnes climbed out, opened up the rear doors and grabbed a rucksack and a rifle then walked over to where Mike, Shaw and the rest of them were standing. "Changed my mind. Thought a little trip might do me good."

Mike and Shaw shot each other concerned glances, but it was Hughes who spoke. "Barney, mate, don't you think you should be with Beth and Annie? I mean, Jesus, she's just lost her little brother."

"Beth's not left the bedroom since yesterday. She and Annie need to be alone right now, and I need to be doing something."

Hughes looked towards Shaw then back to Barnes. "Okay, mate. I understand. It will be good to have you aboard."

Mike and Shaw looked at one another again, and Mike gave him a barely perceptible nod. "I'll go tell Lucy that I'm heading out with you. If I'm not back in five minutes, come looking for me, and bring a needle and thread, I'll probably need my bollocks sewing back on."

11

"Jesus, Mary, and Joseph, how do these people live like this?" Angel asked as she and Troy climbed back into the caravan.

"You've been living the sweet life too long, princess. I'd say these people are doing pretty well for themselves. Everyone has a roof over their heads and food in their bellies. On top of that, they put up a pretty good defence against us the other night."

"Why, Troy, you sound like you admire them."

"I do. They've achieved something pretty impressive here."

"Having second thoughts?"

Troy smiled as he sat down. "You can admire your enemy and hate them at the same time."

"You hate them?"

"No, actually. They're just in my way."

Angel smiled. "So are you going to tell me now just exactly what the plan is?"

"It's still forming."

Angel went to sit down by his side. She crossed her legs and looked down sadly at her designer jeans that had been deliberately stained with mud and dirt to make her look more like a refugee and less like a Hollywood actress. "Okay, but talk to me about figures."

"Figures?"

"How many of us are there going to be?"

Troy let out a long breath. "Why don't you just leave all that to me?"

"Look, Troy, none of this would be in motion if it wasn't for me. You wouldn't have your little fleet, and we wouldn't be sitting here right now."

"Tell me you didn't just say that. Tell me you don't think all this is down to you."

"Damn straight it's down to me. Who else could have made all this happen?"

"Seriously, Angel, I thought your husband was deluded, but damn if you haven't got your very own God complex." Troy stood up. "I'm the one who made all this happen. I'm the one who put the fleet together, who trained the crews, who devised the raids. I did it all." He stopped as he saw something approaching hurt on Angel's face.

"I just need to know, Troy. What we're doing is no small thing. What I'm doing is no small thing."

"What you're doing is running out on your husband. Millions of women have done it before, don't make out it's something special or unique."

Angel's eyes narrowed. "Don't belittle me. I won't have you belittling me. You know damn well this is much bigger than that. We're leaving most of those people on board that ship to die a slow death."

Troy knew that wasn't true. He had a plan in place, and only the ones closest to him knew what it was. The people on *The Ark* would not die long, lingering deaths at all. Noah would not die a long, lingering death. As much as Angel complained about her husband, he knew she would never be on board with the plan Troy had in place, so he played along. The last thing he wanted was for Angel to go to pieces behind enemy lines.

"Those people have got as much chance as

anyone."

"With no fuel? With no food?"

"Those people have been happy for minions to run around after them for most of their lives. They're about to find out what life is really like now."

"Will you at least tell me this—will we have enough people to survive, to build a community like they have here?"

"Yes and more besides. We should have about four hundred men and women all told. Every last one of them sick to the teeth of running around after those over-privileged pissants, every last one of them willing to do whatever it takes to survive. A lot of them were mercenaries who went into private security, but we've got a few who are just servants, nannies to the wealthy, but with good skills. The kind of skills we'll need. We've got crew and engineers, useful people, people in charge of the supplies. A lot of them have been in the forces and then found regular jobs. But most importantly of all, we'll have the arms cache. That's the only currency worth squat now. That and fuel."

"You say good people. Would good people really be thinking about doing this? About invading, occupying somebody else's land?"

"It's the apocalypse, Angel, or haven't you been keeping up with the headlines? It's survival of the fittest, and these people have lasted longer than I'd have given them credit for, but Jesus, communal breakfasts and suppers? A roof over the head of every straggler who wanders into this place? That kind of red liberal commie bullshit will be the end of them. And if it wasn't us doing it, it would be someone else."

"Spoken like a true Christian."

"You can mock me, but this place will be our fortress, and by taking the food from *The Ark*, we'll have time to settle ourselves before the next growing season starts. We'll keep the fishing boats running and, who knows, maybe we can send out the odd hunting party, get ourselves some prime highland venison."

"You make it sound idyllic, but it still means we're putting the people we set sail with from Texas to their deaths."

"No. It doesn't mean anything of the kind. We're not killing them. We're just making them work. They'll have every chance to escape that boat and fend for themselves." *I will never be able to tell her the truth, so let her believe one last fairy tale.* "Hell, they've still got some fuel, enough to get to shore. They could get themselves another fleet, who knows, they might even find a place like this. But they're not our responsibility. We need to think about ourselves. Hey, if you're getting cold feet—"

"I'm not getting cold feet, it's just…"

"Just what?"

"Noah and me. For a long, long time, it's just been a business arrangement between the two of us. I've had my lovers, he's had his, although the last few years he hasn't really been interested in that. We've led separate lives. We've loved each other, we've hated each other, we've tolerated each other, but if ever one of us was in trouble, I mean real trouble, we've stood our ground together. Oh, don't get me wrong, I know that's a pretty screwed-up idea of what a marriage should be, but it's worked for us up until now."

"The now being that you're going to leave him on board that ship with the rest of them. Don't get me wrong, Noah's always been alright by me, even when you and I had our thing, but I can tell you he wouldn't have the stomach for this. This is about survival."

"But he does. He signed off on your fleet. Granted, he didn't know all the details, but I think he figured out that we weren't just being gifted food parcels by generous benefactors and when he learned exactly how we did it, he didn't say anything."

"I don't mean that. I mean this," Troy said, gesturing around him. "Taking over a settlement by force then leaving all his rich pals, all his flock."

Angel was about to protest but then thought better of it. "His flock? Honey, have you been to one of his prayer meetings lately? He barely has fifty people in that auditorium most nights. I suppose you're right. So, what do we do? We just going to sit in this tin can all day long?"

"No, we're going to be model citizens, grateful to our new hosts. We're going to get out there and be about as helpful as we can be."

"Why?"

"We have three missions here. Figure this place out. Figure these people out. Figure their defences out. The next time we attack will be the last time, and you can be sure we're going to win."

"I still don't understand. We've got that huge arms cache. We could outgun these people a thousand times over."

"It's all that simple to you, isn't it? They aren't making any more bullets. I want to keep that cache to defend this place for the next five, ten, twenty years. If we do this right, we can win with barely a bullet being fired from our guns."

"Twenty years with you? I might just need to save one of those bullets for myself."

*

Mike and Hughes pulled the motorboat onto the narrow beach, while Ryan and Barnes held all the equipment. They were only going to climb the ridge to get an elevated view of Kyle before sailing into port, but experience had taught them time and time again that even the most straightforward missions could run into all sorts of problems. Hughes hitched the boat to a formidable boulder, and the four of them began their hike up the steep incline.

They travelled in silence, well aware that there was a chance they could run into infected at any moment. They eventually reached a plateau and shuffled their rucksacks and weapons from their shoulders.

"Oh shit!" Hughes said, staring through the

binoculars.

"The attack was days ago, what are they still doing here?" Barnie asked as he looked down the sight of his L115A3 sniper rifle.

"What's happening?" Mike asked.

Hughes handed him the binoculars and Mike aimed them towards the dock. There was a single fishing vessel at the end of the long pier. The vessel had a small crane on the deck, which had hoisted what looked like a modified shark cage onto the wooden dock. The door to the cage was raised, and directly behind it was a second cage.

Mike handed the binoculars to Ryan. "What the hell is this?" Barnes asked.

"I don't know, but they've taken three of the larger fishing boats I was hoping would still be here," Ryan replied, "and the town is swarming with those things."

"I'm guessing that means the mission's off then," Hughes replied.

"Let's just watch a minute, I'm curious," Mike said, taking the binoculars back from Ryan. More than a minute passed.

"Come on," Hughes said, "this is a waste of time. Let's head back."

"Hang on. I think I've figured this out," Mike said.

"Figured what out?" Ryan asked.

"This is how they gather the RAMs. They lure them with live bait and probably something like loud music or maybe another siren. They have somebody in the cage behind the one with the open door. The RAMs walk into the first cage, someone lowers the gate, and, hey presto, they're trapped. And that diagonal metal lip that's been fitted to the back of the boat … that's how they release them. They raise the cage, the lip angles it downwards, the door comes up, and they all fall out. Then the boat heads back out to sea and the infected head towards the lights and noise beyond the shallows."

"So how come the gate's open on that cage? And

where's the crew?" Hughes asked as Mike gave the binoculars back to him.

"I think this one didn't quite go to plan. I'm guessing they got overrun."

"That's too—" A rifle crack thundered, echoing around the entire bay. "Jesus, Barney! What the hell are you doing, mate?" Barnes fired again and again. Each time another creature fell.

"Barney, what are you doing? This is just wasting bullets," Mike said.

Barnes kept firing, and Mike, Hughes and Ryan all looked towards one another, not understanding what was going on. "Barney, mate, this is mad," Hughes said.

"No more," Barnes said under his breath. "No more."

"Barney. What do you mean?"

Barnes turned towards Hughes. "No more," he said again before returning his attention to the RAMs on the dock.

12

Mike grabbed the binoculars back and aimed them towards the boat on the dock. The bodies were really starting to mount up.

"Barney, what the fuck are you doing? For Christ's sake, you're scaring me," Hughes shouted.

"No more."

Hughes, Mike and Ryan all looked at each other again as Barnes fired another shot.

"Barney?" Mike said.

"No more," Barnes said again, a little louder.

"Barney, come on, mate, what are you doing?" Hughes asked again.

Barnes did not answer; he took another shot then reloaded the weapon. Another full minute passed, and Barnes fired four more times, then he climbed to his feet. "There. We're done," he said, walking past the other three men and heading back down to the beach.

Mike, Hughes and Ryan all threw each other concerned looks then followed him.

*

"Hi," Lucy said as Emma appeared around the corner.

"Hi."

"How come you're not with Sammy and Jake?"

"I've left them with Tabby."

"She seems nice."

"Yeah, she is."

"But I think after everything that's happened, and you being away so long, they'd want to be with you."

"You're right. I know you're right, and I've literally just popped out. I'll be heading back there before they even realise I'm gone."

"Okay," Lucy said, placing a few bottles in her doctor's bag and fastening it up. "So what can I do for you?"

"I wanted to go and see Beth and Annie. I know Barney's with them, but—"

"Barney's not with them. He went down to Kyle with Mike and Hughes."

"Whoa! Back up. They've gone to Kyle?"

"Yeah, with Raj, Talikha, Ryan and April. Ryan thought that a few of the small boats down there might be useful for us."

Emma's brow furrowed for a moment. "Err … okay, but Barney going with them. That's a bit weird, considering what's just happened."

"Shaw told me that he thought Beth and Annie needed some alone time and he needed to stay busy."

"Okay, well, alone time or not, I want to pay my respects. Beth, Annie and John were with us from the beginning, and it's only right—"

"I'm heading up there now. You can come with me if you like."

"Yeah. That would be good."

The two of them left the ward and climbed into Emma's Jeep. "Look, I'm sorry if I was a little frosty with you the other day."

"Don't worry about it. I deserved it."

The car left the outskirts of the village and wound along the coast road. The sun was shining, and as Emma drove, she remembered why this had been such a special place to live.

"Pull the car over," Lucy said.

"What? Why?"

"Just pull the car over; I need to talk to you."

Emma looked confused but carried on to the next passing place and pulled in. "What's all this about?"

Lucy took a deep breath. "Okay, I'm not meant to be telling you this, but ... I..."

"You're starting to worry me."

"Listen, Mike is the most important person in the world to me, and he wanted to keep this a secret for a while because of everything that's gone on, but I'm scared to death about your reaction. I'm worried you won't take it well and that will just kill him, so I need to tell you now so you can get used to it."

"Okay. Now you're really scaring the hell out of me. What is it?"

"Mike asked me to marry him, and I said yes." There was no joy in Lucy's face as there had been when she had spoken to Jenny, only apprehension.

For a moment, Emma's expression was unreadable. Then she broke out into a big, beaming smile, took her seatbelt off and leaned across to hug Lucy. She didn't let go for a full minute. "I couldn't be happier for either of you."

"You mean it?"

"Of course I bloody mean it," Emma replied, wiping her eyes. "Nobody deserves happiness more than you two, and I'll finally get to be an aunt."

"Ha. Just hold your horses there."

"I should probably start knitting some little booties. What do you think, blue or pink?"

The pair of them laughed. "Thank you. I was worried."

"I understand why, but I am seriously okay with this. Better than okay. It's wonderful news."

"Just remember to act surprised when you're told

officially."

"Mum's the word ... hopefully."

"Oh, God."

They both laughed again, but the smile soon disappeared from Lucy's face. "Are you okay?" Emma asked.

"I'm sorry, sweetie. I just started thinking about Charlie."

"Hey, look, if Charlie was still around, I know she'd be happy that you're happy and I'm sure there's nothing she'd want more than a little brother or sister."

Lucy looked across to Emma and smiled sadly. "I suppose you're right."

"Of course I'm right. If she came from you, then she had a good heart."

Lucy reached her hand across and squeezed Emma's. "Thank you."

Emma squeezed back before starting the car again and resuming their journey.

They were travelling for less than five minutes before they took a right turn into the well-hidden driveway. Beth and Barnes had taken great pride in restoring the once ramshackle fisherman's cottage. Barnes had even scavenged enough white paint to cover the outside of it, making it gleam in the afternoon sun.

Emma pulled on the handbrake and turned off the engine. Both of them remained in their seats for a moment, staring towards the bottle-green front door. "This isn't going to be easy," Emma said. All joy from the previous conversation now dried up as she contemplated seeing Beth.

"No, no, it isn't."

They climbed out of the car and slowly walked towards the door. Lucy tried the handle and stepped into the kitchen. "Beth, it's Lucy," she called as Emma followed her in. "Beth!" There was no reply and Lucy and Emma looked towards one another.

"She's probably asleep. I slept for days after Mum

died."

The two of them made their way through the house. When they reached the master bedroom, Lucy knocked on the door. "Beth. It's Lucy. I've brought someone to see you." Still there was no answer. She knocked once more. "Beth?"

The door swung inwards revealing Beth and Annie sitting up in bed. Beth had a cradling arm around her younger sister. There was no colour in their faces, and their eyes were closed.

"Beth? Annie?" Emma cried as she and Lucy ran to the bed.

Lucy immediately placed her fingers against Beth's neck, withdrawing them just as quickly before doing the same with Annie. Emma started to sob, and Lucy slumped down onto the bed, taking a tight hold of Annie's cold little hand in hers. There were two empty pill bottles on the floor and two mugs containing a powdery residue of something mixed with drinking chocolate.

"Such a sweet little girl," Lucy said as tears began to pour.

Emma flopped down on the bed next to Beth. She placed her head in her hands, and a heaving rasp left her as she began to cry too. They had all been through so much together. Beth and Annie had lived through that terrifying ordeal back in Leeds. Beth had stood up to Fry in Candleton then she had lived through the torture he had inflicted on her when she was taken hostage.

She had lived through it all and come out fighting, but this was obviously one tragedy too many.

The two of them sat crying for more than five minutes before either could talk. "I understand. I do, I understand if she wanted to leave, to step out, but why take Annie? She was only twelve for God's sake."

Lucy blew her nose. "I'm guessing she just didn't want her to grow up in a world this cruel."

"Barney's going to be devastated."

"Em, at a guess I'd say this happened last night. Barney already knows."
"But…"
"I know."

13

Barnes had already got the boat in the water as Mike, Shaw and Ryan reached the beach. They were all apprehensive about Barnes's state of mind. It was only when they heard the motor start and saw the dinghy begin to chug away that they realised just how bad the situation was.

Mike burst into a sprint, tearing across the sand, through the shallows, and managed to dive into the small craft before it picked up speed. Barnes tried to manhandle him overboard as the motor continued to chug. "Get out," he shouted. "They need to pay. They need to pay for what they've done."

Mike fought back, grabbing hold of his friend's wrists. "Barney, they're dead, they're already dead, what else are you going to do?"

"I'm going to kill them … kill them all."

"I understand. I understand, but there's no justice or vengeance to be found here. Those things don't think or feel; they just are."

"They killed them. They killed them," Barnes screamed as the boat moved into deeper waters still. His eyes were wild, and Mike suddenly realised that there was something else behind Barnes's motivation.

"Barney, what is this? What are you talking about?"

"They killed them all," he said again through gritted teeth then finally stopped struggling.

Mike loosened his grip around Barnes's wrists. "You need to calm down, mate. You can't take stupid risks. Beth and Annie are going to need you more than ever now.

Barnes looked at Mike and began to chuckle, then laugh, until the sound was so loud it could be heard onshore. "You don't get it, do you? They're gone. Beth and Annie are dead."

*

Noah had his suite, but as the front for this entire operation was The Noah Jackson Evangelical Church, he had an office as well. In the early days, when there was still a minute hope that things would get back to normal, he used it quite frequently, but as time went on, he realised that things would never get back to normal, and but for one night in the last twelve months when he'd had enough of Angel's shenanigans and made it his bedroom, he had not set foot in it. Now, though, he had been summoned to a meeting with the CEO of IFG Shipping and Holdings.

"We've been more than patient, Noah. We've been drifting around this same stretch of goddamn coast for the last two weeks, now what the hell is going on? We've got a right to know."

Noah knew that the "we" he was referring to was the group who had put the money together for this venture. They were a collection of the most immoral, avaricious, scheming, self-centred people he had ever met, and now, as fully self-aware as he had become in recent months, that was saying something.

"Everything's in hand, Thomas."

"Everything's in hand? Everything's in hand? You've been saying that to me for the last goddamn six months. If I have to eat one more fish dinner, I'm gonna puke. We want to see results."

"Listen. We might have found somewhere. That's why we've been in this area for so long."

"Might have found somewhere? Might have found somewhere? What in hell and damnation does that mean?"

"We're establishing whether it's suitable right now."

"Establishing whether it's suitable? You're not establishing shit. You're in this office talking to me, and from what I can tell, when you're not in here, you're doing diddly squat." Thomas Madison had brown eyes but rarely did anyone see more than just slits. He seemed to scowl most of the time, even when he was happy. Right this minute, though, he was not happy. Not by a long way.

"Look, I've got people on it."

The smile that crept onto Madison's face was a mocking, cruel one. "Listen to me, and listen good. We want results. I'm not interested in your wife and one of her boyfriends going on an early honeymoon before she dumps your ass once and for all under the guise of a scouting mission."

Jackson looked shocked. "That's not what—"

"Thought I didn't know? I know everything that goes on here. I have eyes and ears everywhere."

"If that's the case, you'll know that it's not just anybody over there, it's Troy."

It was Madison's turn to look surprised now. "That I didn't know."

"You should have a little more faith."

"Well, regardless, we want to start seeing results. If you think we don't know what our fuel and supplies situation is, you're very much mistaken. We emptied the last JKC supertanker two months back. Time's running out, Noah, for all of us."

"I have a good feeling about this place."

"Feeling? I don't give one damn about your feelings, good or not. Listen, this is getting us nowhere. When Troy and Angel get back from their trip, I want to see them. 'Bout time I started talking to the organ grinder and not the monkey." Madison stood up and marched out of the office, swinging the door closed behind him.

Noah remained seated, just staring at the empty chair that had been occupied by Madison a few seconds before. These people were truly abominable. For so long Noah had been there to do their bidding, but just being in the same room as them sickened him now. He opened one of the drawers and pulled out a bottle of scotch and a glass. He poured a double and took a drink.

He was about to close the drawer again when he saw his Bible. Not the one he used on stage, not the one he had carefully put together by a props team for his live telecasts in years gone by, but his Bible, the one he had owned as a child, the one his father had given him. He took it out of the drawer and placed it down on the desk. How many times had he found sanctuary in it as a boy and young man?

He flicked through the pages until they fell open at one of his favourite passages. Noah took another drink before beginning to read out loud. "*Jesus said unto him, Thou shalt love the Lord thy God with all thy heart, and with all thy soul, and with all thy mind. This is the first and great commandment. And the second is like unto it, Thou shalt love thy neighbour as thyself.*" He sat back in his chair. "What are you doing, Noah? What have you become?"

There was a knock on the door. "Sir, is everything okay?" Doug asked, popping his head around the corner.

"Everything's fine."

"It's just I thought I heard you talking."

"Just reading out loud from the good book. Sometimes when you hear the words, it gives them a new perspective."

"Yes, sir. I'm sorry to have interrupted. I'm right outside if you need me, Mr Jackson." Doug closed the door behind him.

Noah flicked through the pages again, and this time

the book fell open at Revelations. "*But as for the cowardly, the faithless, the detestable, as for murderers, the sexually immoral, sorcerers, idolators, and all liars, their portion will be in the lake that burns with fire and sulfur, which is the second death.*" He closed the book and sat back once more. Virtually everyone on board this ship was guilty of one if not all of those things, himself included.

His heart sank further as he thought about all he had done, all he had sanctioned. Why had he allowed Angel and Troy to create that damned fleet of ships? He had bowed to the pressure of Madison and men like him. He knew the supplies were dwindling, he knew the ship was dying, slowly, but why did that make it acceptable to steal and plunder? Love thy neighbour, not murder thy neighbour.

A single tear ran down Noah's cheek as he continued to look at the Bible. He had forsaken his Lord, his faith, everything. He had been lured by a demon from his father's shoe shop, a modern-day Dr Faustus selling his soul to the devil for wealth and bodily pleasure. Yes, he deserved to be on this ship with these people. This was Hell, and none of them deserved to escape.

He reached out, placed his palm face down on the tatty bottle-green cover, and whispered, "I'm sorry, Lord."

*

Barnes was virtually catatonic on the return trip to Safe Haven. Hughes and Mike had taken him down to one of the cabins. They had tried to talk to him, to find out what had happened, but he just lay still, staring towards the ceiling; eventually, the pair of them headed above deck.

"What else did he say to you?"

"I've told you. He said that Beth and Annie are dead. I couldn't really get any more out of him."

"You think suicide?"

Mike looked out across the blue waves. "Beth's been through more than most. She's always been tough, but when I found her the other night… It was like a different person. Grief can do strange things."

"Jesus. Barney was devoted to her."

"I know. We're going to have to keep a close eye on him too."

A nervous smile appeared on Hughes's face. "What, Barney? Barney wouldn't kill himself."

"Until today, I'd have said the same about Beth."

"Shit!"

"I know."

"I'm sorry about your friend," April said, coming up behind them with two mugs of tea. They both accepted them gratefully. "It's a terrible thing. Loss can break the strongest souls."

Neither of them was in the mood to exchange platitudes or discuss their friend with a virtual stranger. "Thank you for the tea, it's very kind," Mike said.

April looked at them both for a moment then rolled her sleeves up and showed them her wrists. The two thick scars were old but prominent. "When my husband died, I couldn't see the point in going on. I couldn't see what was left for me. A friend found me in the bathtub, got an ambulance, saved me, even though I didn't want saving. She stayed with me through those dark months. It wasn't easy." She rolled her sleeves back down. "Like I said, it can break the strongest souls." She smiled weakly and disappeared below deck once more.

"When we get back, we'll get Lucy to take a look at him," Mike said. Hughes nodded and started walking away. "Where are you going?"

"I'm going to be outside Barney's room if you need me."

14

It was still an hour before daybreak when Troy visited the cove just around the corner from the dock. The good folks of Safe Haven had been spending all their time and resources looking for ways to bolster their sea defences while still taking in refugees. He, Angel and the others they had arrived with had settled in without an eyebrow being raised. The good thing about having an international force of mercenaries was there were more than enough British volunteers for the mission. Eight or nine Americans all coming in at different times would have looked suspicious. But one South African, one American man and wife, and seven Brit refugees went unnoticed.

He had sent out signals from this cove each night. Even though he did not get any back in return, he knew they were being received. Jacobs had never let him down. He looked at his watch. "Any minute now," he muttered to himself.

Then he saw them, like seal heads bobbing out of the water, ten frogmen and women. They emerged from the sea, immediately removing one of their oxygen tanks, followed by their masks, then headed straight towards him. "Good to see you, sir," the leader said.

Even though this was not strictly a military concern, and these people were no longer soldiers, most still addressed Troy as sir, and he referred to them as his army.

"Good to see you, Ashton. Is everything in place?"

Ashton removed what appeared to be a backup oxygen cylinder but was, in fact, a plastic storage container. He opened it up, and Troy saw a pistol, magazines, and knives, but it was the two radios his eyes focused on. Ashton handed him one of the handsets along with an extra battery. "The teams are in position at the two checkpoints as you asked, sir. They've been there since last night, and they're ready to move on your orders."

"Excellent. And everything on board *The Ark*?"

"All systems go, sir."

Troy smiled. "Okay. Make yourselves scarce and listen for my signal. I'll see you boys and girls later." He began to head back to the campground where Angel was still fast asleep under the covers, but then he stopped and looked back.

None of his soldiers were looking towards him. They had each removed the second dummy oxygen tank from their backs and were sliding out of their suits. He knew he didn't have to worry, these were his people, professionals; they would do what he asked. Soon Safe Haven would be his. He allowed himself a smile then carried on.

*

When Noah woke up, it was as though a sixth sense was telling him something was wrong. Angel had been gone for several days, and that was nothing unexpected or worrying, quite honestly, he was grateful for the peace. But there was something ... something he could not quite put his finger on. He climbed out of bed and walked across to the windows where he flung the heavy velvet curtains back.

His mouth fell open in shock. Normally he would see a vast array of tall ships, tugs, fishing boats and other vessels that went to make up Troy's pirate fleet. This morning there was nothing … nothing but open sea. "Sweet Jesus," he said, running across to his neatly folded clothes and flinging them on. He looked at his watch to see it was only six a.m. Most people would not even begin to stir for some time yet, if nothing else he could confirm his worst fears before being assaulted by a barrage of questions from panicked and angry billionaires.

He bolted out of his suite to the one next door, knocked three times and waited. Doug and Viktor had originally been housed in the lower quarters with the rest of the bodyguards, personal assistants and ship's crew. When Noah's neighbour, Andrew Markham, chairman of Markham Industries had found out his wife was having an affair with a common porter, he had gone mad. He had killed her, the porter, his children and himself, thus conveniently freeing up the accommodation next door for Doug and Viktor. There had been protestations about two bodyguards getting a suite when other employees lived on the lower levels, but it wasn't as if *The Ark* was taking on any new passengers, so eventually things died down.

"Mr Jackson?" Doug said, opening the door in his robe. "Is everything okay, sir?"

"No. No, it isn't, Doug. I think we're knee-deep in shit."

Within two minutes, Doug and Viktor had dressed and were following Noah down through the ship to the pantry. It was called a pantry, but ultimately it was a food warehouse taking up hundreds of square metres. The extra two decks that had been used to store food when *The Ark* first set sail were emptied long ago, and now every last morsel was stored here. For some time, the stock levels had been getting lower and lower. They had been replenished to an extent by Troy's fleet, but as the three of them walked past row after row of empty racking, they began to realise just how little time there was left.

They rounded a corner and suddenly heard raised voices. The conversation was in Spanish, so Noah could not understand it, but he could hear and feel the panic in the air.

"Señor Jackson," gasped one of the senior chefs as Noah and his two bodyguards walked around the corner.

"Thiago, what in tarnation's going on here?"

"Sir, I came down here just now and found this." He gestured around to the empty shelves. It's nearly all gone. There is a little food on a couple of the higher shelves. There is fish in the freezer, we have some food left in the galleys, but all our staples they have been taken." Thiago's eyes were wide and terrified.

Noah stared at him for a moment then looked around at the empty racking. "How long?"

"How long for what, Señor Jackson?"

"How long before we're out of food completely?"

"I ... I don't know, sir."

Noah took a breath. "Okay, Thiago, this is what you're going to do. Go wake our inventory officer up. I want a full stocktake of every strand of spaghetti, every baked bean we've got left. We don't even think about serving breakfast until we know what we're dealing with here."

"Yes, Señor Jackson," he said, turning to his colleague and almost running out of the warehouse.

Noah turned to look at Doug and Viktor. "Well now, I knew Angel was a lot of things, but even I never saw this one coming."

"I'm sorry, sir," Doug replied.

"What in hell are you sorry for? I'm the dumb son of a bitch who married her. Look, this is what I need you to do, go get the armoury keys, make sure they didn't get to that. Then meet me back up in my office. When news of this breaks, I'm going to have a lot of pissed-off people banging on my door."

"Yes, Mr Jackson," Doug replied, and both men left.

Noah remained there for a few more moments with his hands on his hips looking around in dismay. "God damn you, Angel."

SAFE HAVEN: IS THIS THE END OF EVERYTHING?

*

The final tidying away was still being done as the council members assembled in the village hall. They had been having regular chats in smaller groups, but now all eight of them had come together with the addition of one extra speaker to discuss how the preparations for the enhanced defences were going, what still needed to be done and what further resources were required.

"I've told you before, I prefer being in the background," George said to Jules quietly as the others took their places around the pushed together rectangle of tables.

"Ah, stop moaning, you old windbag," Jules replied. "Shaw only wants you to give everyone a quick update then you'll be on your way."

Mary Stolt and one of her helpers brought out trays with pots of tea and coffee on them and placed them in the centre of the island of tables. "Like a proper boardroom this," George said with half a smile as he took his place.

"Well, don't get used to it. The only reason you're getting drinks is that we've just finished breakfast and we still had hot water," Mary replied.

"Thanks, Mary. We appreciate it," Shaw said.

"Well, if you don't want anything else, me and my girls will be away."

"No, this is great. Thanks again," Shaw replied.

The council members continued to make small talk until the kitchen staff left. "I don't know what it is about that woman, but she scares the living daylights out of me, and I've done two tours in Afghanistan," Hughes said, causing a ripple of laughter to run around the room.

"Ah, Mary's alright," Jules replied. "You've just got to know how to handle her."

"And how's that?" Hughes asked.

"I'll let you know when I find out."

"Okay, well, first things first, thank you all for coming," Shaw said. "I wanted to get an update from

George as to how everything was progressing, so I thought it was appropriate to invite him; that way, if anybody has anything to ask him, they can question him directly."

"Question him?" Jules said. "It sounds like he's taking the stand."

Shaw smiled. "Okay, ask him politely. How's that?" He turned towards their guest. "Well, George, the floor is yours."

George sat there for a moment looking a little self-conscious before finally taking a sip of tea. "So, things are coming along well," he began. "We've now got five mangonels fitted on board vessels up and down the coast. As you probably heard, the first of the trebuchets was tested yesterday, and everything went as we'd hoped."

"You're being modest, George," Hughes interrupted. "The bloody thing's a marvel." He looked around at the assembled faces. "It can really cover some distance. With a dozen of those up and down the coastline we're never going to have to worry about an attack from the sea again."

"Well, that's not really—"

"Credit where credit's due, George," interrupted Shaw. "I was there too, remember? You've done incredible work."

"It wasn't just me," he said, looking at the faces around the tables then finally settling on Ruth. "Richard and David did just as much as I did. They helped draw up the plans, and they were with me for the building of the prototype."

"Well, if they were here, we'd thank them too, but just take some praise where it's due, old man," Jules said, placing a friendly hand on his arm.

George smiled, more than a little embarrassed, but then continued. "Well, anyway, the tests were successful, and we started work straight away on building the next one. In the interim, the other team has been working on the giant crossbow, and we're hoping to have the first of those ready this afternoon for a test."

"Wow!" Lucy said. "You really don't mess about, do you?"

"I'm working with good people."

"Obviously, what you're doing is of the utmost importance, and all our resources are available to you. Is there anything you need that will speed this process up or make things easier for you and your teams?" Shaw asked.

George pondered the question for a moment. "Well, I was thinking about something, and it is just a thought, mind." He turned to look at Emma and Lucy. "Up at your place there's a kiln, isn't there?"

"Yeah, that's right," Emma replied. "Gran used to make earthenware."

"Well, I was wanting to do a little experiment."

"What kind of experiment, George?" Shaw asked.

"Obviously, the trebuchets, fire boulders, stones, rocks, whatever we can fit in them. We can cover them in oil and set fire to them, but what if we could construct a kind of giant Molotov cocktail? Y'know, like a big hollow cannonball that we could fill with something flammable."

"For such a sweet old man, you've got a bit of a dark side," Lucy said, and everyone around the table laughed.

"Well, it was just a thought," George said.

"Whatever you need. You'd be welcome to come down and experiment whenever you want," Emma replied.

"That's an interesting idea," Shaw added. "But shouldn't our priority be building these weapons first?"

"Of course, but it was just something that I'd been pondering ... a way to enhance their effectiveness."

"We really need to find you a nice lady to spend your evenings with. You've obviously got far too much time on your hands," Jules said.

"I've got a nice lady to spend my evenings with."

"Wren's your granddaughter, that wasn't the kind of lady I had in mind. Plus, I think she might be a bad influence on you."

George smiled. "Well, I can't really argue with that."

"So, George, before we let you get back to work, do you have any kind of timescale in mind as to how soon we might have all this completed?" Shaw asked.

George raised his eyebrows. "We've only just begun."

"Sorry, I didn't mean it to come out like that. I just wanted an idea, not to put you under pressure."

"The siege crossbows are going to be faster to construct than the trebuchets. Once we've got the first one done, I was thinking about splitting the team into two and getting another couple of helpers and then having two production lines."

"Good ... excellent."

"The trebuchets, they're a little different. The sheer size, scale and complexity mean that they're a little slower to put together."

"Slower?" Jenny said. "You don't seem to have been hanging around to me. You've got this done in an amazing time."

"Well, as I said, I have a good team. But anyway, we'll probably be able to build two or more giant crossbows for each trebuchet. As successful as the test-firing was yesterday, there still needs to be a little bit of fine-tuning and—"

The double doors to the village hall swung open and in walked five men. Everyone sitting at the tables turned to look. The men headed straight towards the assembly. "Err, breakfast's over I'm afraid," Shaw said, climbing out of his chair.

"That's too bad," said Troy as he continued towards them.

Puzzlement continued to reign on the faces of the council until all five of the men withdrew sidearms. "What the hell?" Shaw said as both he and Hughes reached for their own weapons and jumped to their feet simultaneously.

"Don't even think about it," Troy boomed, aiming his gun towards Lucy's head.

Shaw and Hughes stopped dead. "What is this?" Shaw demanded.

The doors swung open again, and Angel walked in. "I told you to keep watch," Troy said as he turned to see her bolting the entrance.

"You know I don't take orders, hun."

"What's going on?" Shaw demanded again.

"Well, shug, in business terms, this is what we call a hostile takeover."

"I don't understand."

"Don't worry, you will. Now, why don't you just go and sit yourself down and stop getting your panties in a twist?" Angel said as two of the men who had accompanied Troy took Shaw's then Hughes's sidearms.

"Okay, tie 'em up," Troy said, sweeping his weapon around to point at Shaw. Another man stood back with his pistol raised, ready to put down anyone who tried to resist. The council continued to look on slack-jawed and bewildered; the other three soldiers cable-tied the council members' hands, using the narrow hole in the back of the plastic chair to bind them to their seats. Each one had the same impulse, to struggle and to fight back, but they realised it was futile.

Before they reached her, Lucy quickly delved into her pocket and retrieved a stainless-steel paperclip. She placed it between her index and middle fingers. She held her breath and prayed as her hands were bound together through the rectangular gap in the back of the plastic chair. She relaxed again when the guard moved on to his next captor. A paperclip ... one single paperclip. It wasn't much, but it was something.

"Are you going to tell us what the hell this is about?" Hughes said.

"In good time," Troy replied. He stood there, his

gun not wavering for a moment as it pointed directly towards the bridge of Shaw's nose. When the three men had finished securing the last of the cable ties into place, they retreated from the table and raised their weapons. Troy lowered his and placed it in the back of his jeans.

"Okay, you've got our attention," Shaw said.

Troy laughed. "Your attention. Oh boy, by the end of today we're going to have a lot more than your attention. Now, I think it's about time you just shut up and stop acting like you're still in charge because as of now you're not in charge of anything."

Shaw looked around at the rest of his friends. All of them were as stunned as he was. "Now listen," Angel said, taking over, much to Troy's irritation. "If you play this thing just like we ask, not a single hair on anybody's head is going to get ruffled today."

"Who are you people?" Lucy asked.

"That's not relevant. What we want is," Troy said with a menacing smile.

"Look, we want what you've got. We want this place ... Safe Haven, and I mean what I say. Every last man, woman and child can walk out of here unharmed if you give it to us," Angel interjected once more.

"Give it to you?" Lucy replied incredulously. "This is our home. We've got hundreds of people living up and down this coastline."

"We know. That's why we're not unrealistic with our demands," Troy continued. "We realise it's going to take a little while, but we're here to help you with that."

"You came in the other day. We housed you, we fed you," Ruth said.

"Well, that was your problem. You keep an open-door policy at a time like this? You're lucky you've survived as long as you have," Troy snapped.

"We do it to prove there's still good in the world, that the people who need help can still get it. If we closed our doors to refugees and the desperate, what would that say about us?" Jenny asked.

"That you had good sense," Troy said with a wide grin that made him look like a man who had just won the world chess championship.

"You're mad," Shaw began. "Five of you against hundreds? Okay. You've got those guns, you could kill every last one of us in this room, and then what? You're insane if you think—"

"Oh boy, well, you just don't have a clue, do you?" Troy pointed to the radio handset that was sitting on the table in front of Shaw. "You're going to get on that walkie-talkie and tell all your units to stand down. My fleet is just waiting for my command, and then this place is going to be a whole lot more crowded."

"Ships? You're the marauders?" Emma said.

"Marauders?" Troy laughed a little. "Well, yes, I suppose that's what you'd call us."

"You're totally insane," Shaw said. "I'm not going to give that order. Never in a million years. You can kill me, but there's no way I'll let you take Safe Haven."

"Listen, what Angel said was the truth. We're going to let everyone walk out of here alive."

"What, like you did in the Kyle of Lochalsh?" Emma spat.

Troy smiled again. "You might not like my methods, but they're effective. Right here, right now, the smart play for everybody is to do as I ask. We're not monsters. We don't kill people for the sake of it, but make no mistake; we don't have a problem killing if it helps us get something we want. Now, we don't want infected running around in a place where we want to settle down, and we don't want a bloodbath where we use up some of our valuable, yet considerable resources. There is no benefit to us in killing all of you people."

"Wow! You're real fuckin' saints," Jules said, boring holes through Troy with her eyes.

"Trust me, you don't want the alternative," he

replied before turning back towards Shaw. "This is the deal. My ships come in here, and every man woman and child gets marched out of Safe Haven unharmed. You all go off and start a new life somewhere else."

"This is our home. We've built our lives here," Jenny said.

"Past tense. Was your home. You leave here with the clothes on your backs. You leave all the food, vehicles, weapons, supplies, medicines… You leave it all behind, but at least you leave."

"But we've got sick and old people. We've got people who aren't up to making any kind of journey," Lucy said.

"Well, that's just too bad," Troy replied. "This is the deal, take it or leave it."

Lucy turned towards Shaw. "We'd be putting those people to death."

Shaw stared at Troy then Angel; then he looked at the other four men. "There's no reason we can't come to some kind of compromise. This is a long stretch of coastline. We can all find a place to live here."

"You don't listen too good, do you?"

Suddenly Hughes lifted his chair off the floor with his feet and flew backwards, crashing it against the wall. There was a loud crack as plastic split, but the chair did not shatter and free his constraints as he had hoped. He collapsed to the ground, writhing and wriggling, desperate to break free from the cable ties that were bound tightly around his wrists.

Troy and the other men raised their weapons towards the sudden movement, but when they realised Hughes was going nowhere, they lowered them again, just watching and laughing, cruelly. They let Hughes struggle for a few more seconds before two of the men dragged him and his chair back to the table.

"Now y'all should listen to what Troy says." Angel looked at the women for what seemed like an age. "Some chance of life is better than no chance of life."

"Chance of life?" Lucy said. "Walk out of here with no food, no shelter, and no weapons. Walk out of here with those sick people with no meds? What chance of life will they have?"

"More than if you don't do as we say," Angel replied.

"I'm fed up of jawing," said Troy. "Now, I'm going to press the talk button on your radio, and you're going to tell all lookouts to stand down, you're not going to fire up your siren, and my ships are all going to enter the bay unencumbered."

"That's a big word for a piece of shit like you," Lucy hissed.

Troy's eyes flared, and he walked across to where she was sitting. He grabbed a handful of her thick hair and pulled her head back, placing his mouth up to her ear. She could feel his rough stubble brush against her lobe as he spoke. "I know lots of big words, darling—disembowelment, decapitation, dismemberment." He let go of her hair as quickly as he had clutched it and her head fell forward.

Lucy looked across towards Shaw. "You can't do this. You can't give that order. If they kill every last one of us in this room, you can't give that order. It would be the end."

A heavy silence hung in the air for a few moments as her words sunk in. The nine friends all looked at one another. This meeting had started so routinely and now there was a good chance none of them would be leaving.

Troy pulled a knife from his belt and marched across to Shaw. "Now, are you going to do as I ask and give the order?"

Shaw looked at each of his friends before lifting his head to look at Troy.

"Go fuck yourself!"

15

"I don't think you understand, shug, we—"

"No, you don't understand." It was George who interrupted her, and every head in the place turned towards him. George, the mild-mannered, logical, thoughtful engineer behind so many projects that had improved life for the citizens of Safe Haven; George, the kind-hearted old gentleman who never had cross words with anyone. "Everyone around this table has stared death in the face a hundred times before. It's nothing short of a miracle that we've lasted as long as we have. You can kill us one by one, but we'll never kowtow to people like you, and if your ships show up, then everyone in town will come out to fight. We've faced down tyrants and bullies before. We're not scared of the likes of you."

There was not a member of the council who did not swell with pride as George spoke, despite the dire situation they were in. "Well, ain't that just adorable," Angel said, smiling.

Troy's face remained like stone, and he looked towards two of the men and nodded before turning back towards the table. "You can't say you weren't warned."

The two guards dragged Hughes, chair and all, over

towards the stage that had been the platform for speeches, public meetings and even the odd children's nativity play in its time. Now, though, it was merely an elevated position to make sure the captive audience had a full view of what was going on. The two burly men lifted Hughes, despite his kicking legs. Then, when the chair was up on stage, they climbed up too.

"Come on, you fuckers. Don't be a pair of little mummy's boys, take these restraints off and I'll give you a fair fucking fight."

"I'm afraid that won't be happening any time soon," Troy said.

"Tell you what, three against one. I win, you let us all go. I could take down a bag of shite like you in a heartbeat."

Troy laughed. "None of you understand yet, do you? But you will in a couple of minutes."

"What, you think torturing me will make a difference?" Hughes asked as the two men tried to secure their prisoner's feet. As one of them bent down, Hughes brought his knee up hard. It smashed into the face of his captor, and the guard stumbled back, falling off the stage.

The man hit the floor with a heavy thud and let out a pained groan. Troy removed his weapon again and raised it towards Shaw and the others. "Go help him tie up the prisoner," he said to another guard, utterly disinterested in the man in agony on the floor who was trying to scramble back to his feet.

The third guard went to join the other on stage. He managed to avoid Hughes's kicking legs and, eventually, with cable ties and a short length of rope around the prisoner's midriff, they secured him to the chair properly.

"What, you're going to torture us one by one until we give in to your demands?" Shaw asked.

"To be honest, I've never found torture to be that effective, and I can tell that I'd probably get bored long before you gave me what I want, so let's call this a demonstration. Yes, that's what this is. Mercer, do the honours, will you?"

Mercer was the one who hadn't fallen from the stage. He had worked as a mercenary in Africa for thirteen years after coming out of the United States Army. He had seen the most horrific sights and done things that, no matter how he tried, he would never be able to forget. Today was no different, and as he reached into his belt bag and removed a syringe there was no sadness, or regret, or shame on his face for what he was about to do, it was just business as usual. He looked across to Troy who gave him a nod, and Mercer immediately plunged the needle into Hughes's neck.

Hughes let out a small grunt as the metal punctured his skin, and the icy liquid entered his body. "What's that? You're giving me some kind of truth serum? You want to find out our secrets? Well, good luck with that, you fucking pricks."

Mercer withdrew the needle and replaced the protective cover before placing it carefully on a trestle table at the back of the small stage; chances were he'd be using it again before the day was over. Then he and the other guard watched. Troy leaned into Shaw. "Now remember, all this could have been avoided, you've only got yourself to blame."

"What is this? What's going on?" Shaw asked.

"Shh," Troy said, placing a hand on Shaw's shoulder. "The show's about to begin."

Shaw continued to look at his captor, still baffled, until he heard a loud cough come from the stage. He immediately turned to look at Hughes, whose expression of belligerence had disappeared and had been replaced by one of fear. "What's happening to him? What did you give him?" Shaw demanded.

"All in good time."

The entire council was transfixed in terrified silence as they watched the colour drain from Hughes's face. His cheeks twitched, and his body convulsed as he tried to fight what he realised was happening to him. He grimaced and gritted his teeth as he felt the infection taking over. This was it; after everything he had been through, this was his end. A deep sadness overwhelmed him, and as much as he wanted to shout, and kick, and scream, and damn his captors to hell, it was taking him all his time not to cry. He didn't want to give them the satisfaction of knowing how scared he was that this foreign, dark, cold menace was invading his body, consuming him from within.

He began to shiver as he looked towards the council members. Horror and sadness painted their faces in equal measure. His eyes fixed on Jules. Why hadn't he had the guts to tell her how he had truly felt about her? From the first day they had met, he had been smitten. Now it was too late, but if there was any image he wanted to take with him before this malevolent thing inside devoured him once and for all, it was her face. Not as it was at this moment in time; not with wide-eyed terror and floods of tears blurring her beautiful eyes, but with that smile. That smile of hers was what he wanted in his head.

He could feel the cold spreading quickly, but he needed his petrified brain to do him this one last service. Just remember. Remember the way the corner of her lips curled up before she used to say something funny; remember that laugh—almost like a little girl's laugh, he wished he could hear it now. Remember the warmth and caring in her eyes whenever she spoke to him. What he wouldn't give for one last word. But as he looked at her now as even more tears flooded onto her cheeks, he knew that it was all over.

Hughes continued to fight as he watched her. He continued to shake and shiver. He could feel his eyes starting to close, not by choice—his body belonged to something else, some other entity. Tears ran down his face, he was so afraid, so sad, so alone. But then he heard a sweet sound, the voice of an angel, and he fought with every last ounce of strength to focus. It was her. It was Jules.

"Don't fight it, darlin'," her voice was quivering as she continued to cry. "Just go to sleep now. Close your eyes and go to sleep. We'll all see you again on the other side. We'll all be together again soon."

Hughes froze for a moment. His face had been contorted with pain for the best part of a minute, but as he closed his eyes one last time, the thinnest of smiles stretched his lips. A pause, two, three, four, then dark red blood dribbled out of his mouth and over his chin. His eyes flicked open once again, but they were not his eyes anymore. What sat in that broken plastic chair on stage was no longer Hughes. It was a monster.

Whereas Hughes had writhed and struggled in a vain attempt to fight off the infection, the creature now wriggled and thrashed, desperate to break its constraints and feast on the bountiful warm flesh in front of it. Within a few seconds, its wild movement had toppled the chair over. It continued to convulse, doing its best to shuffle its way across the stage. It had no concept of the physical limits the restraints bound upon it; it had just one goal, a single purpose.

Shaw looked at each of his friends. Tears were flowing from every pair of eyes. He turned his head towards Troy. "You people are monsters."

"I told you. This was on you. It could all have been avoided. If you'd have just got on that radio and—"

"Don't you dare put this on any of us, you piece of fuckin' shite," hissed Jules. "All we've ever tried to do is live our lives. Yet people like you keep showing up."

"As I was saying"—he turned his head towards Shaw once again—"you needed a demonstration."

"To what end? There are quicker ways to kill someone," he replied, looking back towards the growling figure on stage.

"I don't need lessons in how to kill, and that's not what this was. Now, this is how it's going to play. You're going to send a message out to your people. The rest of my team is already in position. Across at that library of yours, you've got at least a dozen youngsters." He turned towards Jenny. "You must have the best part of twenty people over in that pub car park of yours, sawing away to your—" he turned towards George "—specifications, so you can give those darn marauders a lickin' the next time they show up." Troy glanced across at Angel. He could see a renewed respect for him on her face. He was in charge now. Women like her, they liked that. They liked men of power. He unclipped the radio from his own belt. "One word from me and my team spring into action. Within a minute, we'll all be gone, and you'll be shoulder-deep in death stink."

"Troy!" shouted one of the men from the stage.

Troy turned to look. The Hughes creature had managed to shuffle its way across to the edge. A few more centimetres and it would drop to the floor. The fall would have the potential to finish off the broken chair once and for all and free the creature. "Well, good God, man, do I need to tell you to tie your shoes as well? Finish it off."

The guard marched across to the beast. He pulled out a knife from his belt and plunged it through the Hughes creature's head. Despite Jules, George, Emma, Lucy, Ruth, Jenny, Raj and Shaw all knowing that it was no longer their friend lying there, they let out gasps as the steel blade plunged through the monster's temple.

"I hope you burn in hell," Jules said.

Troy carried on. "Anyway, as I was saying. You get on that radio and say what I want; otherwise, there's going to be a hell of a mess here. You're going to have infected everywhere."

"You wouldn't do it," Lucy said. "You'd be just as screwed as the rest of us."

"Oh, darlin'," Angel said. "We won't be here when it all happens. We'll hop in our little dinghy and just head out. We'll leave it a few days then we'll do a clean-up like we always do. We'll put one of our sirens in position outside of town, set a nice big fire, lure all them monsters away, and then, yes, we might have to use up some valuable resources to get rid of them, but it'll be worth it."

"So, you just want us to make it all easy and convenient for you?" Lucy replied.

"It's not like you wouldn't be getting anything in return. Like Troy said, you'll all leave here, living and breathing. Now isn't that better than what happened to your poor friend over there?"

"Why should we believe you?" Jenny demanded. "Why should we believe that you'll let us go and you won't kill us?"

"Darlin', haven't you been listening? There'd be no point."

"She's right," Troy said. "I don't care what happens to any of you, but I'd rather march everyone out of here without wasting a single round of my valuable ammunition than the alternative. So, the question is a very simple one." He turned back to Shaw. "Do you people want to live or die?."

16

Talikha opened the door for Mike as he carried the case of freshly distilled alcohol into Ward One. He took it through to the small store cupboard and placed it carefully on the shelf.

"Lucy and Raj aren't back yet?" he asked, crouching down to make a fuss of Humphrey.

"No, I was expecting them before now."

"Poor George must be getting the third degree." He ruffled the Labrador's furry mane, kissed him on the head and stood up. "Well, I'd better be getting off, I've got another delivery to make."

"You're making deliveries?"

"Yeah, I told Jules I'd do the supply runs for her this morning. I knew she'd have the meeting. I've already done the North Ridge. You were my second stop. I've just got East Ridge left, and then I promised Wren and Sammy that I'd go out foraging with them this afternoon."

"Foraging? You?" Talikha had always been well-mannered. She was very quiet, but the people she allowed to get to know her best found out that she had a real sense of humour and a mischievous side.

"That is just what Wren said. What's wrong with

me foraging?"

"As I understand it, it requires a lot of patience."

Mike laughed. "I can't believe I'm getting dissed by Talikha Chakrabarti. What happened to that lovely, polite, quiet veterinary nurse I met in Candleton?"

"She got to know you."

"And again. Y'know, if I told anyone, they wouldn't believe me."

Talikha smiled. "That is what makes it so enjoyable."

"Just for your information, I have plenty of patience."

"Michael, please do not take this as an insult when I say that is a dirty, rotten lie." Mike burst out laughing, and Talikha couldn't keep her deadpan expression any longer, she laughed too.

"Okay. You've got me. But it was really important to Sammy."

"You are a good brother, Mike."

"I try to be. I don't always get it right."

"None of us get it right all the time." There was a pause of a few seconds before Talikha spoke again. "How is Emma?"

"Em's okay. We had a long chat, cleared the air."

"And how are you?"

"I'm better now she's back."

Talikha smiled. "I can tell. It is like a giant weight has been lifted from your shoulders. You are young again."

"Err ... you do realise I'm only twenty-two. I mean in my culture that's still pretty young."

"Ah yes, but when Emma was gone, you were the oldest twenty-two-year-old I had ever met."

Mike shrugged. "Yeah, I don't suppose I can argue with that." They walked back down the short hallway and into the main living area of the static caravan. "How come there are no patients?"

"We have just one at the moment, in Ward Two. If

this prolonged bout of good health continues, I will be made redundant."

"I'm sure it will change come winter. Do you remember—" The radio handset at the nurses' station crackled to life, causing Mike to stop in mid-sentence.

"This is Shaw. Please listen carefully. This is not a drill. This is not a hoax. I am speaking on behalf of the council, and I need everybody hearing this broadcast to do as I say." There was a long pause then finally he continued. "We need to evacuate. We need to head out of Safe Haven with the clothes on our backs. We're taking the coast road north. All vehicles, boats, weapons and supplies must be left behind." There was another long pause.

"What the hell is this?" Mike said.

"This next bit is the most important. A fleet of ships is heading towards us. They'll anchor in the bay, and their crews will be ferried to land. Under no circumstances will they be fired upon or interfered with. We are leaving Safe Haven. That's the only thing that any of us need to focus on. The rest of the council and I will remain here at the village hall until all citizens of Safe Haven are outside of the settlement boundaries. We will then be driven to safety. Under no circumstances must anyone try to reach us. The results would be catastrophic. The crews from the ships will be armed, and they will escort those not already heading to the North Ridge out of town. Anyone left in the boundaries of Safe Haven by the end of the day will be shot on sight. Those of you hearing this please spread the word and organise the evacuation. We have no other choice. There will not be another broadcast. We will see you later on tonight."

The radio went dead. Mike and Talikha looked at one another in a state of shock. "What the fuck?" Mike said.

"I don't understand," Talikha replied.

"Yeah, you and me both."

*

"Nicely done. For a minute there, I thought you

were going to lose it and shout out a warning, but no," Troy said, pulling the radio away from Shaw's mouth. He brought his own radio up and hit the talk button. "Jacobs, it's Troy. You there? Over."

"I'm here, Troy, pass your message. Over."

"We are a go! Repeat, we are a go. Over."

"Yes, sir, I roger that. We'll see you real soon. Over and out."

Troy clipped his own radio back onto his belt and brought Shaw's radio up, hitting the talk button. "Now, you heard what Shaw here had to say to you all. My name's Troy and I'm running this show." He looked towards Angel and winked. "You'll all leave this place today, never to come back, but you will leave. I've got operatives already in situ who are making sure that you do as asked. If there is any sign of anything other than complete adherence to Shaw's instructions, people are going to start dying. Your beloved councilmen and women will be first. Any attempt to breach the village hall will be met with deadly force, and, trust me, it won't just be visited on the ones stupid enough to try to rescue these people. We'll be unleashing a whole lot of hurt on everyone. Around about now, the first of my teams will be arriving at the checkpoints to the east and to the north. We've done our research, don't take us for fools. If anybody tries to smuggle anything out of here there will be consequences, and if you're wondering what those consequences might be, refer to my prior warning.
Now, the sooner you people start organising yourselves, the sooner this will all be over. Here the message ends."

"You're enjoying this," Shaw said, not hiding the disdain in his voice.

"I don't like losing. When I can turn a loss around into an emphatic win, I get a buzz like you wouldn't believe, so, yes, I'm enjoying it."

Jules looked towards the thing that had been Hughes, just lying there on the stage. "You're a fuckin' lowlife," she said.

The smile left Troy's face, and he almost charged to where she was sitting. He moved his head so close to her face that she could feel his breath against her skin as he spoke. "You'd better be nice to me, sweet-cheeks, or I might just kill one of your friends to show you the importance of manners."

Jules swallowed hard. She could take any punishment this monster dished out to her, but she couldn't let her temper cause the death of a friend. She closed her eyes to fight back more tears. "I'm sorry," she whispered before starting to cry again.

"I've just figured out where I know you from," Lucy said, glaring at Angel.

"You're mistaken, shug, you and I have never met."

"No. No, we haven't, but you're Angeline Jackson."

"Why Angel, you're famous," Troy said, the smile reappearing on his face.

"You really know her?" Ruth asked, remembering back to the first time Lucy had said she thought she recognised the woman.

"Her husband ran a sham evangelical ministry."

"Now, weren't you listening to Troy when he was talking about playin' nice?"

Lucy ignored her and turned to look at Ruth. "They made more money than you would believe. There was lots of talk about how their church laundered cash for some of the country's biggest arms manufacturers and dealers. Y'know a contract for supplying weapons to the United States Marines is something a company can shout about. Selling those same weapons to terrorist regimes, well, the pay's even better, but you don't really want that stuff going through the books."

"I said it's time for you to shut up," Angel said.

Troy brought his sidearm up to Raj's temple. "Say another word and Osama here buys it."

A snarl started on Lucy's lips, but she managed to

subdue it just in time. "I am Hindu," Raj said defiantly.

"Say what?" Troy asked.

"You called me Osama. Osama Bin Laden was a Muslim and a Saudi. I am Hindu and I am Indian."

Troy looked at his men, and they all burst out laughing simultaneously. "Well, pardon me. I didn't want to cause you any offence." He pressed the gun a little harder against Raj's skull and glared at Lucy. "Say another word and Gandhi gets it." Lucy dropped her gaze to the table in front of her. "That's better." He bent down and brought his mouth close to Raj's ear. "Now listen to me, you worthless, towelhead, bhaji-eating motherfucker. I'll call you whatever I damn well please. If I say you were one of those pieces of shit that flew planes into the twin towers, then that's what you fucking are. I'm running things, and right now, the only god you need to worry about is the metal one that's pressing against your skull. You understand me?"

"I understand."

"Good then. We're going to get along just fine, Osama. Oh, wait a minute," he said, looking worried and animatedly patting Raj down. He turned to look at his men again. "Don't worry, boys, we're safe, no suicide vest." Troy's men burst out laughing once more, and this time Angel joined in.

"Oh, Troy, you're just terrible." She looked at him, and he looked at her. That feeling was coming back. He could tell. The sparkle in her eyes from the early days.

Troy winked at her. "Don't you just know it?"

*

"What are we going to do?" Talikha asked with a look of worry in her eyes the likes of which Mike had never seen.

Mike slumped down onto one of the beds. He remained silent for a moment; the cogs in his brain were turning slowly, trying to digest what he had just heard. "Okay, first things first." He stood up and disappeared out of the ward for a moment. Talikha heard the boot of his car close before he returned a moment later. There was some rustling and a thud in the entrance hall before Mike reappeared.

"What are you doing?" Talikha asked.

"Don't worry about it," he replied, walking up to her. "Talikha, I've got a big ask. If you move quickly, you'll get to George's place before anybody's had time to react. Speak to Richard and David. Get them to organise the march north. Tell them to form a team and make sure that every house along the way is evacuated. Then I need you to take the car and head to my house. Sammy, Jake, Wren and Tabby will be there. They won't have heard the message. I need you to explain everything to them. Leave the car at the house and start walking towards the North Ridge, then on to Torridon. It should be safe there. Take Daisy with you; walk her up one of the hills before you get to the checkpoint. These bastards will think she's livestock. Do that for me, please. Do it now."

"But—"

"I need you to do this, Talikha. I need you to keep my family together and safe. I need to know you're with them. Whatever happens, please stay with them."

"What are you going to do?"

"I'm heading to the pub. They'll probably have heard the broadcast. I'm going to get a team to go door to door and get everybody out of the village. We're probably going to need a couple of the wheelchairs from here, but we need to get everyone moving."

Talikha looked at him. "So, when you have been to the pub, you will catch up? You will join us?"

Mike placed his hands reassuringly on her shoulders. "They've got our families in there, and there is no way these people are going to let them go once we're all out of here."

"How do you know?"

"The council is the community's brain, its organisation. They want rid of us, they want us weak, they want us to die out there. They're not going to hand our best people, our military leader, and our doctor back to us. They'll make sure everyone is out of Safe Haven then they'll just kill them."

Talikha's brow furrowed. "What are you going to do?"

Mike strengthened his grip on her shoulders. "I'm still working on that one, but whatever else happens we need to maintain the appearance that we're obeying their commands."

"Mike, I am scared. I could not live without Raj."

"It's not going to come to that."

"You are just one man, what can you do?"

"This is family, Talikha. I'll do whatever I need to." He let go of her shoulders, bent down and tussled Humphrey's ears. "Look after everybody, boy." Mike stood straight once again and threw his arms around Talikha. "Take care. You're the only person in the world right now who I can trust to get this done."

"Please don't do anything foolish."

He kissed her cheek, picked up the radio and left. As he entered the small wooded area between the infirmary and the Haven Arms, he heard the car engine start. For all his bravado, he knew this was going to be virtually impossible. One man against an army, but while ever Lucy and Emma were still alive, he would never give up.

17

Kirsty had been inside the pub when the first part of Shaw's broadcast had begun. She had run outside with the radio to let the assembled workers listen to the message, and now, rather than heading out of town as the instructions had said, there were panicked and fevered conversations going on. Mike could hear the frightened murmurs before he'd emerged from the woodland, and as soon as he appeared, Kirsty headed straight towards him.

"Jenny's at the meeting, Mike." Jenny was the closest thing Kirsty had to family. He knew how she felt, he could empathise with her anxiety, but familiar feelings had begun to stir in him.

After he'd experienced hallucinations and ultimately what was a psychotic break, Lucy had helped to piece him back together. Part of that process had been relieving him of some of his responsibilities so the weight of the world was not on his shoulders. Part of it had been a concerted effort to react with more thought and less emotion to situations. Mike felt that during this time he had matured greatly, but he could also feel the pressure building once again.

"I know. Lucy and Em are across there too," he said to Kirsty before climbing onto a bench. "Listen to me, everybody." He projected his voice loud enough to be heard even at the back of the car park. "We need to follow the instructions we've been given. We don't have a choice in this. There are only a few radios dotted around, so there'll be a lot of people who didn't hear the broadcast. I need you to split up the village, go door to door and then head towards the North Ridge."

"But this is our home," shouted a voice.

"You don't think I know that? They're holding all the cards here. We've got to do as they say, and the sooner the better. So, please, no more discussion. Alert the rest of the village then head north on the coast road. There's another team evacuating all the properties on the road north. It won't take long for you to catch up with them and then you can give them a hand too. I know how hard this is for everyone, but we have to do as these people say."

Mike caught movement out of the corner of his eye. It was someone lurking behind a tree that bordered the car park. *Was that one of them? Was that one of the enemy?* Safe Haven had an open-door policy. They took in refugees on a regular basis and, providing they were happy to have the physical examination to check they hadn't been bitten or scratched and that they were willing to work at whatever job they were given, they were given accommodation and food. There were often faces Mike didn't recognise, but, given the circumstances, he wondered now if this was one of the spies the voice on the radio had warned of. He climbed down off the bench and headed into the pub. Kirsty followed him.

They entered the main lounge and Meg, Jenny's dog, lifted her head up, looked at the two of them and brought it to rest once more on the thick rug in front of the fireplace. Even when there was no fire burning, that was her favourite place to while away her days. "So this is it then?" Kirsty said. "Everything we've worked for, we're just handing it over."

Mike carried on walking. "Maybe," he replied as he began to climb the stairs to Jenny's flat.

"Err, Mike, where are you going?"

He didn't respond but reached the top of the flight and walked along the hallway to the main bedroom. He stopped just back from the window. The crowd outside were talking and pointing in various directions, dividing up the village to spread the grave news. "You see that guy?" he said, gesturing to the far corner of the car park and the figure he had seen two minutes before.

Kirsty sidled up beside him. "Yeah."

"You recognise him?"

"Well, it's difficult to see him properly, he's not exactly out in the open, but, no, can't say I know him, why?" The men and women in the car park began to disperse and almost as soon as Kirsty had stopped speaking, the mystery man vanished behind the tree and out of sight. She and Mike kept a vigil for a few more seconds, but he did not re-emerge.

Mike turned to look at Kirsty. "Whoever these people are, they're well organised. I thought that when they talked about having spies, they might have been bluffing, but I'm pretty certain they're not."

"I don't understand why we can't take the vehicles, it would be much quicker."

"I told you they want everything. You know how precious fuel is, they want that too. I sent Talikha to organise Richard and David then get to my family almost as soon as the broadcast had finished. I figured there'd be a few minutes' grace. They'd appreciate not everyone would have heard the instructions, but I wouldn't want to press our luck."

Kirsty looked confused. "I don't understand. You sent Talikha? How come you didn't go?"

Mike brushed his hand over his face. "Lucy, Em, Jen, Raj, Jules, George, Hughes, Shaw, none of them are making it out of that hall alive. They've got a few hours while we get everyone out then that's it."

"But they've said if we try anything, all bets are off."

"That's why I can't make a move until everybody else is safe."

"Mike, that's madness. They're coming in on those big ships, there's going to be a whole army in Safe Haven before long. What can one man do against an army?"

"I suppose we're about to find out."

*

"He specifically asked for Richard and me to do this?" David asked again.

The men and women at George's workshop were already making preparations to leave when Talikha had pulled up outside.

"For the third time, yes. Now, it is of vital importance that you do this. Mike has put his faith in you," Talikha replied.

"Oh, goodness me." It was Richard who spoke this time. "I can feel my hives are getting ready to break out."

"Look, you are very methodical, very thorough, and that is just what this requires. It is of paramount importance that this is done with all possible haste."

"Maybe we should draw up a plan," David said.

"No!" Talikha even shocked herself with the sternness of her tone. "No," she said again, softer this time. "There is no time. We must start this now. I have to collect Sammy, Jake and Wren, and then I will join you." She looked towards Richard then David. "We have been through a lot together. We have always depended on others to guide us, now it is their turn to depend on us."

There was a short pause as the enormity of Talikha's words sank in then a knowing nod shared between all three of them.

"You're right," Richard said. "You're right."

"I will see you shortly," Talikha replied then turned to leave.

*

SAFE HAVEN: IS THIS THE END OF EVERYTHING?

Mike had formed a plan in his head long before leaving the pub, in fact soon after he had given Talikha her instructions. There was no way he could have told anyone else. There was no way he could even have spoken it out loud for that matter. Just the thought of carrying it out made him shiver, but it was the one chance, the one glimmer of hope he had.

There was no way he could have been seen by spies or anyone as he slipped out of the back door of the Haven Arms and into the woods. He arrived at the infirmary to find that it had already been evacuated and all that remained were four empty static caravans.

Mike kept his eyes peeled to make sure there were no mysterious strangers looking in his direction before breaking cover and running across to the entrance of Ward One, where he had said goodbye to Talikha just a short time before.

He climbed the steps, opened the door, and there in the corner where he had left it was his rucksack. Just carrying it would be a death sentence if he was seen. The crisscrossed machete handles protruding from it would have been enough to signal his intent, but if anyone opened it up to look inside it, they would see a shotgun, shells, Lucy's Glock 17, a couple of spare magazines as well as screwdrivers, a crowbar and a couple of knives. Up until a few days ago, it had been gathering dust in the back of their car, but now the familiar backpack had been forced out of retirement.

Mike slid the straps onto his shoulders, returned to the door, and scoured the landscape before sprinting back across to the woods. Where he was going nobody would think of looking for him.

*

Talikha brought the car to a stop and pulled on the handbrake outside of Mike's house. She turned to look at Humphrey. "I know, boy, I'm scared too," she said then reached across and gently stroked his head. "Come on."

She opened the door, climbed out, and Humphrey followed her. They had only just reached the garden gate when the front door swung open, and Wolf bounded out towards the Labrador Retriever. The two greeted each other, wagged their tails and disappeared into the house. Wren was waiting at the door with a smile on her face.

"Hi," she said, "there's only me, Sammy, Jake and Tabby here if you're looking for Mike or Lucy."

"No, I have come to see you."

"Sounds ominous," Wren replied, still smiling, but as she looked into Talikha's sad and frightened eyes, the smile washed off her face. "What's happened?"

"I need to speak to you and Tabitha away from the children."

"Okay, but you're starting to scare me. What's going on?"

A few minutes later, Talikha had relayed the events to Wren and Tabby in the kitchen while Sammy and Jake were entertained by Humphrey and Wolf in the living room.

"Oh my God!" Tabby said.

"Grandad's there."

"I know, Wren. Raj is in there too."

"Where's Mike now?" Wren asked.

"I have no idea. He asked me to come here and make sure that the four of you got to safety."

"But he's not leaving?"

"I don't know what Mike is doing; I am just doing what he asked me to."

"I don't understand. If they gave these instructions, and he tries something, then it doesn't make any difference if it's one man or all of Safe Haven, they'll retaliate."

"Wren, please, I have no idea what he has in mind, but I know that he would never do anything to jeopardise the safety of those nine people who are being held hostage or any of us."

"Well, by the sounds of it, if they see him, he already is jeopardising their safety."

"Look, I understand your concerns, I share them equally; however, the best course of action we can take is to do as he has asked."

"I'll go get the children ready," Tabby said, leaving Talikha and Wren alone.

"I have known Mike for a long time. I trust him with my life. I trust him with Raj's life. If there is a chance, he is the one who will find it."

Wren stared at Talikha. She remembered back to the first time she saw Mike, trapped in the snow, on the verge of being made mincemeat by a horde of rampaging infected. "I suppose you're right." Almost as if he sensed Wren's distress, Wolf appeared at the door. "I'll go get Daisy and then we can set off." Wren headed out of the kitchen and Wolf followed.

A few minutes passed, and when she did not return, Talikha went outside to see what the hold-up was. She walked around the house to the lean-to that housed Daisy, Mike's gran's beloved goat. The animal was happily bedded down, chewing away on some grass. "Wren?" Talikha called, but there was no reply. "Wren?" she shouted this time, running to the side of the house to get a view of the track leading up to the road, but there was no sign of anyone. Talikha clenched her fists and closed her eyes. Part of her wanted to jump in the car and go looking for Wren; part of her wanted to scream and cry at the top of her voice, to shout to the gods to protect her husband; but she did neither. She coaxed Daisy out of her little home, attached the short length of rope around her neck that was hanging by the shelter door, and made her way back around the front of the house to where Tabby, Sammy, Jake and Humphrey were all patiently waiting.

"Where's Wren?" Sammy asked.

"She's going to catch up with us later," Talikha replied sadly, knowing it wouldn't be the last lie she told that day.

18

Noah stood in front of the window, looking out over the glimmering sea and massaging his temples in the hope that the gentle action might relieve the hammering headache he had been suffering since soon after waking up that morning.

The luxury ship was in an uproar. Breakfast had still not been served. Madison and dozens of others had demanded to see Noah but to no avail. He had sequestered himself and his two bodyguards away in a vacant cabin. Eventually, he turned around to look at Doug then Viktor. "Okay, take it from the top, one last time, because as much as I want to stay in here for the rest of the day, at some stage I'm going to have to go out there and explain what's going on."

"Sir, the inventory officer isn't on board; he must have helped them and gone with them. His deputy and the head chef reckon we might have three days' food left at the most."

"Yeah, yeah, that much has sunk in. Go over the rest of it again."

"Mr Jackson, we're missing a lot of the crew. My guess is there'll be a lot of pissed-off people out there who are missing members of their entourage too. This was well planned, sir. Both the ship and the lifeboats have been drained of fuel, and even if that wasn't the case, the engines and controls have been sabotaged. This ship isn't going anywhere. The armoury looks just like the pantry, lots of empty shelves and very little else."

Noah turned back towards the window. "Angel, what have you done to me?" he asked under his breath. He looked at his watch. "Shit, it's getting on towards lunchtime and we ain't even served breakfast. Do me a favour." He turned back around. "Viktor, head down and tell the chef to start serving breakfast. Then go find Madison. Tell him to round up his cronies and meet me in the dining room."

"Yes, sir," Viktor said, immediately disappearing out of the door.

"What do you want me to do, Mr Jackson?"

"I need you to stay the fuck with me and make sure your weapon's loaded. When they find out what my wife's done to us, they're going to want someone's blood, and even money I'll be that someone."

*

The radio hissed to life. "Troy, this is Santos. Over."

Troy unclipped the handset from his belt. "Santos, this is Troy. Go ahead. Over."

"The village is nearly clear. They're emptying the last few houses now. What do you want us to do? Over."

"When everyone's out, post two guards on the north approach. We've already got our team in place on the east approach, so we don't need to worry about that. It's going to take them a few hours to make that trail. When the reinforcements arrive, have a team do regular sweeps up and down the coast in a vehicle. Make sure everybody sticks to the plan. You know what to do if they try anything. Stay in regular contact. Over."

"Message received and understood. Over and out."

The radio went silent and Troy slid it back onto his

belt. "Well, it looks like your friends are all playing nice."

"They didn't really have a lot of options, did they?" Shaw replied.

A cruel smile curled up the corners of Troy's mouth. "Everybody has choices."

*

Mike sat down on the sturdy wooden bench. He had lost count of how many times he had been to the cemetery. He had helped dig more than his fair share of graves, and now, as the outlines of the first tall ships appeared on the horizon, he wondered if he would ever dig another. There was a sad resignation to what he was doing. He knew that the chances of his actions allowing him, Lucy, Emma and the rest of them to escape into the sunset unharmed were a million to one, but doing nothing was not an option. He couldn't join the rest of them on their march out of Safe Haven.

Talikha was an intelligent woman. She had a sound medical knowledge and a sensible head on her shoulders. Wren had survived out there for months by herself, she was a fighter. As long as Sammy and Jake were with them, they would be okay. But the chances of everyone surviving without the infrastructure that had been put into place in Safe Haven to protect them were slim.

Mike reached into his rucksack and pulled out a bottle of water. He took a drink then regarded it for a few seconds. This was from the well at home. It was probably the last water he would ever drink from it. As much as it tantalised him, as much as he would like to drink it all as the sun beat down upon him, he knew he would need it later, so he screwed the top back on and returned it to his backpack.

He sat a while longer, enjoying the serenity. The cemetery was well off the beaten track. There were no houses around, and it was on a long-neglected road. He watched the flotilla of ships and boats move forever closer. Tick-tock, tick-tock, tick-tock.

He finally stood up and walked to the rickety shed in the far corner of the burial ground. He opened it up and there in the corner was a selection of spades. He grabbed a long-handled stainless steel one and headed back out to a freshly laid plot. There was a large wooden cross sunk deep into the dry brown earth. It read, "JOHN MASTERS, MUCH LOVED BROTHER OF BETH AND ANNIE. MAY HE REST IN PEACE."

A wave of guilt swept over Mike as he read the words. He wished John could rest in peace, but, unfortunately, that wasn't going to happen.

*

Thiago and his vast team had sprung into action as soon as the word had come down from above that breakfast was to be served. The bakery had long since delivered the bread, possibly the last bread that would ever be served on *The Ark*. The massive galley was a throng of activity as trolleys started to be wheeled out. Steam rose from various urns, plates clattered, orders were shouted down the line, and every member of staff in the place was doing their best to subdue the angry growls from their almost empty stomachs. They had taken hurried and hungry bites from rolls and croissants while preparing a much slimmed down breakfast experience, but the passengers, especially these passengers, were the most important ones.

As more and more trolleys of food and drink made their way out of the doors, Thiago started to relax a little. He was down quite a few staff that morning; he could only assume they had disappeared in the night as well, so he found himself mucking in wherever he was needed. Right now, he was scooping strawberry jam from a tin, which was about half the size of the average beer barrel, into bijou terracotta serving pots. This was his second trolley. The first was already being pushed out to the dining room.

"We should be starting lunch now, never mind breakfast," said Timo, the man doing the same job on the opposite side of the preparation table.

"We shouldn't be starting anything. We should be rationing what we've got more than ever," Thiago replied.

"The bread was already made. It's not like we could let it go to waste."

"It wouldn't go to waste. In three days' time, when there is nothing left but tomato ketchup and mayo, trust me, these people with all their airs and graces would kill for a piece of stale bread."

"It won't happen. They'll come up with a plan. They always do."

Thiago shook his head. "You have too much faith."

"They gave us the scavenger fleet, didn't they? They will sort something out."

Thiago looked across at Timo to see if he was joking, and when he saw he wasn't, he shook his head again with more frustration this time. *Am I the only one who can see what's going on here?* He returned to his work and, aware that there would be lengthening queues at the buffet tables, picked up his pace. A big glob of jam spilt over the sides of the pot he was holding and landed on his thumb. "Dammit," he said, wrapping his lips over the red splodge then wiping the rim of the small pot. He carried on to the next and was about to fill that when he stopped.

Despite all the noise going on in the kitchen, Timo noticed that the rhythmic clink from across the preparation counter had come to a stop. "What is it?"

Thiago looked at him, confused for a moment. "The jam. It tastes funny."

"Funny how?" Timo asked.

"I don't know … coppery … rusty … just funny."

"Maybe you had something on your hand," Timo said, dipping one of his own fingers in and sucking the globule of red jelly into his mouth. He swilled it around for a moment like he was wine tasting then cringed a little. "No, you're right, there is definitely something wrong with it." He looked across at his friend who was now just staring dead ahead. His eyes almost seemed glazed. "Thiago? Thiago, are you okay?" A few seconds passed by then a few seconds more. Then… Thiago coughed, and a spray of blood left his mouth and spread over his white uniform. "Thiago?"

*

There were long queues at the breakfast bar even before any food appeared. Noah and Doug had not got ten feet into the colossal dining room when Madison and a small army of entitled wealthy patrons and their various henchmen and women made a beeline towards him.

"What the fuck is all this about?" Madison hissed, his face barely three inches away from Noah's.

"Thomas, I need you to back up now," Noah replied, not breaking eye contact.

"I'll goddamn well back up when you give us answers, you little shit."

Noah knew this was coming and he was prepared. He was about to address Madison and the rest of the group with a brief and well-rehearsed summary of what had happened when a piercing scream sliced through the noise hushing every single conversation in the place. Noah, Doug, Madison and the rest of the large group all turned their heads in the direction of the sound. It was followed by another shriek then another. "Holy Jesus, what is it, a fire?" Noah asked. "Doug, go find out what's happening."

"Yes, sir." While everyone else was glued to the spot, Doug ran towards the sounds coming from the galley. He had not got far when the double doors burst open to reveal Timo, or what had been Timo. His Mediterranean colouring had been washed away. His skin was pallid, his eyes grey, and the bright red blood that painted his mouth and uniform told the story of what he had become. For a moment, Doug froze in shock, but then, as Timo pounced, leaping on one of the female serving staff and disappearing from view behind one of the long tables, he realised what this was. A fire on board a ship was never a good thing, but in that split second, Doug would have given anything for it to be a fire rather than this. He drew his Sig Sauer P320 as more and more screams and howls rose into the air from next door.

The Timo thing reappeared. Terrified screams erupted all around Doug as passengers saw the bloody flap of freshly torn flesh protruding from the creature's lips. Doug took aim and fired. Everything fell silent around him for a moment as he watched the bullet enter the beast's forehead. The monster collapsed to the ground. The rest of the serving staff, having got over their initial horror, began to flee in any direction that was clear, as did the passengers. Any hunger pangs were forgotten as more creatures burst through the doors.

Doug turned to look at Noah. The crowd that a moment since had been so eager to confront him now fled like frightened children, their security details covering them as they ran. The growing army of monsters surged forward, making the buffet tables cartwheel. Bread buns, brioche and croissants flew into the air like they had been fired from a cannon. More shots began to echo around the vast dining room as some of the security personnel started to realise the only way out of this was to contain the outbreak while it was still in its elemental stages. Doug took aim at the young waitress Timo had attacked as she vaulted over chairs and upturned tables towards him.

"Watch out, Doug!" screamed Noah, just as the bodyguard squeezed the trigger, but it was too late.

The bullet went astray as Doug was knocked from his feet. He hit the floor heavily still managing to keep a firm hold of his weapon. He brought it up as the creature's mouth closed in on him and fired. The freshly turned beast's face imploded, and Doug exhaled a relieved breath, but then the relief turned to abject fear as he tasted the monster's blood in his mouth. He spat it out, but still more splashed on his skin. Chaos was unfurling all around him, though he was deaf and blind to all of it. He threw the creature off him and rolled away. "Water. I need water to rinse my mouth," he shouted to anyone who was listening, but nobody was.

He looked towards Noah, who was still standing in the same place he had left him. "I'm sorry," Noah mouthed, and Doug saw genuine sadness in the preacher's eyes as he spoke.

"Run!" Doug shouted. "Run, sir!"

Noah tore his eyes away from his loyal bodyguard to view the hellish scene unfolding around them. When he looked back towards Doug, he saw him coughing blood, and his skin was beginning to drain of all colour. Noah did not run, but he turned and walked out of the dining room for the last time.

19

Wren knew the woodland and landscape surrounding Safe Haven better than anyone. She and Wolf made good time sprinting through the trees. Mike would be angry that she had not done as instructed, but he didn't make her choices. They were just a few hundred metres out of the village; this was where the real danger began. If what Talikha said was true, being spotted would result in Wren's end plus who knew what for the nine prisoners.

She paused to catch her breath and think. Mike would not just burst into the village hall guns blazing. As impulsive as he was, he would not do anything to risk the lives of his sister and Lucy. Wren thought back to the stories she had heard about him, and there had been plenty of stories.

Hughes had told her about the time when Mike first showed up in that village and was ready to fight him to find out whether his family was there. Jenny had once regaled the story of the first encounter with Fry and how, against all odds, they had beaten back his forces due to Mike's heroics. Beth had told her about how he had saved her from Fry's mad hands at that farm.

Suddenly, a light bulb switched on over Wren's

head. Up until this point, her sole focus had been to get back to the village to help Mike, but she had not thought for a second where he would be. Now she knew exactly.

"Come on, boy," she said, turning towards Wolf. "We've got some way to go yet." The German Shepherd cocked its head slightly, then the pair of them set off at a sprint once again.

*

Talikha held Sammy's hand, who in turn held Jake's. Tabby walked by Talikha's side, and Humphrey trotted along in front of them. Up until here, the path had been winding but relatively flat; however, they had reached one of the many steep inclines on this coastal route, and their pace had slowed.

When Talikha had given Sammy and Jake the Disney version of events, there had still been tears, but Sammy's unwavering faith in her brother meant she would do as she was told. Whatever Sammy did, Jake always followed. Wren disappearing had not helped the situation and saying goodbye to their gran's beloved goat had resulted in more than near hysterics, but as the journey had progressed, a resignation to the task had set in.

The ascent of the hill was slow going, and at first, when they stopped halfway up, Talikha presumed it was due to fatigue. She looked at Sammy whose eyes had grown wide. Talikha turned towards the ocean to see a fleet of ships on the horizon. This was it, the invasion was underway.

"Don't look, children, just carry on walking. We have a good distance yet to cover," Talikha said and tightened her grip around the young girl's hand. They reached the brow of the hill, and Humphrey stopped and turned to look back. He let out a bark.

Talikha, Tabby, Sammy and Jake all turned at the same time to see Richard and David leading an emerging crowd. Even from this distance, Talikha could recognise villagers as well as people from the outskirts. As they stood and waited, more and more emerged from around the bend.

It took the two librarians a few minutes to lead the rag-tag mob up the incline, but when they reached them, both men uncharacteristically threw their arms around Talikha, who happily reciprocated. They had all been through so much together, and their torments were far from over, but being back with old friends, being back with people who had suffered the same trials made them feel a little better.

"I didn't think we'd manage to catch up with you," David said. "Do you think we should wait for the rest of the village or should we just carry on?"

"Mike wanted me to get Sammy and Jake out of here as quickly as I could. That is what I promised him, that is what I must do."

David nodded slowly. "Okay then, fair enough. I suppose we'll all meet up on the other side anyway."

Tabby shot him a sharp glance. "You don't rate our chances then?"

David looked confused for a moment then chuckled. "Bad wording. I meant on the other side of the checkpoint."

When the last of the group reached the brow of the hill and had the chance to regain their breath, they continued their march. "Err, where's Wren? I thought she was with you," Richard said.

Talikha gave him a sideways glance. "She was with us. She isn't now."

"Oh, dear. That's not good."

"There is nothing good about any of this."

"No."

A horn sounded behind them, taking the whole group by surprise. It was the school minibus. The crowd edged towards the verge, and it slowly trundled forward. It pulled up by the side of Talikha, Richard and David. The window lowered, and a man with black hair and soulless eyes nodded curtly. He was wearing a military uniform with an insignia on the sleeve that Richard didn't recognise. "Rest up when you get to the bottom of this hill," he ordered in an American accent.

Richard looked beyond him to the armed men and women behind. "I thought we were meant to get out of here as quickly as possible."

"Look, buddy, you've got a group of about two hundred coming up behind you, and I don't want to spend my entire day rounding you people up like I'm corralling a herd of cattle. Now, take a breather when you reach the bottom and wait for them. Me or one of my colleagues will be back this way soon." The window closed, and the bus set off once more.

"I suppose this is really it, isn't it?" David said. "It's the end of everything we worked for."

"While ever we are alive, it is not the end," Talikha replied as they all began to move again.

They reached the foot of the hill, and some of the older people sat down on rocks while others stood watching the incoming fleet. Nervous conversations fluttered around, and the mood gradually worsened. Richard, David and Talikha all moved away from the rest of the crowd and spoke in hushed tones. "Did Mike give you any inclination as to what he was planning?" Richard asked.

Talikha shook her head. "He told me he did not believe they would let the council go when we had reached the checkpoint." A tear appeared in the corner of her eye. Up until now, she had needed to be strong for the children, strong for the people who looked to her, but in the company of old friends, she could be herself.

David let out a long sigh. "I think he makes a fair point. Knowing what these people have done, there's no reason to believe they'd do anything that wouldn't serve their own purpose. I mean look at us," he said, gesturing towards the already tired and drawn looking faces. "No food, or water, and when we set foot out of Safe Haven boundaries, things will only get harder. What happens when we run into infected with no weapons and old and infirm people to take care of? Ruth is like my sister. I love her, and there's nothing I want more than to see her again. I'd love to believe that these people would keep their word, but I can't, and this ... this walk to freedom. It's nothing but a death march."

*

Mike could feel the sweat running down his bare back as the sun continued to beat down on him. He'd already dug several feet, but there was still a lot of earth to remove before he could think about taking proper rest. He reached over for his water bottle and took a drink then suddenly caught movement out of the corner of his eye. Without indicating he had seen anything, he placed the bottle back in his rucksack and grasped hold of the handle of one of his machetes. This wasn't going to be easy. He was standing chest-deep in a grave. Vaulting out of it and over to the bushes before someone had a chance to make their move was a tough ask.

"Relax," called a familiar voice. "It's me."

"What the hell are you doing here?" he asked, climbing out of the hole.

Wolf broke cover from the bushes first then Wren stepped out into the open. "Yeah, nice to see you too."

"Did you not see Talikha?"

"I saw her."

"And she told you what I said?"

"Yeah."

"Which brings me back to my question, what the hell are you doing here?"

"I don't take orders from anyone, Mike. My grandad's in that village hall, just like your sister and girlfriend. I've got as much to lose as you and I'm not prepared to just walk out of town and hope for the best."

Anger flared in Mike's eyes, but it was fleeting. "It's not safe, Wren. This—" he gestured to what he was doing "—it's a Hail Mary. Some of them have already arrived, but soon we're going to be overrun, and when our people have reached the North Ridge, I'm pretty certain they're going to kill the council. What I'm doing, it might provide the tiniest diversion, the slimmest chance, but that's all it is. I couldn't just leave them in there and do nothing."

"Yeah, well, me neither. I've lost my parents, I've lost my sister. I'm not going to lose my granddad ... again."

"I didn't want anyone to be taking this risk but me. And you, you, in particular, I wanted with Sammy and Jake."

"Why? Why me? 'Cause I'm a girl and only sixteen?"

"What? No. Because you're one of the bravest, smartest and most capable people I've ever met. Because if I wanted anybody to look after my family, it would be you."

Wren felt a sudden urge to cry but managed to hold it back. "Err, that's really nice of you to say."

"It's the truth. You might be a sarky little bastard, but I'd trust you with my life ... and my family's."

Wren let out a small laugh. "Thanks."

"Oh well. You're here now. Not a lot I can do about it. How did you find me anyway?"

"Well, I asked myself what I'd do, and when that didn't work, I asked myself what's the maddest, most dangerous, suicidal thing anyone could do, so here I am," she said with a smile.

"I'm impressed."

"Don't be. I used to watch lots of documentaries about delving into the minds of serial killers."

"In fairness, I've always been more of the spree killer type. Serial killing requires a level of effort I'm just not prepared to commit to," he said, crouching down and making a fuss of Wolf.

"Well, I beg your pardon."

"How long had you been in the bushes?"

"A couple of minutes. I was trying to figure out what I was going to say to you without you going off on one."

Mike looked towards the hole he was digging once more. "It's a good job Beth's not still here. She'd never forgive me for this."

"There's nothing to forgive. It's just flesh. That body isn't John."

"I suppose you're right."

"It's rare that I'm not."

"You must have been so popular in school."

"I was probably about as popular as you were in prison."

"It wasn't prison it was ... alright, it was a prison. And, as a matter of fact, I *was* popular, eventually."

"What, in the showers? Yeah, you strike me as that sort."

"Funny ... funny girl. If I'd have known you were going to show up, I'd have brought my sunglasses so I wouldn't be so dazzled by your sparkling wit."

"Come on," she said, jumping down into the hole. "You look like you could do with a break. Let me dig for a while." She grabbed the spade and began to shift more earth without even waiting for a reply. Suddenly, the impossible task ahead of Mike seemed a little more possible.

*

Shaw continued to stare at the remains of his oldest friend. In his life, he had never felt so helpless. His captors were only paying the slightest attention to them now. What were he and his fellow council members going to do with their hands cable-tied to the chairs? Troy and the other guards kept throwing fleeting glimpses across to the rectangle of tables before returning to their hushed plans and conversation.

Shaw finally tore his eyes away from Hughes's body and looked towards his friends. They were all preoccupied, lost in their own sad thoughts. Jules, Emma and Ruth had tear streaks running down their cheeks. Raj looked distant, like a man who was waiting for the executioner to flick the switch on the electric chair. They all knew what awaited them, Shaw better than anyone. These people were smart and ruthless, a deadly combination. He glanced towards Jenny, whose eyes were closed. Was she praying? Was she just wanting to block out the reality of what was going on? Was she holding back tears? His gaze then moved towards Lucy and stayed there.

She was not looking towards him; she was staring at Troy. Her face did not reflect the same hopelessness as the others. It was filled with concentration ... determination. She was planning something, but what? As if a sixth sense told her that someone was looking at her, she turned towards Shaw before casting her eyes back towards her captors.

Shaw continued to stare towards her then he spotted it, a micro-movement, no, micro-movements. She was trying to free herself. She knew what he did; that despite Troy's assurances, when the population of Safe Haven were out of town, everyone around the table would have served their purpose and be put to death. Shaw had no idea what plan Lucy was working on, or if she had any plan at all beyond freeing her hands, but now Shaw slowly began to move the stainless-steel links of his watch strap against the plastic cable tie. It would take some time to cut through the thick material, but for the time being, he had nothing better to do.

20

Noah pulled a bottle, two glasses and his Colt Python from the bottom drawer of his desk. He had managed to escape the fate that so many others had suffered so far, but he knew he did not have long left. He poured healthy measures into each glass and then pushed one of the drinks over to Viktor.

Viktor was looking very pale. He had met up with Noah as the mass exodus from the dining room had taken place. He had saved Noah from one of the infected and for his troubles been bitten on the arm, no, more than bitten, a chunk had been taken out of him. He had lost a considerable amount of blood, and even though a tourniquet had been applied, the prognosis was not good. He grabbed the glass of whisky and glugged it like it was water. Noah leaned over and immediately refilled it then grabbed his own glass and took two big gulps. "I'm sorry as hell this happened to you, Viktor."

Viktor took another drink. "Death comes for us all in the end."

"I just hoped it would be later ... much later for both of us. I can't believe Angel would do something like this. I mean running out on me is one thing. Killing me is one thing. Doing this to all these people, well, that's just … it's just evil."

Viktor took another drink and placed the glass back down on the desk. "Sir, I always liked you."

"Why thank you, Viktor, I always liked you too."

"But your wife was a total fucking bitch."

Noah's eyes widened with shock as he looked towards his bodyguard; then finally a smile turned the corner of his mouth up before he guffawed with laughter. "Well, I suppose you got that dead right."

"But, sir," Viktor continued, "This wasn't her." He gestured around as distant screams could be heard from the hallways. "This was someone who wanted to make sure that there was no chance anybody could come after them. This was a tactical move, a clever move, a winning move. Rendering the ship immobile, sabotaging the lifeboats, making sure there was no way anybody could escape. That was check. While ever there were engineers or ship hands on board, there was always the slimmest possibility that some would find a means of escape. But this is checkmate. This was the move of a grandmaster. This was Troy."

"Well, my dear wife, may she rot in Hell, chose him over me."

"Yes, but I know Troy. I know what he did as a mercenary in Mali and Rwanda. I know some of the men he has with him. A very small circle would have known about this, and your wife would not be among them. For whatever she is, she would not be able to reconcile herself to this."

The room fell silent for a moment, and both men took a drink. Noah looked towards Viktor whose face had turned greyer. "Sweet Jesus, we should get you laid down on the couch." He started getting up from his chair to help his wounded bodyguard when Viktor put his hand up.

"No. I need … I need a favour, sir." He looked towards the revolver on the desk.

Noah took an even longer drink. He rubbed his other hand over his face as another scream, nearer this time, echoed down the hallway. He picked up the gun and felt the weight of it in his hand. "The only thing this baby has ever fired at is paper targets."

"Not today," Viktor said. His voice was just a whisper now, and as Noah looked at him, he could see the bodyguard's head start to droop.

"No, not today." Without hesitation, Noah raised the weapon and fired. The bullet disappeared into Viktor's forehead and burst through the back of his skull, decorating the wall behind with a bloody abstract. The loud crack made Noah's ears ring, but he was still able to hear yet another scream. It wouldn't be long before they were right outside his door. He looked over the desk to the grey figure on the floor. If he didn't do it now, if he didn't take his own life, it could be too late. He could be damned to spend eternity on this ship as one of these ... things. He poured one final glass of whisky and drank it down straight. Figures ran by his window. They didn't see him, but it would not be long until one did. He placed the muzzle of the revolver against his forehead and tears filled his eyes. "Please, God, forgive me for what I've done and what I'm about to do."

Noah closed his eyes, and warm streams ran down his cheeks. He smiled; he could not remember the last time he had cried genuine tears. He had done it a thousand times on stage using peppermint oil to start the waterworks. Seeing a preacher cry was always a crowd-pleaser, always made the donation hotlines go into meltdown. This was real though. These were real tears, and, despite everything, they felt good. Noah let out one last breath and squeezed the trigger; then Noah didn't feel anything, ever again.

*

The spade hit something solid. "I think this is it," Wren said, tapping the metal blade against the lid of the wooden box again.

"Okay," Mike said, jumping down. "You've done enough, get yourself a drink, I'll finish this off. He reached across and took the spade from Wren who struggled to pull her eyes away from his brown, glistening bare chest and shoulders.

Oh, God. "Okay," she said, colouring up and hoisting herself out of the hole.

Mike cleared the rest of the earth from the top of the coffin, or what passed for a coffin. It was not decorative or even varnished. It was the type of wooden box he had seen in Western movies after a gunfight. It served a purpose, no more, no less. The smell from within was already seeping out of the cracks, but it was a smell Mike was familiar with and used to now. He reached across to his rucksack and retrieved a straight-edge screwdriver then got to work levering the lid. When there was a big enough gap, he shoved the blade of the spade in, twisted and pulled. Some of the wood splintered, but the lid opened, revealing the rotting body that had once been John. The stink hit Mike like a freight train, but he stood his ground. Wren was standing by the graveside watching, and it was a split second later that the full impact of the odour reached her. She immediately ran off to the side and threw up.

Mike grabbed a pair of gloves from his rucksack, put them on and pulled out a knife. "You okay?" he asked, looking over towards Wren.

"Oh yeah, I'm fine. Having a ball."

"Okay, dumb question."

"Do you think?" she said, standing up and returning to the side of the hole.

Mike bent down and pulled open John's shirt. He inserted the knife into the grey skin a few centimetres below the boy's – the creature's – ribcage and began to carve a cantaloupe-sized hole. When he was done, he peeled back the disc of flesh, revealing the gory contents within. Wren's eyes widened and she ran off to the side once again to be sick.

"For someone who was out there so long by yourself, you've got a poor gag reflex."

"Yeah, well, funnily enough, I never cut one of

these things open. It's not something that ever occurred to me."

Mike straightened up for a moment. "We need something to mix this in."

"What?" Wren asked, wiping her mouth and looking towards him.

"We need something to mix this in."

"Mix it? What are you talking about?"

Mike's head tilted a little. "Wren, what do you think we're doing here?"

She looked towards Wolf, who was sitting patiently at the foot of the grave, then back at Mike. "Well, we're … we… I suppose—"

"Listen. We need this as some kind of solution. This thing's been dead a few days. The flesh is stiff, solid. We need something like a mortar and pestle to mash it up so we can make it usable."

Wren vomited again. She remained bent over for a few seconds then straightened up once more. "That's the grossest thing I've ever heard."

"Hey look, it's not my first choice either. The first time I did this, I used a blender; the second time the infected were still fresh enough to—"

Wren bent over and wretched again, but there was nothing left to come out. "I'm begging you, please stop talking. Do whatever you need to do, but, please, no more commentary."

Mike climbed back out of the grave and placed a comforting hand on Wren's back. "Are you okay?"

"I swear if you ask me that again I'm going to set Wolf on you."

"Wolf likes me."

"Yeah, for a German Shepherd, he's not that smart."

Wolf whined, and their attention was immediately drawn to him. They both looked at the dog who in turn was staring out to sea. They followed his gaze. Both of them had been so preoccupied with the digging of the hole and the contents within that they had not noticed the entire fleet of ships and boats that had made its way into the bay. "Oh shit!" Mike blurted.

The pair of them watched as the smaller boats sailed into the harbour, while the tall ships dropped anchor further out. Even from this distance, they could see the busy crews. "Oh my God, Mike, there must be hundreds of them."

"The more the merrier."

"You really are mad, aren't you?"

Mike smiled. "If I had a penny for every time somebody said that to me."

"This isn't a time to be flippant," Wren snapped.

The grin disappeared from Mike's face, and he took a step towards her. "Wren, right this minute, it's you and me against all of them."

"Err ... yeah, that's what I'm saying."

"If our plan works, we are going to be the last thing they'll be worrying about because the place will be swimming with RAMs."

"Okay, I get that, but they aren't the only ones who'll need to worry about RAMs, Mike. We don't have immunity to them."

"What, really? Damn, we'd better come up with another plan then."

"Look, smart arse, I'm just saying, even if our plan works, the chance of us getting out of here in one piece is like fifty million to one."

"Do you have a better idea?"

"No."

Mike leaned against one of the taller gravestones. "This is why I wanted to do this alone. You say fifty million to one, but it's one more shot than we have at the moment. Look, it's not too late. You and Wolf could still make it out of here. You know the woods and the shortcuts well enough, and at your speed you could catch up with the others."

"I'm staying."

"So we're doing this then?"

She glared at Mike. "We're doing this."

*

Talikha and the others had resumed their trek when the crowd from town led by Kirsty had caught up. Now they marched along the coast road like a slow caravan of war prisoners. They had not seen the minibus again since it had left them and headed north, but they were under no illusions as to who was in charge. Everyone had seen the fleet appear in the bay.

"What are we going to do when we reach North Ridge?" Kirsty asked.

Talikha looked across to Sammy and Jake, who, for the time being, were walking with another group of children. "Mike told me to head to Torridon, wait for them there and then…"

"And then what?"

"And then we move on."

"What if they don't show up?"

Talikha did not answer, she just carried on walking. If they did not show up, it meant that Raj, Mike and the others were dead and if that was the case, then nothing else mattered anyway.

She did not need to speak the words, Kirsty understood perfectly without them. Picking up on the worsening atmosphere, David changed the subject. "Mac's place is coming up over the next brow. We should be able to stop there and get some water at least. If I know Mac, he's going to take some convincing to leave, that property has been in his family for generations."

Nobody responded; they carried on walking. They reached the brow of the hill, and as they began their descent, a fresh gloom shrouded them. "Oh no," Richard said and then turned towards Talikha. "Keep everybody moving; we'll get water from somewhere else."

Even from the road, they could see the door had been forced off its hinges. Richard and David jogged ahead and ran through the gate. As they entered the kitchen to the compact fisherman's cottage, they immediately noticed that the double-barrelled shotgun that usually hung proudly over the fireplace was missing and the kitchen drawers and cupboards were all open. The pair of them looked at one another and then trepidatiously walked towards the short hallway that led to the bedrooms.

Richard came to an immediate halt. "What is it?" David asked. Then he saw it too. There was a stain on the carpet—not just a stain, a spray like a fine mist of blood had been pumped through an atomiser. They edged towards the patch of red, and as they reached the open doorway from where it protruded, they stopped again. It was a full minute before either of them could tear their eyes away. The four hundred plus people they had been marching with began filing past the entrance to the driveway, blissfully unaware of what had gone on inside.

"Poor Mac," Richard eventually blurted.

"Do you think he suffered?"

"He had his throat cut like some halal goat. Of course he suffered."

"What should we do?"

"There's not really anything we can do, is there?"

"We could put him to bed."

"What?"

"We could lay him to rest in his own bed. I think he'd like that."

"David, he's dead for Christ's sake. He doesn't care anymore," Richard snapped and immediately regretted it as he saw an even greater sadness chisel its way onto his friend's face. "Oh, good grief! Get his legs, I'll take his shoulders."

The two of them lifted the old man's still warm body and placed it onto the bed. Then Richard opened the wardrobe, found a blanket and covered Mac's corpse from toe to chin. "Thank you," said David.

"For a man of logic, you defy reason sometimes."

"What sort of people would do something like this?"

"The sort of people we don't want to be anywhere near." The two of them stood in silence for a moment longer, just looking towards the bed.

"I wish Ruth was here."

"David…"

"What?"

"You do realise that we're probably never going to see Ruth again."

David had a tendency to be overly sentimental sometimes, but he wasn't an idiot. He knew what was going on. "Why are we bothering? Why are we bothering with any of this?" he said, gesturing out towards the road.

"Because there are families, children, friends out there who are counting on us. Because the people in that hall, Shaw, Hughes, Ruth, Lucy, Emma, Jenny, Jules, George, Raj, their deaths can't be in vain. They'll know better than anybody that they're not getting out of this alive, but if we can help lead our people to safety; if we can at least try to save them, then it won't have been in vain."

David looked back towards the bed and let out a comical honking sound. Richard immediately turned towards him, baffled as to what he was doing, but as he looked towards his friend, icy despair embraced him. David was crying, he let out the humorous sound again, but there was nothing funny about it. It was his desperate attempt to suck in air while combatting streaming tears and problem sinuses. Richard walked across and placed a comforting arm on his shoulder. "I'm not ready to lose Ruth, Richard. I can't. I don't want to carry on without her."

"We have to carry on. For her, we have to carry on."

21

In the tiny shed, Mike had found a pickle jar that was crammed with everything from galvanised fencing staples to padlock keys. He emptied it out and wiped it clean with an old cloth. Placing it on the corner workbench, he poured in some of their last remaining water and the handful of zombie sushi he had chiselled out of John's stomach. The tissue floated down to the bottom, not even causing the clear water to discolour slightly.

"This isn't going to work," Wren said.

"Trust me, it'll work." Mike grabbed his knife and straight-edged screwdriver. He pinned the flesh to the bottom of the jar using the screwdriver then slowly carved. Gradually, the water started to turn pink then red. When he had sliced as much as he could, he placed the glass container on the floor, reached for the sweeping brush leaning against the wall, turned it upside down and placed the dome-shaped end inside, squashing and melding the tissue, blending it with the water until it was a gloopy red mess.

"That is the grossest thing I've ever seen in my life."

Mike picked the jar up and screwed the lid on. "I wish I could say the same."

"You've seen something worse? What could be

worse than that?"

Mike thought back to the siege in Candleton, when he sliced chunks of fat from John's mother who had also had the misfortune of becoming infected. He remembered Emma and Jenny putting the flesh into a blender and hitting the button. "Trust me, you don't want to know."

"I'll take your word for it. So, what's the plan?"

"Huh?"

"The plan with this," she said, pointing to the jar.

"Well, that's going to be the tricky bit."

"Oh good, there's a tricky bit. 'Cause with the hundreds of armed soldiers heading into shore, the fact that my grandad, your girlfriend and sister as well as a load of our friends are being held captive and the rest of our friends are being frogmarched out of town into God only knows what kind of hell, everything was looking so boringly straightforward. So come on, Einstein, enlighten me, what's the tricky bit?"

Mike smiled. "You know sarcasm is the lowest form of wit."

Wren turned to the German Shepherd. "Wolf, get ready to rip his balls off on my command."

Mike ignored the comment and carried on. "When we did this in Candleton, we had hollow-point bullets. We put the mixture inside and sealed it with wax. When we went up against Fry, we had tennis balls with nails through them that were covered in entrails and all sorts of shite. As of this minute, the only thing I can think of is me dipping my blades in this stuff and stabbing the fuckers. The really tough part will be stabbing them but not killing them. They need time to turn."

"Okay, I see your problem… You're an idiot."

"You've obviously been spending way too much time around Emma."

"No, you just irritate me sometimes. We're in this together, and the answer is right in front of your nose," she replied, pulling one of her crossbows from her backpack.

"We dip the bolts, so no hand-to-hand stuff is necessary."

"Okay, that might work."

"Of course it'll work. I've got some bolts with wooden shafts. We'll carve divots near the heads and that way even more tissue will enter the body."

"Okay, that's pretty clever."

"It's pretty simple, but at the side of your idea, it's positively genius."

Mike let out a long breath. "I really wanted to avoid getting you involved in the front-line stuff."

"Look, Mike, I understand why you are the way you are. I heard about what you went through growing up … the way you protected your mum and your sister. It was admirable … heroic even. But I'm not your mum or your sister. I can take care of myself, so there's no need to treat me with kid gloves. I lasted out there for months. I've faced death a hundred times, and I'm not afraid to do it again, especially when my family's at risk." She pulled a Swiss army knife from her pocket and levered open the blade. "Now come on," she said, dumping a dozen bolts down in front of them, "let's get to work."

*

Jacobs smiled as he stepped out of the Rodman 1250, one of the prizes they had claimed from Kyle. His team was busy unloading crates of weapons and ammo as Troy grasped his number two's hand and shook it hard.

"Everything go smoothly?"

"Like a well-oiled machine," Jacobs replied.

They both turned to look at the larger vessels out in the bay and the smaller ones heading in with more personnel, more food, more supplies, more everything. The village was already bustling with armed men and women, many of whom were a little disappointed that there would be no grand conquest, that not a bullet would be fired to claim this strategic piece of coastland.

"Our base of operations is across at the village hall, but the check-in for all the new arrivals is the pub. We'll head there now; then I'd be grateful if you'd come back here and oversee the rest of this side of the operation."

"Of course."

The pair of them walked through the village as familiar faces greeted them, grateful to have solid earth beneath their feet. Mercer was in the car park of the Haven Arms. Several tables had been dragged outside, and clipboards covered them all. His deputies surrounded him as the new recruits filed into the car park to be allotted assignments and temporary accommodation. He broke away as he saw Troy, or the Admiral, as he had been respectfully nicknamed, approach.

"How are things going here?"

"Well, sir, I've got another team across at the campground. We've stripped out eight trailers and designated those for supplies, although I don't think that's going to be enough. We might need to use the tall ships for storage until we can sort something more permanent out."

"And housing?" Troy asked.

"Sir, for the time being, we're giving everyone temp digs at the ground. I think after we get today out of the way we can do a proper assessment of what's available."

"Excellent! Good work, Mercer. And the evac?"

"Shep's on top of that, sir."

The three men looked over to a tall woman with tied back blonde hair. She was wearing khaki and looked every bit the soldier she was. She had served in the army and then like so many been lured by well-paid opportunities in Africa and the Middle-East until going to work as the head of security for a rich banker who had played a pivotal part in the subprime mortgage disaster. She had finally taken a lucrative role on the bodyguard team for a petroleum executive. Elizabeth Shephard, or Shep as she was known, was not someone to be trifled with, and when she was given a task, everyone knew it would get done.

"Shep," called Mercer.

Shep looked across and seeing Troy and Jacobs

went to join them. "I was just asking how the evac's going."

"Sir, a full sweep of the village has been carried out, and I can confirm it is clear. The east and north checkpoints have been vacated and are now under our control. I currently have one vehicle patrolling the coast road. It will be arriving back with us shortly and then I'll be taking over. The evacuees number nearly five hundred by our estimates, but the going is slow. There are a number of wheelchair-bound as well as some older and less mobile individuals who are just slowing the whole thing up."

A smile crept across Troy's face. He could sense the irritation in her voice. "Well, Shep, it sounds to me like you're doing everything you can, barring shoving a rocket up these people's arses."

"Well…"

"What is it, Shep?"

"These people, sir, it's just delaying the inevitable. In here they were protected; out there, they don't stand a chance. It's survival of the fittest, let's just—"

"Put them out of their misery?"

"Yes, sir."

"Let me think about it." Shep nodded and went back to work. "Jesus Christ! Boys, let's hope none of us ever get sick, we know where we'll end up." Mercer and Jacobs both laughed. "Right, I'm heading back to the hall. You're both doing outstanding work. Keep it up." The two men nodded, Jacobs and Mercer walked back to the tables, and Troy retraced his steps to the village hall. There were just two armed guards watching the prisoners now.

He walked back inside to hear raised voices. Angel had tight hold of Lucy's hair. "Cheap hooker? Cheap hooker? You just keep talking, you fucking bitch, we might just keep you back for entertainment for the boys. We'll see who's a cheap fucking hooker then."

"Get your hands off her, you fucking old slapper," Emma shouted.

Angel's eyes flared even wider. She released Lucy's

golden hair and almost ran to the other side of the table. "Oh, you think you're funny, you little shit. Well, let me tell you—"

"ANGEL!" Troy boomed. "Stop this!"

"You don't tell me—"

"You do just as I say. Stop this now."

Angel was shaking with anger as she glared first at Emma then at Lucy and finally Troy. She stood there for a full minute before marching to the office, bursting through the door, and slamming it shut behind her.

"So, you thought you'd have a little sport with Angel while I was gone?" he said, making eye contact with Lucy. She did not respond, but there was a defiant smile behind her eyes, which enraged him. But of course, Troy being Troy, he did not show it, he simply smiled and brought the radio up to his mouth. "Shep, this is Troy, come in. Over."

"Sir, this is Shep, go ahead. Over."

"Shep, I've been thinking about what you said. All those lame and old folks who are slowing down the convoy—give them an expedited pass to the other side. Over." The entire council turned towards Troy, convinced that he was merely tormenting them or the term *expedited pass* meant something other than what they feared.

"Sir, to be clear, are you telling me to kill them? Over."

"That's what I'm telling you, Shep. Contact me when it's done. Over and out."

"You can't do that," George hissed.

"You people just aren't learning, are you? I can do what I want. I told you to stay quiet, I told you not to antagonise me. I'm gone for a few minutes and you've got poor Angel into a rage."

Emma's eyes narrowed into slits as she regarded Troy. "You're a monster. If you think you're unique, you're not. We've met your kind before. There are thousands like you, self-serving serpentine little pissant. Let me guess, abused by Daddy? You think the world owes you something?"

The smile on Troy's face broadened, and he sauntered around to where Emma was sitting. He grabbed the chair and dragged it across to the stage. "Put her up there," he said, nodding to the spot where Hughes had been injected with the deadly concoction.

The room fell silent, and despite the warmth outside, a chill shivered through it. "I'm sorry," Lucy said in a panic. "I'm sorry, it was my fault. Don't hurt her."

Troy walked back to where Lucy was sitting and grabbed her hair the same way Angel had held it a short time before. "Apology accepted, but this is your last warning. You people piss me off once more and your attractive friend over there is going to get the needle."

Lucy ignored the pain she was in. She could feel strands of hair being plucked from her skull, but that was nothing. Tears appeared in her eyes. "I'm sorry. I'll stay quiet. I'm sorry."

Troy unclenched his fingers, and Lucy slouched forward. Her tears dripped onto the grey Formica surface of the table, and she wept in silence.

*

The former residents of Safe Haven continued in one long procession towards the North Ridge. The minibus that had checked in on them made another appearance. "That layby up ahead, stop there. We're sorting out transport for the old and disabled. No kids. Just old and disabled. Anybody struggling to walk, anybody in a wheelchair, we're going to take care of them."

Talikha nodded. "Thank you, that is very gracious."

The man stared at her to measure if she was being sarcastic. When he was happy she wasn't, he smiled. "Sure … gracious, that's us all over, isn't it?" he said, looking back into the minibus. Laughter erupted from behind him and for a moment Talikha looked confused but then considered her language and thought that, given the circumstances, gracious may have been a bit of an overstatement, so she smiled too. "Mind what I said now. Next layby and someone will be along directly to give them a helping hand."

The minibus sped off again, and Talikha and the rest of the townsfolk carried on as instructed.

She, Kirsty, Richard and David halted there and passed on the message. They realised due to the sheer volume of people that not everyone would be able to fit in the layby, so, after a very brief respite, Talikha, Kirsty, Sammy and Jake continued while Richard and David spread the word among the others. In the end, there were over thirty wheelchair-bound, differently-abled and old folks left. Richard and David stood with them. The news that transport was going to be provided was gratefully received. Some of these people had chronic back complaints, and the time they had already spent in their wheelchairs had meant that most of the journey had been agonising.

David glanced at his watch. "It's been a while, but they probably won't be much longer. Look, there's no point in us both waiting here. You go ahead. I'll catch up when they've gone. You never know, they might be good enough to drop me off."

"These people don't exactly strike me as good Samaritans," Richard replied.

"No, maybe not, but they want us out as quickly as possible, so it would be in their interests."

"True ... I suppose. Okay, are you sure you'll be all right here?"

"Of course I will. Now, chop, chop, Talikha and Kirsty need you."

"I'll see you soon then."

"See you soon," David replied. He watched as his friend jogged to catch up with the others. Richard turned back once to wave, and David reciprocated.

"You're like a fucking married couple, you two," blurted Angus Macdonald.

David smiled. "I realise friends are a foreign

concept to you, Angus, but that is all we are—very, very old and dear friends."

"Still say you act like fucking Terry and June," he replied, pulling a hip flask out of his pocket, unscrewing the top and taking a drink before handing it over to David.

"Don't mind if I do," David said, accepting the silver flask and gulping a mouthful of the peaty flavoured whisky. He handed it back to Angus. "Nice drop."

"Yeah, well, I don't suppose we'll find any more of it, so enjoy it while it lasts."

"Come on now, Angus, you never know what the future might hold."

"What, like being made to leave the house and the village where you've lived all your life, where you brought up your children? Being made to go on a death march into the unknown to face God only knows what, that kind of future? Yeah, I suppose you're right."

"You're very much a glass-half-empty type, aren't you?"

"No, I'm a flask-all-empty type," he said, finishing the remainder of the whisky and flinging the engraved silver container over the road. It skimmed across the surface like a pebble on a lake then disappeared over the edge to the waiting rocks and sea below. "Last scotch I'll ever taste."

"Come on, Angus, we don't know that."

"I fucking know it."

David caught a glimpse of an elderly woman who was listening in on the conversation. She rolled her eyes and David smiled. He loved the people of this town. There were all different types. Some grumpy, some sweet, some happy, some sad, but deep down inside they were the same. They were good people who had been through hell and come out on the other side, and he felt sure in his heart that they would be doing that again. So they had to leave their beloved Safe Haven behind. A place wasn't what made a town, it was people who made a town, and there was no town that he would rather be a part of.

A few minutes passed and polite conversation fluttered around. They wanted to talk about anything other than what was happening to them. The talking stopped as the drone of an engine became audible. A few seconds later, the by now familiar sight of the minibus came into view. It pulled up on the opposite side of the road, and the front and back doors opened. Eight men and women climbed out; the leader, a blonde-haired woman in sunglasses, walked across the tarmac. She angled her head to look over the top of her sunglasses at David.

"This everybody?"

David was transfixed by the huddle of guards on the other side of the road. "Err, yes, these are the people who are struggling a little." He looked around her towards the minibus. "I think it's going to need a few trips if that's all you've brought," he said with a weak smile.

The woman raised an eyebrow and looked him up and down. "You look okay. Why are you here?"

"Well, I said I'd stay, just in case. I was hoping you could drop me off but, given the circumstances, I'll catch up with the rest of them on foot."

"Go on then. Catch up with them."

"I can give you a hand helping the older ones in if you like."

The woman smiled. "Well, aren't you just a sweetheart? No, we'll take it from here. Get going." The smile disappeared.

"So are the rest of your team going to stay here while you ferry the others? You know, in case they need anything."

"Jesus H Christ, you are dumber than a bucket of rocks. Now, get out of my sight before I lose my good humour."

"I don't understand."

"Go, David," Angus growled. "Go for God's sake." David looked back at him. "Don't you see, son? They're not here to help us; they're here to kill us."

SAFE HAVEN: IS THIS THE END OF EVERYTHING?

A flurry of frightened murmurs ran around the small crowd. The woman who had smiled at David earlier began to sob. Angus's words were confirmation; it seemed that David was the only one who did not understand the gravity of the situation. He turned back towards the blonde-haired woman with a nervous smile on his face. "You're not going to…" He couldn't finish the sentence, her eyes said it all.

"I'm giving you one last chance to get out of here," she said, pushing the glasses back up to the bridge of her nose.

"No. You don't have to do this. Look, we can reach the checkpoint. It might take us a bit longer, but … you don't need to do this."

The woman shook her head, turned and walked back to the waiting minibus. "Do it!" she said, climbing into the driver's seat.

The guards immediately raised their weapons and issued a controlled volley of shots. A few seconds later, all that could be heard were the echoes of the final cracks. David was the last to fall. Sadness overwhelmed him. He stumbled and looked down to see a rapidly growing red patch spreading over his T-shirt. Then he turned to see friends and familiar faces lying dead. Finally, he focused on Angus. The old man had been right; they had both drunk their last whisky. David's legs were starting to feel weak, and with his remaining energy he looked back towards the firing squad. They had lowered their weapons and were all looking towards him with mild amusement. He staggered forward, one, two paces then collapsed. The side of his face smashed against the tarmac, and he felt his cheekbone fracture, but there was no accompanying pain. He felt nothing but cold.

"Now what?" asked one of the guards.

"Now, tip 'em over the edge. I don't want to be seeing that sorry bunch of assholes every time I drive past."

There was still a little life left in David, although his thoughts were incredibly jumbled, as someone grabbed hold of his ankles and dragged him to the edge of the cliff. Sharp pieces of gravel tore at his flesh as he was pulled across the road. Then suddenly he felt himself being lifted. There was a rush of air beneath him, and his body spun. He was flying. Was this what death was, living childhood fantasies of flying without wings? His body flipped and somersaulted, and then David understood precisely what was happening. He saw the jagged black rocks rushing to meet him. He tried to scream, to wake himself from this terrifying nightmare, but couldn't, and in that instant, before a craggy wedge of granite smashed through his skull like a turbocharged axe blade, a single tear of sadness for what Richard, Ruth and the others were about to face appeared in his eye.

22

The whole procession came to a stop as the shots rang out in the distance. Richard had only just caught up with Talikha and Kirsty and now, as frightened screams and worried mumbles spread through the gathered throng, his heart began to beat faster.

"What was that?" he asked, wide-eyed.

Humphrey whined, and Talikha looked at him. She knew exactly what it was. She had seen the worst in mankind before. When the man in the minibus had pulled alongside them, Talikha had felt in her bones there was something untruthful about his words, but she had been alone in that thought as others believed it was the most natural thing in the world. The echo of the shots that rang out over the bay told a different story, however. She had been right all along. "We must carry on," she said. "We must carry on and get to the North Ridge as fast as we can."

"But David's back there."

"Richard…" She wanted to tell him that David wasn't back there, that he would never see David again, but she could not. "We need to carry on."

For the time being, nobody was going anywhere.

They were just standing, looking around at each other. Some of the children began to cry. "I'm going back," Richard said.

"No, please. Think rationally. Whatever happened is over now. It is dangerous not to obey the demands of these people. We must carry on, all of us."

Richard looked at Talikha and Kirsty then turned back to the direction the gunfire had come from. "I'm sorry. I've got to see for myself." Without even waiting for a reply, he started to charge down the coast road to the layby where he had last seen his friend.

*

Mike and Wren finished adapting the last of the bolts and walked out into the slowly setting sun. The majority of the fleet were now crowded into the harbour, leaving the tall ships out in the bay. The cemetery gave them the perfect cover. They were high up enough to get a good overview of the village and dock through the woodland but close enough to be able to gauge the size of the foe they were about to face.

"So, this is it then?" Wren said.

"Not quite."

"What do you mean?"

"They won't have reached the North Ridge yet."

"How are we going to know when they have?"

Mike twitched involuntarily. "We need to get hold of one of their radios."

Wren looked towards the one clipped to Mike's belt. "Can't we tune in using that one?"

"I've been through all the bands and haven't heard a peep."

"Okay, so how do you propose we get hold of one of their radios exactly?"

"I'm working on that."

"You do realise that, as far as plans go, this is one of the worst in history?"

"In my defence, yes I do."

"And yet you seem so proud of it."

"Look, Wren, when I came here, all I knew was that I had to do something. I was going to piece the rest of it together as I went along."

"How's that working out for you?"

"Pretty well. At least I'm not going to die alone."

"Well, we're not going to get hold of one up here are we?"

"I don't suppose we are."

The pair of them collected their belongings and started out along the stone path that led back to the road. "I don't understand why they didn't build a proper road to this place. Why do the coffins have to be carried so far?"

"When I meet the guy who designed it, I'll be sure to ask him."

"Smart arse."

"Sorry. I know up until we got here that cemetery hadn't been used in at least twenty years, probably for that very reason. Plus, it was getting a little crowded. The one near the community hall was where most village burials took place."

"So how come you started using this again?"

"I suppose..." Mike stopped in his tracks and turned towards the sea. "Look at that view."

"Yeah, it's beautiful, but the people who are buried here don't really get the benefit of it, do they?"

"I know what you mean. We buried my gran near the house, but you can understand why people would want their family to spend eternity here. It's kind of like carrying the coffin all that distance from the road is the toll, the price you pay for your loved ones being allowed to rest here."

"Y'know, for an atheist you sound very spiritual sometimes."

"Maybe I can just appreciate other people's viewpoints."

"Oh yeah, like you appreciated that priest's viewpoint? The one you put in intensive care."

Mike laughed. "I draw a line in the sand when it

comes to people spewing hate-filled nonsense, regardless of what they believe in."

"Yeah, you're a real Renaissance man."

"That's me."

They continued along the path with Wolf following, ever vigilant. Finally, they reached the gate and the small parking area.

"If we turn right, we could climb the trail to Dead Man's Pass, avoid the lookout point at the East Ridge and escape to safety. If we turn left, we head down towards the village, imminent danger and an excellent chance of premature and fairly brutal death. So, what's it going to be?" Wren asked.

"Has anyone ever told you that you have a really dark side?"

"Coming from you that is saying something."

"We need to head across the road. Get into the trees and not break cover."

The three of them stepped out onto the tarmac, checking in both directions to make sure the coast was clear before proceeding to the other side. They carried on into the woods for thirty metres before turning left and heading down the incline towards the village. Mike stopped and thrust his hand out, taking hold of Wren's arm.

"What is it?"

"It's not too late, Wren. You and Wolf could head up the pass. You could get out of here. Nobody would blame you."

"I'd blame me, knowing that I could do something and instead doing nothing. I wouldn't be able to live with myself."

"There's something else."

"What is it?" Wren noticed that Mike looked a little edgy … nervous.

"I know you were uncomfortable with some of the things I did in Loch Uig."

"That was a long time ago, Mike."

"Yeah, that may be so, and I'm the first to admit I've changed a lot since then, thanks to Lucy. But make no mistake, Wren, there is nothing I won't do to try to save her ... nothing. If you're coming with me, you need to understand that."

Mike's nerves were gone, and he set a steely gaze upon Wren. In a heartbeat he had changed, and it was Wren who now felt nervous. "Okay. Okay, Mike, I understand."

*

It was a little less than a mile to where Richard had left David. He had never been much of an athlete, but there was no part of the route where he was not running flat out. Back in Skelton, he, David and Ruth had been best friends, oddballs, always on the periphery of normal society. They were the geeks who parents were eternally grateful to for introducing their children to reading. They organised Harry Potter theme days at the library and had floods of eager children and enthusiastic middle-class young mother volunteers to help out. People were happy they were there doing the job they did but not *so* happy that the three of them would be accepted into the fold, that they would be invited to book clubs and social events outside of the library. People liked them ... but there was a limit.

So, Richard, David and Ruth found solace in each other's company, learning to mock the world outside, not care about how they were viewed, and just enjoy life the way they wanted to live it. When the outbreak began, their safe haven had been the Skelton library where they had spent the happiest days of their lives. They would have ended their days in that place too if it had not been for Mike. Richard knew in his heart that Ruth was already gone. Losing David too would mean he had nothing left, no more family.

Richard rounded the last bend. The sweat was pouring down his forehead, and he was getting shooting pains through his legs and lower back, but he did not care. He stopped in mid-stride, and his mouth fell open.

The layby up ahead where he had left David and

the thirty or so other Safe Haven citizens was empty. For a little while he didn't move, he just stared. He was still a hundred metres back, but it wasn't as though they could all be hiding behind a rock waiting to jump out and say peek-a-boo. He cautiously advanced, taking in everything, anything that might give him a clue as to what had happened. His heart was still racing from the run, but as he noticed red streaks painting the road and shell casings glinting in the lowering sun, it began to beat even faster.

He walked across to the spot where he had said his last goodbye to his friend. There was a spray of red blood decorating the broken white line. He followed the thick smudges across the narrow carriageway to the edge of the cliff, pausing to take a breath before he dared look over.

"Oh, God, no!" he cried as he saw the hellish picture below. Wheelchairs, bodies, white wake turned pink with fresh blood and there, seemingly wedged between two jagged spikes of granite, was his friend. "Oh, God, no." He whispered this time and sat down on the edge of the cliff, dangling his legs over the side. This was it. This was the end.

*

The sun was getting lower and lower in the sky, and although no one was dilly-dallying, Talikha was concerned that they would not reach Torridon before nightfall. This was a long stretch of coastline and people were tired, scared and hungry. Even Humphrey, over the moon that he'd been reunited with his pal Meg, kept casting worried glances towards his mistress. Making the trip to Torridon on foot in daylight was one thing, doing it at night with no weapons and God only knew what lurking in the shadows and tree line was something else completely. Ryan, April and Tabby had caught up with Talikha and Kirsty. Everybody's mood was becoming grimmer by the minute.

After hearing the shots, after seeing the normally measured and reserved Richard sprinting back to the layby like a mad person, and after him not returning, everybody was beginning to wonder what horrors were still to be unleashed on them.

"Is there a plan for when we get to where we're going?" Ryan asked.

"You're asking me?" Talikha said. "Mike asked me to get everyone to Torridon. That is all I am trying to do. I don't even know if our people based at the North Ridge will be waiting for us or whether they will have gone their own way. All I know is what I was told."

"Okay, what's at Torridon?"

"Not much. But I know it is one of the villages they swept. It should be free from infected. There is a freshwater loch there and a river with fish."

"I suppose that's something. Listen, the second we get out of this place I suggest we arm ourselves."

Talikha turned towards Ryan. "You seem like you know what you are doing. Mike simply tasked me with getting his family to safety. I am not a leader, and I am more than happy for you to take charge of things."

Ryan smiled. "Well, for someone who isn't a leader I'd say you've got an awful lot of followers. All I'm saying is big branches, sharp sticks, jagged rocks, if everybody grabs something then at least we can put up some sort of fight if we're attacked."

"Yes! You will help with this?" Talikha replied.

"Certainly."

"Thank you."

"I've known Emma quite a while now. She's a pretty resourceful woman. I wouldn't give up hope on her or on any of them while she's around."

Talikha smiled sadly. "You are right, of course."

Tabby carried on walking in silence. She had lived among the people of Kyle for some months before Emma had come along. She knew how special Emma was, but she was a realist too and these invaders did not possess an ounce of mercy. In her heart she knew she would never see Emma again.

23

Wolf stopped dead in his tracks, making Mike and Wren almost trip over him as they halted too. The German Shepherd stared dead ahead, raising his head a little to sniff at the air.

Mike drew the two machetes from his backpack and Wren grabbed one of her crossbows.

"Give me the jar," Wren whispered.

"No. It's too soon."

"So what then, we just let ourselves get discovered?"

"Keep quiet and keep your eyes peeled," Mike said, crouching. They stayed in position for over a minute but heard and saw nothing. Mike glanced towards Wolf, who was still staring directly ahead. There had to be something there, dogs didn't get this kind of thing wrong. "Stay here."

Before Wren had the chance to reply, Mike had disappeared through the trees like a jungle animal. "How come you are the only man in my life who doesn't treat me like I'm still in primary school?" Wren asked. Wolf turned to look at her and angled his head. "Come on, boy; let's see what's going on."

Wren and Wolf glided through the trees like ninjas,

barely breaking a twig as they went. It was only a few seconds before they stopped again. Mike was up ahead, kneeling behind a leafy shrub, watching something, but what?

Wren and Wolf advanced carefully, eventually nestling down by Mike's side. "Keep quiet," he said, almost as if he'd expected her.

A man and a woman were up against a tree. Neither was clothed below the waist, and if World War Three had broken out at that moment in time, it was doubtful that they would have noticed. Even from this distance, the sheen of sweat and the joyous looks of ecstasy emanating from their faces proved that not everyone was having a lousy day.

"I knew you were a lot of things, but I never had you pegged as a perv," Wren whispered. "You enjoying yourself? You want me to ask if you can join in?"

"As a matter of fact," he said, crouching down further and turning to look at Wren, "I am enjoying myself. Look what's next to the guy's trousers."

Wren raised herself slightly to look above the branches of the shrub. "It's a radio," she said excitedly, ducking back down to join Mike.

"Well done. There's obviously nothing wrong with your powers of perception."

"How do we get it?"

Mike didn't answer; he gave Wren a look that made her arms prickle with goosebumps despite the warm weather. "So, do I have to guess?"

"Wait here," Mike said calmly. He kept in a low crouch and speedily circled the perimeter of the opening in the trees where the two lovebirds were reaching greater heights of euphoria.

Wren watched; that was her job, after all, to make sure whatever happened she was ready to spring into action. She watched as the khaki shirt turned darker as more sweat poured down the man's back. She watched as his smooth olive buttocks thrust, again and again, driving the woman to a level of bliss Wren did not even think humanly possible. She watched, her eyes growing wider, her heart beating faster, and then she saw movement from the opposite edge of the clearing. Mike sprinted out, carrying a heavy branch, a few inches longer than the average baseball bat but just as thick. The woman's eyes were closed; the man's lips were excitedly sucking on her neck and shoulder.

"Don't stop! Don't stop!" she moaned loudly.

Mike took the branch in both hands, wound it back around his shoulder, and then, coming to a stop next to the tree, swung with all the power of a jackhammer. There was a loud noise that shot around the clearing like a rifle crack. In an instant, the man's head caved in, his upper incisors and canines sunk into the woman's shoulder and a jet of blood exploded over her face, then the man crumpled to the ground. The woman screamed first in pain then in shock. Her khaki shirt was open, revealing her bloodstained breasts and torso. Instinctively she threw her hands up. Tears came quickly. A few seconds before, everything had been right with the world.

Mike dropped the branch, balled his fist, and punched the woman hard in the face. Her head ricocheted off the tree, and she fell unconscious on top of her already dead lover.

Wren emerged into the clearing in a state of bewilderment. "What ... what did you do?"

"I did what I had to."

"But ... couldn't you have..." She stood there with her mouth agape as more blood pooled from the man's head onto the forest floor. "Is he dead?"

"I'm pretty certain I felt his skull cave, so if he isn't, he soon will be," Mike replied matter-of-factly.

"And her, you killed her too?"

"Not yet." But then he pulled out one of the machetes and brought it down hard and fast through the woman's skull.

"Oh, God!" Wren said, looking away, horrified. It

was a full minute before she turned around. "We could have done this differently." Her voice quivered as she spoke.

"What, and give them time to get to the radio to put out a distress call?"

"They'll miss them soon enough anyway."

"You've seen it down there. There are hundreds of people; they can't keep tabs on everyone."

"If he's got a radio, he must be someone important."

"He doesn't look important to me. Go get Wolf, we need to move."

Wren didn't like taking orders, but Mike's tone had changed, and now he was that man she had feared back in Loch Uig—the man who had no problem killing someone in cold blood. He walked across to the radio and smiled as he saw two pistols, both with spare magazines, still in their holsters. He bundled them into his rucksack and then clipped the other radio next to his own.

Wren beckoned Wolf and knelt down to give him a hug. The dog licked her face with his broad tongue, sensing she needed reassurance that he would protect her no matter what. He always knew how to make her feel better. She sighed and looked over at Mike, who was perched on a log with his back to her. "Part of me daren't ask, but what now?"

Mike looked up through the canopy of the trees towards the sky. "Now we wait a while."

*

It had been a long hike up the coast road. Talikha did not even want to think about what had happened to Richard, David and the others. She didn't want to think about Raj, the council members, and what would happen now. The end of the first leg was in sight. They were coming up to the checkpoint and they could already see a good number of armed guards waiting for them. Sammy slipped her hand into Talikha's as if the child could sense her despair, sense her sadness. "Don't worry; Mike will make sure nothing happens to Raj."

Talikha looked down at the little girl and swallowed hard in an effort to hold back her tears. Eventually, she managed to smile. Even after all this, after everything they had been through, this young girl still had faith. "I'm sure you are right, Sammy." She squeezed the young girl's hand and smiled then looked across to Jake, who was holding Sammy's other hand, and smiled at him too. It felt like a betrayal, a betrayal to her beloved husband to humour such fantasies, but what else could she do? Shatter a child's hope to make herself feel better just so she wasn't the only one feeling like this?

"Hold it right there!" said a giant of a man with military insignia tattooed on his arms. "This is how it's going to work. Ten at a time." He pointed towards ten guards spread across the road. "Everyone will be frisked. Nobody leaves here with anything but the clothes on their backs. No weapons, no food, those were the orders. Now pass that down the line. First ten, you're up."

Talikha's stomach began to churn. This was really it. They were leaving Safe Haven forever. This time it was Humphrey who brushed up against her leg as if trying to take some of the weight of her sadness. She crouched a little as she walked to ruffle the soft fur on his neck.

"Arms and legs spread like you're about to do a star jump," shouted a woman from the side of the road. There were another six guards with weapons raised ready, waiting for any sign of trouble.

Jake began to cry. "It is alright," Talikha reassured him, "just do as I do." She assumed the position and closed her eyes as a tall, blonde-haired, blue-eyed man with a red face frisked her. Nobody other than Raj had ever laid hands on her. She got a sense this man enjoyed the power immensely. She tried not to squirm as he moved his hands around her legs, up her thighs, across her buttocks, then over her back and between her breasts. It was the most degrading thing she had ever experienced, but she had been bestowed with a task and she had to carry it out whatever the cost to herself. "Nice ass," he said, slapping her on the rear. "Next!"

That was it. The humiliation was over for now. The first ten were done, and it was on to the next. Everyone was checked; men, women, children, dogs. As distasteful as she found the experience, as much as she hated these people, yes, hated, a word she rarely had a need to use, she could not deny their organisational skills. But then again, that was not something necessarily to be admired. The Nazis had excellent organisational skills, she certainly didn't admire them. The way the Turks carried out the systematic genocides of the Greeks, Assyrians and Armenians required phenomenal organisational abilities and she had not one iota of admiration for them either. It was difficult to find anything positive about monsters inhabiting human flesh, for these people were certainly that and more.

"Where now?" Ryan asked as Sammy slipped her hand back into Talikha's.

Talikha looked up at the sky. Darkness would not be long in coming. "We still have a few miles to go."

"Well, one way or another we're going to find out if your friend Mike was right about this area being clear."

*

The radio hissed. "Troy, it's Blaze, come in. Over."

Troy unclipped the radio from his belt and hit the talk button. "This is Troy, go ahead. Over."

"Troy, they've finally got their lazy, slow asses here. We're processing them now. I'll update you when it's done. Over."

"You be sure to do that, Blaze. Over and out."

The sound of the radio made Angel reappear from the small office. She could tell by the smile on Troy's face that the plan was all falling into place. "I'm guessing that's good news?" she said, the animalistic rage from before forgotten.

Troy clipped the radio back onto his belt. He

looked towards Emma, who was still cable-tied to the chair on the stage, then back towards the rest of the council. "It seems that our time together is coming to an end," he announced with a bitter smile. They all looked at him; they all wanted to say so many things. They knew they were beaten, they knew they were going to die, but they would prefer a clean death – a bullet to the head, not what Hughes had suffered, not what they had threatened to do to Emma – so they all stayed silent and just hoped.

"Do you think we could keep this one a while longer?" Angel said, walking up behind Lucy and stroking her hair.

Troy looked towards Lucy then Angel. If he did not hold the supreme power he now possessed he knew Angel would not be interested in him, but thirty minutes before, when he had gone into the back office to talk to her, she made it clear how much she thought of him, in words and in deeds. "Sure. Why not?" he said with a smirk.

"Aww, hear that, shug? We're going to get to spend some quality time together soon."

Lucy did not show fear or dread, she kept her face stern. There were a thousand things she wanted to say to both of them but she couldn't. They had proved they were willing to carry out their threats, and she would never risk Emma's life. When the end finally came, she had one last card to play, she was sure she had etched and gouged enough of the plastic cable tie to snap it and at least try to throw a punch, grab a gun, something, anything, but that time hadn't arrived yet.

Troy turned to the two guards. "Will you get that thing out of here?" he said, nodding towards the creature that had once been Hughes. "It's stinking the place out. And can we get some of these lanterns on? It's getting hard to see in here."

The two men placed their rifles down. They turned on the solar lanterns that were positioned strategically all over the hall, picked the rotting creature up and carried it towards the door. "I really need to go to the toilet," Jules said.

"You went earlier. You're going to have to hold it. Won't be too long now," Troy replied.

"I've been holding it. Jesus, you've had us here all day. I'm busting. If you don't want to be sloshing around in a lake of piss you really need to let me go."

"Wait a minute. When my men are back, we'll figure something out."

*

Mike and Wren had doubled back a few times. There were people everywhere, it was a miracle they hadn't been spotted up until now, but they had the advantage of the home ground.

They had seen from the cemetery earlier that the pub car park was the main hive of activity and that was originally where they had been heading to unleash their bio-weapon, but then they had heard the broadcast and realised they were almost out of time. They had altered course and made their way straight to the village hall. They both crouched down behind the wall next to an old BT cabinet. From their position, they could see people on the main road, but in the grounds of the hall there was no one. The light had started to fade fast, beckoning another cool autumn night.

Suddenly, the double doors of the hall burst open, and a man backed out, struggling to carry what at first looked like a bulky, cumbersome sack. Another man came through carrying the other end; they followed the building around towards the rear car park.

"It looks like a body," Wren said, squinting. When there was no response from Mike, she turned towards him to see a blank expression on his face. "Mike, what is it?" He turned to look at her, still unable to speak. Tears welled in his eyes. "Mike, you're scaring me. What is it?"

When he spoke, it was in a broken whisper. "It's Bruiser."

"No. No, it can't be," Wren said, turning back to look at what the two men were carrying.

"Wren, it's Bruiser."

"How can you be sure?"

"The bracelet," Mike replied, "it's the one Sammy made for him for Christmas. He's never taken it off."

Wren was convinced Mike couldn't be right. Bruiser was a member of the council. If he was dead, that meant… She squinted even harder and then she saw the multi-coloured bead bracelet. "Oh, no." She began to sob too. They were too late, too late to save their families, and now they were trapped behind enemy lines.

Mike watched the two men for a few seconds more as they disappeared around the rear of the building; then the tears of sadness turned into something else. He wiped his eyes with the heel of his palm, and when Wren looked at him again his face was contorted into an image of raging hatred. He leapt over the wall and sprinted towards the men carrying his best friend's corpse. Reaching over his shoulders, he withdrew the crisscrossed handles of the machetes and continued his lightning charge.

Wren was caught entirely unaware. She remained glued to the spot, stuck in a cinema seat while the most terrifying 3D horror film unfolded around her. A growl started in the back of Wolf's throat, sensing that things were only going to get worse from here.

Mike threw a glance to his left, beyond the entrance to the village hall car park and out to the road. There were at least five soldiers who had spotted him, but so unexpected were these events that they lost a few seconds before they began to respond. That was all Mike needed. He too vanished behind the single-storey community hall that had housed everything from town meetings to Christmas parties. The two men were still oblivious to his presence, but then one caught movement and immediately dropped the end of the creature he was carrying. He reached for his sidearm. At the same time, the other guard dropped the beast's feet and began to turn.

Mike grunted as he flung one of the machetes. It whistled through the air, slicing the first man's forehead, eye and cheek. He immediately fell to the ground, and Mike was on the second guard before he had the chance to turn around fully. He slashed at the side of his head, nearly decapitating him with the first blow. The man started to scream, but in the end it was merely a wheezing high-pitched gurgle that came out. He collapsed to the ground like his compatriot, but that was not enough for Mike. He brought the machete down over and over; blood-splattered then caked his face and clothes. He could taste it on his lips, and he began to scream. Not a frightened scream but a yawp. A final battle cry.

He reached back into his rucksack to retrieve the pump-action shotgun, and less than a second later the first of the men from the road came running around the corner with his weapon raised.

Mike was about to squeeze the trigger when the side of the man's head exploded. He fell to the ground, but momentum carried him another few feet across the tarmac before he came to a stop. A split second later, a second man emerged, and the same thing happened to him.

Mike wondered if he was going mad. Was he imagining this? Was Fry about to come walking around the corner next, laughing his head off at the big joke he'd played?

Another soldier came to a running stop, but this time he didn't turn towards Mike, he looked towards the trees opposite. The back of his head erupted, spewing bone, blood and brain tissue. Mike heard something other than his blood rushing. There was a soft *pfft* sound. He had heard that before, the familiar sound of a silenced rifle. He heard two more muffled shots and then nothing. He just stood there, waiting. The blood continued to drip down his face, trickling over his lips and off his chin. Finally, a figure emerged from the trees. It was Barnes. He looked towards

Mike then shouldered his rifle and ran across to where the bodies were strewn. He pulled the first one around the corner, out of sight from the main road, before Mike came to his senses and understood what was happening.

He placed the shotgun back in his rucksack, levered the other machete out of his victim's head and ran across to help Barnes. "Looking good, Mike," the soldier said under his breath.

Mike looked down at his blood-drenched clothes. "You saw that was Hughes?"

Barnes nodded sadly as he dragged another body around the corner. "I've been watching the place most of the day. These are the first two I've seen leaving in a while." He tapped the radio on his belt. "I heard the broadcast this morning and came straight here. I knew it was going to be my last mission, but damn it if I wasn't going to take a few of them out with me. I was waiting for the right time to cause maximum casualties. You kind of made me bring my plans forward."

"We managed to get hold of one of their radios. Our people have reached North Ridge."

"We?"

"Me and Wren." Mike looked to where Wren was still crouched down and signalled for her to come out. A few seconds later, she sprinted across to join them with Wolf by her side, all the time looking towards the road to make sure it was clear. They dragged the final body out of sight then stood facing each other.

"So, do you have a plan?" Barnes asked.

"We did," Mike said, taking the bottle of water from his backpack and giving his face a quick rinse. He turned towards Wren. "You need to go."

"What? What are you talking about?" she demanded.

"Our plan is redundant. We were going to create utter mayhem as a cover so we could try to save our people." He nodded towards Hughes's body. "Our people are already dead. God knows what twisted games they've played before then, but they're dead. You need to go. Go through the woods, head out past the East Ridge and go join Talikha and the rest of them in Torridon. They need someone like you."

"And what about you?" Wren asked.

Mike and Barnes shared a knowing look. "We're going to get a little payback before we call it a day."

"What? No! Look, we've lost. We're too late, but we can get out of here together, the three of us."

"You are one of the most amazing people I have ever met. There's nobody alive who I would rather have as a role model for Sammy and Jake. Now go."

Wren watched as the two men walked around to the entrance of the village hall. Barnes leaned his rifle up against the wall; Mike pulled the shotgun from his rucksack. They paused for a second then charged.

24

Barnes and Mike were stunned by what they saw. They expected a room full of guards and a pile of bodies. They were going to start shooting and not stop until someone stopped them. Instead, there was one man with a radio in his hand, one woman who looked like she belonged on a shopping channel selling makeup and jewellery, and an almost full council bound to chairs around a rectangle of lantern-lit tables. The woman screamed, and the man standing behind Shaw immediately brought the radio up to his mouth and drew his sidearm. He was about to hit the talk button to issue orders when Shaw planted both feet firmly on the ground and lurched backwards on his chair, knocking the man off balance. They both crashed to the floor, and the pistol skidded towards the wall, clattering against the skirting board.

Realising there was no way Shaw could fight, Mike charged towards the tables and leapt up. Stride, stride, dive. The man was beginning to gather himself when the shoulder of the human cannonball made contact with his ribcage. There was a sound like thick twigs snapping, and the man let out an almost deafening cry of pain as Barnes ran to join them. Backup, just in case.

"Troy!" the woman screamed.

Troy collapsed back to the ground; the radio flew from his hands and skidded across the floor. Mike had not even thought about landing, only inflicting maximum damage on his target. He rolled and skidded until he eventually came to a stop. As he climbed to his feet, he saw the shopping channel woman start to run to the door.

"Like hell!" Lucy shouted, straining hard against the weakened cable tie and breaking through the plastic. She sprang to her feet, and before the woman could get anywhere near the exit, Lucy had grabbed her and thrown her hard against the wall. "This is for John." Whack! A loud crack and Angel's nose disintegrated beneath Lucy's knuckles.

"No, please. Not my face."

"This is for Hughes." Crunch!

"Aaarrgghh!" One of her front teeth broke, sliding over her already bloody lip onto the ground. "Nooo," she began to cry hysterically.

"This is for all our other friends that you murdered today." Smash! Smash! Smash! Thud! Angel slumped down to the ground, her fingers reading her broken face like braille, her baying cries sweet music to Lucy's ears. "Well, what do you know? The Angel has fallen."

"Please no more. Please no more," she begged.

The picture of Hughes being injected then turning into one of those things flashed in Lucy's head, and she booted Angel hard in the stomach, winding her and making her cry out in agony once more. The other council members watched on in disbelief. This was not like Lucy.

While so much attention was focussed on the two women, Troy launched himself towards the radio, sliding across the floor on his side, minimising the pressure on his cracked ribs. Mike, although as surprised as anyone by Lucy's actions, was waiting for the next move, and as Troy's hand reached out for the handset, Mike grabbed one of the machetes from his rucksack and brought it down like Thor's hammer.

The room fell silent until, "Aaarrrggghhh!" Troy brought his arm up. He had witnessed it but still could not believe it. Blood sprayed like a fountain into the air where his hand had been.

Barnes stooped down, picked up the radio and stepped back, desperate to avoid getting the pooling blood on his boots. The internal doors to the village hall burst open with a clatter and every pair of eyes turned towards them.

*

Darkness was getting closer by the minute. Richard did not know how long he had been sitting on the edge of the cliff, he was lost in his thoughts, in his sadness. He had never felt so alone in his life, and as he looked down to the rocks and the waters below, they seemed more inviting than ever. He had lost the people in the world who had meant the most to him, and now he had a choice.

He could start again with Talikha and the rest of them or he could end his suffering. He stood up and took off his jacket, folding it and placing it neatly on the floor beside him. *No point causing unnecessary wind resistance with that extra flapping material.*

One, two, three. He closed his eyes.

*

Talikha did not know how many people had already been processed, but they were all on the move again. There was not enough room for several hundred men, women and children to amble around while the others got searched. She kept looking back to make sure there was a steady line following.

"Don't worry," Ryan said, "it's not like they can get lost. This isn't Spaghetti Junction, it's one road."

"No, of course not," Talikha replied with a smile.

They followed the first long bend around, and after another three hundred metres, when they were well and truly out of sight of the checkpoint, Talikha stopped. By the side of the road, there was a tree branch. She walked across and picked it up. It was a bit crooked at the sharp end where it had presumably been snapped by the wind. It came up to chest height and was a little thicker than a cricket bat handle.

"What's that for?" Jake asked.

Talikha lied, "My legs aren't young like yours. They are tired, it is to help me walk."

A smile broke on Sammy's face, and she sought out a smaller branch. "I think I want one too," she said, giving Talikha a knowing look.

"You are very old for a young girl," Talikha said under her breath.

"That's why I need a stick," Sammy replied, and they both laughed. They carried on their journey and others began to collect sticks, branches, stones, rocks, anything that could be used as a makeshift weapon, just in case. When night fell, who knew what fresh hell would be lurking in its shadows?

*

"Grandad!" shouted Wren as the doors swung shut behind her.

"Wren?" George called back, half excited, half confused.

Mike was caught off guard for a moment by Wren and Wolf's dramatic entrance, and despite the agony he was in, Troy used the confusion, managing to unleash a powerful kick. He missed Mike's head but made contact with his shoulder, and the younger man flew back onto the floor. Troy began to wriggle towards the gun he had dropped earlier, but Mike gathered himself and was on top of him, pinning him down in the blink of an eye.

Troy took a swipe at Mike with his one remaining fist and made contact with the side of Mike's ribcage. Despite having lost a lot of blood, the mercenary still had tremendous strength. Mike's rage numbed him to the pain, and he unleashed an explosive round of punches to Troy's face. Realising there was no way out Troy wanted to push the knife in one final time. "Your friend, he cried like a little girl when he knew he was dying, it was sickening." Troy's lips were bleeding, he'd bit his tongue, but he used all his energy to speak. A wicked smile started on his face, and Mike sat there on top of him for a few seconds, looking down, letting the hatred consume him.

"You mother fucker. YOU MOTHERFUCKER!" he screamed, and Mike wasn't a man any longer, he was a wild, wounded animal. He climbed to his feet and lifted the pummelled figure off the floor like he was some lifeless shop mannequin. Troy's arm trailed by his side as still more blood spewed.

"Mike! Mike!" Lucy called, seeing that look, knowing what they had been through to rehabilitate him after the incident at Loch Uig.

Mike looked across at her then back towards the feeble, beaten figure with the sickening smile on his face. "Don't worry, Luce, I'm not hearing voices, there's no one whispering at my shoulder. This is all me." He dragged the figure around one hundred and eighty degrees and then charged towards the wall, taking a tight hold of the hair at the back of Troy's head. The plaster buckled inwards, and blood spattered against the dirty magnolia paintwork as Mike used Troy's head like a battering ram. After the first strike the smile was gone from Troy's face, and his eyes started to lose focus. After the second smash his nose was virtually flat, his forehead and eyebrows were bleeding, and his bottom lip swelled up like a giant blood-filled leach.

"Please," Troy whispered, although his face was so malformed now it came out "Pweef."

"Hughes—" smash "—was one of the—" thwack "—bravest men—" thud "—I ever met," crack. Troy's skull caved, but by nothing short of a miracle his eyes were still open. Mike pulled the broken body around to face him. "I want you to know before you die that whatever great general, great mastermind you think you are, you're not. Your people are all going to die, just like your girlfriend over there, just like you. You're a fucking zero, and you've lost.

For all your planning, all your smart ideas, you've lost." Troy's body began to convulse, and Mike smelt something pungent in the air. He looked down to see a wet patch form around Troy's groin. And a broad grin swept across Mike's face. "Oh, and I'll make sure your soldiers know you wet yourself before you died, you piece of shit." Troy continued to shake as Mike pinned him against the wall.

"It's all over, mate," Barnes said softly, placing a gentle hand on Mike's shoulder.

There was still recognition and understanding on Troy's face, and Mike could see the fear in his eyes. "Oh yeah, it's all over now," but he wasn't talking to Barnes. "It's all over now. Everything's starting to go dark. Scary, isn't it? What's facing you after this? Where do murdering cowards who piss themselves when they realise their time is up go when they die? My guess is nowhere good." Mike released his grip and Troy slid down the wall, his body still convulsing violently. A few more seconds passed, and eventually the shaking stopped. Mike stood there a moment longer, hatred still engrained on his face. He felt another gentle hand on his shoulder and turned expecting to see Barnes again, but it was Lucy, his Lucy.

"It's okay, sweetie. He's gone." She flung her arms around him, and he reciprocated. He breathed her in, making sure she was real and this wasn't some wonderful madness his mind had concocted.

"Err... I genuinely couldn't be happier to see you, Mike, and watching you and Lucy cuddle is making me go all gooey inside, but I really, really, really need a piss. Could someone please fuckin' untie me?" Jules said.

Mike turned towards where the rest of the council were sitting and smiled. Wren, Barnes and Lucy went to work clipping the cable ties while Mike climbed onto the stage to free his sister.

Upon being freed Emma hugged him tight. "I didn't think I'd ever see you again."

"Ditto," he replied.

"Sammy, Jake, Tabby?"

"All safe. Heading out with Talikha and the rest of them."

"Actually, I know this should be a really sweet, tender moment between us, but I really need to pee too," Emma said, jumping down off the stage and running into the back.

"And me," George added, breaking his hug with Wren. Gradually the rest of the detainees all drifted into the back realising they needed to use the facilities.

Mike remained on the stage a moment longer then spotted something on the trestle table. He went across and grabbed it, holding it up to the lantern light before placing it quickly in his rucksack and jumping down off the stage to join the others.

"Okay, so what's next?" Barnes asked as he Wren, Wolf and Mike stood there waiting for all the others to return.

"Well … err … what was your plan?" Mike asked.

"You don't want my plan. My plan was a one-way mission."

"Well, our plan was a variant of what we did in Candleton but on a smaller scale. We've got like ten crossbow bolts. We thought—"

"Wait a minute. In Candleton we put Beth's infected mum in a fucking blender. What the hell were you planning on using?" Barnes asked, glaring at Mike.

Oh shit! "We—"

"We found one," Wren interrupted.

"What do you mean you found one?"

"Must have been from when the first attack took place. It was caught up in barbed wire on Isabel Sinclair's croft, really wrapped up good and proper."

The suspicious look left Barnes's face, Wren wasn't a person to lie. "That was lucky."

"Tell me about it," Mike replied.

"I don't think ten bolts are going to cut it. I think

we need something on a bigger scale," Barnes said.

The others began to filter back through. Shaw was first. "So, what's the plan?" he asked.

"You're the tactician. You tell me," Mike said.

The radio crackled. "Troy, come in, this is Blaze. Over."

"Shit!" Emma said. "That's the guy from the checkpoint. Whatever plan you're going to come up with, you'd better think fast."

"Mike, the stuff, where is it?" Barnes asked.

"Stuff? What stuff?" Shaw replied.

Mike unhitched the rucksack, pulled out the pickle jar full of zombie smoothie, and placed it on one of the tables. He turned to Lucy, handing the Glock to her, and placed down the other two weapons and spare magazines he had lifted from the lovers in the woods. Emma picked up one, Jules picked up the other. Shaw walked over to the far side of the stage and grabbed his and Hughes's sidearm. He looked at the remaining unarmed people, George, Jenny, Ruth, Raj. It wasn't a hard choice. He handed it to the Hindu veterinarian. "Remember how to use one of these?"

"Alas, I do." He took the weapon, shoulder holster and all, and strapped it on.

"Troy! Come in, this is Blaze. Over."

"I'm guessing most of these people are going to be in the campground?" Barnes said.

"From what we could see when we were in the cemetery, most new arrivals were heading towards the pub," Mike said and immediately got a glare from Wren.

"What were you doing in the cemetery?" Barnes asked.

We were digging up the dead body of your girlfriend's brother so we could weaponise his zombified corpse. What do you think we were doing? "Err ... we..."

"We figured it was the best vantage point while maintaining some cover at least," Wren said.

"That was pretty quick thinking with everything

that was going on," Shaw said.

"You have no idea," Wren replied and gave Mike another irritated look.

Barnes walked to the table and opened Mike's rucksack, withdrawing the pump-action shotgun. "I know that look, Barney," Shaw said. "You've had an idea."

Barnes turned to look at Mike. "You were a fast bowler, right? Where did you field?"

"Err … Deep Cover, Deep Mid-Wicket, Third Man, wherever I was needed."

"No offence, Barney, but what the fuck does cricket have to do with the situation we're in?" Jules asked.

Barnes ignored the interruption and continued. "So, you've got a strong throwing arm?"

"It's not bad. Why?"

Barnes handed Mike the jar. "Not exactly a match grade corky ball, but do you think you could give it some height?"

Mike measured the weight of the jar in his hand as the globby liquid sloshed around inside. "I reckon I could get it up there," he said with a smile, only now understanding what Barnes had in mind. Barnes returned the grin. It was the first time anyone had seen him smile since the death of his beloved Beth.

"I don't know if this is some male bonding thing or some kind of in-joke, but would one of you please tell me what the fuck you're talking about?" Jules snapped.

"This is Blaze, I need a radio check. Over."

They all turned towards the handset. Even Angel had gone silent for the time being as she drifted in and out of consciousness.

The radio hissed. "Blaze, this is Mercer, reading you loud and clear. Over."

"Mercer, do you have a visual on Troy? Over."

"Negative. Over."

"I can't reach him. He might be having radio problems. Do me a solid. Head on over there and put him on, will you? Over."

"Jesus Christ, Blaze. I am knee-deep in all kinds of shit here. I don't have time to start running errands. Over and out."

"Jesus H. Is anyone one else picking up out there? Over."

"I've got you, Blaze. This is Jacobs. Give me five and I'll head across. Over."

"You're stand-up, Jacobs. Appreciate it. Over and out."

"Hey, Blaze, you still there? Over."

"I'm still here. Go ahead, Jacobs. Over."

"Did Balotelli show up with you? He was meant to be taking a spare radio to the other checkpoint, but I've not been able to raise him. Wondered if you've seen anything of him. Over."

Mike and Wren looked towards one another, both knowing immediately who Balotelli was and where he was.

"Na, I've not seen him over here. You ask me, these radios have seen better days. That should be one of the first things we put on our shopping lists when we get straight. Over."

"Yeah. Guess you're right. Thanks anyway. Over and out."

"Okay. We don't have much time," said Shaw. "Whatever we're going to do has to happen in the next five minutes or we're all screwed."

25

Richard wanted to jump more than anything, but there was a part of him – the part that Mike had found and nurtured – that wanted revenge for what had happened to his friends. A gentle breeze picked up, and for the first time he raised his eyes. Despite the sun having set, he could still make out the diminishing shapes and figures below, slowly being washed away by the wake. But now his attention was caught by something else. The coast road swerved and weaved along the cliff face. There were sections no more than a hundred metres away that were invisible from where Richard was standing. Conversely, there were other stretches miles further down that he could see—in daylight or when a vehicle was travelling with its headlights on, like now. He picked up his discarded jacket and wrung it in his hands as though it was a stress toy. *What should he do?*

There was no intellectual basis for revenge. When it came to studying it as a concept, Richard and David had the perfect lab rat in Mike, the single most vengeful and, quite frankly, terrifying person they had ever met. Now though, Richard got it, he understood. It was nothing to do with intellect; it went much deeper than that. It was to do with love, the deep feelings of brotherly friendship that he possessed for David.

He would not waste his life by flinging himself off the cliff. He would try to give it at least some meaning, and if in that act he died, then so be it, but he would not just give up.

*

"We can't leave her here like this, we need to tie her up," Wren said, pointing towards the battered Angel.

Mike looked at Lucy. "She's one of the ringleaders of this?"

"She's sly, a manipulator, never gets her hands dirty, but yeah, she's in this up to her neck."

Mike looked down at Angel. Her eyes were narrow slits as bruising made the skin puff all around them. "She was here when they killed Bruiser?"

"She didn't push the plunger, but yeah."

Mike grabbed Angel's hair and lifted her off the ground from her slouched position against the wall. "Nooo! Nooo!" she screamed, weakly trying to bat his hands, terrified of what punishment would come next.

Mike withdrew the hunting knife from his belt and sliced her throat deep, immediately unclenching his fingers and letting her drop once more.

"No!" Wren screamed and buried her head into George's chest.

Angel's eyes opened wide, not believing what was happening. She slumped back against the wall, clasping her slit throat in a panicked attempt to stop the bleeding. She tried to speak, she tried to cry for help, but rasping gurgles were all that came out.

Ruth looked away, almost as horrified as Wren, but the rest felt no pity. For what these people had done, they deserved everything they had coming to them, and that would amount to a lot before this day was over.

Mike and Lucy stood there a few seconds longer until Angel stopped struggling. "I suppose my Hippocratic Oath's all shot to hell now. I could lose my licence for this one."

"Tell me it wasn't worth it."

"I can't."

Mike took hold of Lucy's hand and squeezed it. "We need to go."

"Yep," she said sadly, knowing only too well what was facing them outside.

"Okay. Everybody knows what they're doing. If the alarm's raised before we finish this, we're all dead. Good luck everyone," Shaw said before leading them through the doors and out into the evening.

The sun had gone down, but there was enough light for them to see what they were doing. They knew this village intimately, and the darkness would be their ally … for a while anyway.

They stopped again on the steps to the village hall and Shaw turned to Mike, then Barnes and finally Wren. "I didn't thank you."

"I tell you what, get us out of here and that will be thanks enough," Mike replied.

Shaw put out his hand, and Mike took it, pulling his friend close and giving him a hug. "Good luck, mate."

"Good luck, Mike."

"Fuck me! Do you two want a moment alone?" Jules asked.

Mike pulled back to see Shaw smiling as widely as he was.

"I'm begging you, please take her with you," Shaw said.

"Screw that. You're my friend, but there are limits," Mike replied.

"Aren't you two a pair o' fuckin' comedians now?"

"Who's joking?" Shaw asked.

"Come on," Barnes said. "We need to go."

*

The road was eerily quiet as the displaced citizens of Safe Haven continued their march to Torridon. The shadowy woodland looked more ominous than ever as the sun set behind them.

"When was the last time your people came here?" April asked.

"I think a few weeks back. Why?" Talikha replied.

"A lot can happen in a few weeks."

"Hell! A lot can happen in a few hours these days," Ryan added.

"How much farther to go?" April asked.

"Still a few miles. There is a big hotel there. That would be a good place for us to base ourselves, although I think we may already have stripped it of anything useful," Talikha said.

They carried on walking in silence. The night was shaping up to be little better than the day. Yes, they were out of enemy territory, but with no food, no water and still several miles to travel, their prospects were bleak at best.

Suddenly, Humphrey and Meg stopped. As they looked straight ahead, a low growl started in their throats.

*

It had been a long day for Shep. After being cooped up on a cruise ship for what seemed like an eternity, it felt great to get behind the wheel of a vehicle again, but she would be glad when she could climb into her newly designated mobile home and crash. This was her last trip up the coast, the final changing of the guard at the north checkpoint until morning.

She looked into the rearview mirror and caught a glimpse of Jack staring back at her. She and Jack had worked on the security detail for one of JKC Petroleum's senior executives. They had got closer and closer, and now that they were here on land, in what seemed like relative safety, they might have some kind of chance at normality, or whatever masqueraded as normality for two former mercenaries.

She unleashed her killer smile, teeth glinting blue-white in the dashboard light. Jack winked at her, and she winked back then quickly checked to see if anybody else had noticed. They hadn't; they were all preoccupied with their own thoughts about what this new start could give them.

The first rock did not hit the sixteen-seater minibus, but its appearance in the full beam of the lights shocked Shep enough to tug the wheel left in desperation to try to avoid it. The tyres shrieked, and a gasp went up from several of the passengers. These narrow roads carved into cliffs did not leave a lot of room for error.

When a dozen more rocks all struck the windscreen, the bonnet and the roof of the van at the same time, Shep screamed, jammed on the brakes and dragged the wheel in the other direction. The glass had shattered in several places. Spider web fractures and tiny holes let in the frigid evening breeze, and now Shep was not the only one screaming as everyone felt the wheels leave the tarmac. Rocks continued to clatter on the roof as the vehicle veered further. There was an ear-splitting metal on metal screech as the bus hit the antiquated knee-high crash barrier.

The back door burst open with a powerful shoulder barge. Shep caught sight of a figure escaping before she felt the minibus bank and start to roll, only there was nowhere to roll to. It toppled over the barrier like an obese man attempting a Fosbury flop. The metal railing groaned, snapped and fell with the bus. With the back door open, the terrified screams of the passengers rose into the night air like a banshee chorus. There was a deafening crunch, then ... silence.

Dan Wellman was English by birth, brought up in Brighton before moving to the US at the age of twenty-one. He had gone to work as a techy in a private security firm but realised that the security operatives seemed to have a much more exciting job, so he decided to train as one. Despite living in the UK for twenty-one years, he had never visited Scotland. As he picked himself up off the road, looking at his broken and misshapen fingers, he could safely say this was not how he had imagined it.

When he had been sprawled on the tarmac listening to his compatriots' screaming prayers as they plummeted to their deaths, he had seen something black float down to the ground. He slowly limped towards it. As he bent down to pick it up, he registered the fact that not only had he broken several fingers but his ribs had taken a battering too. He let out a groan as he straightened up and pulled out a mini flashlight from his pocket. He flicked it on and held it between his teeth while he examined the gritty garment.

Fragments of stone and soil fell out of it onto the floor, and there were two tears in the material. "What the fuck is this?" He looked up the rock face. He had assumed the falling stones that had made the minibus veer off the road had been part of a landslide, but it was very well targeted for an act of God, and since when did God use North Face jackets as slings for chucking rocks?

Dan dropped the jacket back down to the ground and grabbed his sidearm. He kept his eyes on the cliff in front of him and carefully backed away. Clatter. There was a noise to his left, and he turned sharply, raising his weapon, grabbing the torch from his mouth with his thumb and index finger, the only two digits on his left hand that weren't broken. He panned the light around looking for the man or woman who had killed fifteen of his brethren.

Crack! He fell to his knees before he realised what had happened. Dropping the torch, he reached around to feel the back of his head and discovered a warm, sticky, wet patch in his hair. The Beretta M9 wavered for a moment before it dropped to the ground with a clatter. *What a fucking idiot! Blindsided by someone using the oldest trick in the book.* He started to feel dizzier and dizzier, then—.

Richard watched as the man fell forward onto his face. The adrenaline was pumping through him like it never had before. He looked at the black rugby ball-sized rock he held in his hand and dropped it as he took a step back. It was one thing to kill a busload of people by slinging rocks at them from the top of a cliff, it was another thing to take a rock in your hands and literally bludgeon the life out of someone. He had done it. He had done what he had promised. He'd not given in, he had got some small modicum of revenge for David and Ruth, and on a primal level it did make him feel good.

He felt something on his hands and brought them up in the torch lights to see what it was. It was blood. His hands were covered in the dead man's blood. He started to feel queasy, and the world began to spin around him. He staggered forward; then everything went black.

*

All day the pub car park had been a hive of activity, and the evening seemed to be no different. Although there was still work to do, the lion's share of it had been done, and it was time to celebrate the start of their new life, this new home. Mike, Lucy, Emma and Barnes were silent as they crept through the dark, dingy woods. They simply followed the noise as some of the new inhabitants of Safe Haven discovered that the Haven Arms was still well-stocked with booze.

"I've thought of a problem," Emma whispered.

"What?" Barnes replied as they all carried on walking.

"How are you going to see the jar in this light?"

Barnes stopped. "Holy shit! She's got a point. There was still a bit of daylight when I came up with this idea."

"Have we got a small torch? Could we put one in the jar?" Lucy asked.

"I've got a mini Maglite, but if we put that into liquid, it'll short circuit," Barnes replied.

"Hang on, I've got an idea," Mike said, sitting down on the ground and resting his back against a tree.

"Sweetie, I really don't think this is the time to—"

"Give me a second," he said, undoing the laces of his boot.

"What the hell are you up to?" hissed Emma.

"Trust me."

"That's always the kiss of death."

Mike removed his boot, pulled off his sock, then placed his boot back on and tied it up. The others stood around watching his silhouette, wondering what he was doing. "Give me the torch," he said to Barnes.

Barnes grabbed the small torch from his pocket and handed it to Mike, who proceeded to place his sock over the jar and wedge the flashlight between the glass and the stretched material. He tried to turn it on but soon realised he could not do that through the material, so he pulled it back out, switched it on and wedged it in once more. The sock and the jar lit up like a salt lamp.

"That's a pretty good idea," Emma said.

"Let's face it," Mike replied, "I was due one." He turned to Barnes. "Will this be okay?"

"As long as I can see it, I can shoot it. It will be fine."

Mike climbed back to his feet, removed the torch and switched it off so they didn't get spotted; then they continued towards the sound of the crowd. The noise grew much louder, and they came to a stop several feet before the tree line. Even from where they were standing, they could see there was something akin to a party starting. Lanterns had been placed on window sills and hung from bushes while others sat on the wall at the far end of the car park. There were still a number of pub tables outside, and although it was not the warmest of evenings, the alcohol that had started to flow was beginning to numb people to the chill.

Some were still hastily finishing off scribbling notes on clipboards, there was even a whiteboard on an easel. The man in front of that held a torch in his teeth so he could see what he was doing. Mike brought out his binoculars and peered down them to see what he was writing. "It looks like some kind of inventory. Weapons, Water, Food. They're cataloguing our stuff and theirs. Fuckers! Like they fucking own the town," he hissed.

"Well, I suppose they do ... now," Emma replied.

"By the time we're finished, they're not going to want to be anywhere near this place," Mike said.

"Yeah, but neither will we," Lucy replied.

A cheer went up as a group exited the pub carrying a tray of bottles to the men and women still working. Seeing the levity in the car park and how much these people were already taking their new home for granted made all four of them fume.

"Come on, let's get this done. Remember girls, you're our cover in case we get spotted before we deliver the package," Barnes said.

"Good luck," Emma and Lucy replied at the same time.

Barnes and Mike edged forward to the tree line bordering the busy car park, and each ducked behind a trunk. Emma and Lucy drew their weapons and stood six feet back, scouring their surroundings, waiting for the first sign of trouble, but for the time being, the dark woods were the last thing anyone in the car park was paying attention to. They had won a decisive victory that day. The perimeter was secure, and now it was time for a little fun before another long day tomorrow.

Mike pointed the torch towards the ground and turned it on. A circle of light bled out from the rim that almost touched the soil. "I really hope this works," he said.

"Me too."

A volley of gunshots cracked from somewhere else in the village, and the buoyant conversation and mood in the car park shattered like a crystal vase.

"Oh shit!" Mike said.

"Do it. Do it now or we're fucked," screamed Barnes.

26

Six growling shadows charged towards the crowd. Humphrey and Meg began barking at full volume, alerting their pack to the danger ahead.

"Oh shit!" April screamed. "Everybody get ready!"

Talikha looked around to see some people fleeing into the woods. A slight figure started sprinting to the front to join them. It was Vicky, the woman who had led the band of survivors from Loch Uig. Behind her were Prisha and Saanvi, two Sikh sisters who had also survived Webb's nightmarish prison and come out on the other side. They each clutched branches, which they held in front of them like pikes, ready to fend off the first wave.

The creatures were advancing quickly, and the terror in the air was palpable. Humphrey and Meg darted forward then pounced like lions defending their pride.

Humphrey knocked down the creature on the left flank, Meg the right, ripping into the decaying flesh of the aggressors. "Come on, now!" shouted Vicky. She stormed forward with Prisha and Saanvi following. Talikha, Ryan, April and a few others advanced too, feeding off each other's adrenaline-fueled rage.

"Aaarrrggghhh!" Talikha roared as she charged.

They needed a show of strength, a way to demonstrate to the others that everything was not lost, that while they were still standing there was still hope.

Vicky smashed the first creature over the head with the heavy branch she had found. Prisha swiped at the legs of another, knocking it skidding to the ground, while Saanvi started to batter its head like a whack-a-mole, dazing it before fracturing its skull and then finally turning the lights out for good. Talikha stopped and braced herself. The centre beast, the biggest, lunged for her, and she brought her makeshift weapon up. Despite her diminutive figure, she was a strong woman, but she stumbled with the forward momentum of the hulking beast.

"Talikha!" Sammy cried as she watched her friend, no, more than friend, family member, stumble back and fall onto the tarmac.

Ryan, April and only a small handful of others continued to run forward, already past Talikha, unable to help. Three more creatures appeared up ahead, drawn to the roars and screams. Talikha shuffled back on her hands and buttocks, desperate to climb to her feet as the monster gathered itself and the makeshift spear fell from its shoulder. It leapt again, and Talikha rolled to her left, watching as the silhouette crashed down beside her. She felt the rush of wind as it landed and let out another frightened yelp.

Rather than helping, the people behind her were taking flight, terrified of how many more of these monsters there might be. The beast sprang up again as Talikha edged farther away. She had forgotten how bone-chilling those low-pitched growls were.

"Sammy, take Jake and run!" she commanded as she came to terms with the fact that it was too late for her and one monster would become two. Two would become four, and soon there would be an army. "Run!"

*

A vintage VW campervan was by no means the ideal escape vehicle for eleven people, but without entering the heart of the village, it was the only option they had. George had been working on Mike and Emma's Gran's hippy mobile with Richard and David as a fun restoration project. It had spent some time in George's workshop, but when the new weapons project came along, they relocated it to the librarians' house. There was nothing on the street but houses, and considering how most of the invaders seemed to be concentrated in the pub area, Shaw was convinced he and the others had the easier part of the mission.

They observed the street carefully for a while before climbing over the wall and onto the pavement. The sun had disappeared a few minutes earlier, and although complete darkness had yet to fall, it was difficult to make out much more than shapes. They could see the distinctive contours of the VW campervan, however, and that was their goal.

"Okay," Shaw whispered, "keep your heads low and your eyes peeled."

They tiptoed over the street like a group of cat burglars. The rising sounds of celebration could still be heard coming from the pub area, making them all feel that little bit more secure. George reached the vehicle first and carefully opened the squeaky door, climbing inside and checking the ignition to make sure the keys were present. Vehicle theft was not really an issue in Safe Haven. He nodded to Shaw, who beckoned the rest of the group to hurry up.

A powerful torch beam suddenly hit them like a prison searchlight. "Who the fuck are you?"

A small group of soldiers, men and women, had been sitting on lawn chairs, having their own private party. The one who had sprung to his feet first looked like two rugby prop-forwards with a single head; he spoke with an Australian accent. Other figures rose to their feet around him. Shaw and the others paused in the middle of the road, not knowing whether to continue to the VW or run back to the wall.

"Get in the fucking camper!" Shaw shouted, ducking down and opening fire. Jules crouched too, as did Raj. The men and women in the garden didn't have a great line of sight. The hedges were a significant obstruction, and while they were stuck in the garden, they were fish in a barrel.

One man screamed as a bullet entered his neck, a woman let out a piercing yell as she was hit in the shoulder. They all began to open fire too in the hope that they might get a lucky round in the right direction and that some of their compatriots might come to their aid.

"I can't see a fuckin' thing," Jules shouted.

"Keep firing," Shaw replied. "We only need to pin them down."

The engine of the campervan started, and there were pings as stray bullets bounced off the bodywork. Two guards stormed out of the gate firing, they had barely reached the kerb when the first one fell. "Ricky!" the other shouted, but a second later a bolt entered his chest too. Wren had positioned herself on the other side of the campervan in case the enemy tried to make a break for it onto the road. The ones inside the garden had no idea their friends had been victims of silent crossbow bolts, but seeing their shadows collapse to the ground stopped them in their tracks. They ducked lower, moved back to the house and pointed the weapons towards the gate, waiting for the impending incursion.

"Go, go, go," Shaw said, grasping the fact that they had got the advantage for the time being. The others piled in to the campervan. Shaw stayed outside, continuing to fire until George had manoeuvred the vehicle around. At the last second, he dived in too, and the camper not so much sped as chugged away. A few more shots whizzed and pinged from the garden, but they were out of direct danger for the time being.

They rounded the corner, and the camper picked

up speed. It carried on up the hill, over the brow and down the other side, before pulling into a small National Trust car park that always used to be packed in summer but now was just a dark place surrounded by trees, rarely entered from one month to the next.

"Well, that didn't quite go to plan," George said.

"You can say that again," Jules replied. "Err … I might have a bit of a problem."

It was pitch black in the interior of the camper, but instinctively Shaw turned around. "What is it?"

"I … I think I've been shot."

*

The creature leapt towards Talikha once more. *I love you Raj, I love you Raj*, she said over and over in her head, praying for some kind of telepathic connection. After everything she had been through, this was how she was going to die.

"Aaaggghhh!" For a second she thought the high-pitched cry had come from her own lips, but when she heard the hollow crack accompanying it and when she saw the beast veer off course slightly, she knew that the fight was not yet over.

"Sammy?" The shadowy figure stood above her, still in batting pose. She had swiped at the monster's head as if she was trying to knock a baseball out of the park. The creature had slumped, temporarily dazed, and Talikha knew she had been given a reprieve, albeit temporary if she did not act. She sprang to her feet, grabbing her own weapon from the ground and turning around in one fluid movement. The monster was vertical once more, heading towards Sammy now.

"Help!" the young girl cried. Battles were going on all around as former Safe Haven residents swiped and stabbed and punched and kicked the attacking creatures, but this was the only fight that Talikha was interested in.

She mimicked Sammy's earlier action, swinging her much longer, much heavier branch like a bat. There was a wet thud as it smashed against the side of the beast's head, causing it to stumble to the left. Talikha ran forward, putting herself between it and Sammy as it gathered itself again. She twirled the branch like a baton, turning it the right way up, making sure the sharp end was pointing towards the monster as it ran at them. "Aaaggghhh!" The scream rose from her own lungs this time, and she thrust the weapon towards the creature's face.

She did not see the result clearly, but she felt it as the spear penetrated the attacker's left eye socket. There was a moment of anxiety as the beast remained upright; then it collapsed to the ground with a satisfying thump. Talikha remained there a few seconds more, her breathing was erratic, and despite the chill of the evening air, her palms were sweaty. She turned towards the other jostling figures, and one by one their would-be assailants began to fall.

When the final skirmish ended, a feeling of jubilation swept over the stick and stone-wielding warriors. They had done the impossible. They had gone up against these things in the dark, with nothing but what nature provided to defend themselves, and they had won.

Talikha crouched and placed her spear on the road, opening her arms. Sammy ran into them, and the two embraced. "You are the bravest girl I have ever met. I think maybe Kartikeya has chosen you to do his work," she said, pulling back.

"Who's Kartikeya?"

"He is the Hindu god of war."

"I don't think so. I was so scared."

"Bravery is not the absence of fear, Sammy. Bravery is doing something even though you are scared. What you did was incredibly brave."

"It didn't feel brave."

The pair hugged again before Talikha scooped up her spear once more and rose to her feet. The pair of them walked over to Jake who Sammy had told to hide behind a bush next to the road. He was crying. "I peed myself," he said as if it was the worst thing in the world.

"Don't worry, Jake, I'm pretty certain a lot of people peed themselves tonight," Talikha said, looking around as figures who had run off at the sight of the attackers slowly started to emerge back out of the trees.

"I want to go back home," he said, wiping his eyes.

"We have to find a new home now, Jake," Talikha said, placing a hand on the boy's shoulder.

"I want Mike and Emma."

Talikha hated lying, but to get through this night she knew she would have to. "They'll be here soon, Jake. They'll be here soon."

*

As the first echoes of gunfire began to die down and the occupants of the pub and surrounding grounds realised their celebrations were premature, the car park became alive with movement. The invaders/raiders/marauders, whatever they were, whatever the lowlife thieving, murdering scum wanted to call themselves suddenly put their game faces on. Placing bottles and glasses on the ground and replacing them with their sidearms, a surge towards the car park exit began.

"Now, for fuck's sake, now, Mike," Barnes screamed.

Mike jammed the small torch into the sock, took a split second to measure the weight of it in his hand, ran forward a couple of metres and threw the jar as high as he could. It arced in the air, rising high above the crowd. The few who spotted it had no idea what it was, other than a strange, orange, glowing object rising up into the night sky.

Barnes held his breath and aimed. This was the most important shot of his life, and he knew for the maximum effect he needed to take it before the thing started falling again. Boom!

"Oh shit!" Mike screamed as the jar kept on rising, unblemished by the shot.

Barnes pumped the fore-end of the shotgun as the

first bullets started whistling towards him. Emma and Lucy began to lay down cover fire from their positions further back. Boom! He fired again. "Got you," he said as the jar exploded into a hundred deadly pieces. Infected bloody glass showered the crowd, slicing through cheeks, scalps, arms, shoulders, and, for the unfortunate few who had looked up, eyes and lips.

For a moment the firing stopped as the marauder force realised there was something else going on, a bigger game at play. "Come on!" Mike said, grabbing Barnes's arm.

There was part of Barnes that wanted to stop and fight, just wade into the crowd, firing. But he knew the best revenge he could get had already been served. He handed the shotgun to Mike who pumped it and fired into the crowd while Barnes retrieved his cumbersome but frequently life-saving sniper rifle from the tree where he had left it leaning.

Emma and Lucy started to fire once more as further shots whistled in their general direction. As Mike and Barnes fell back, the two women released one final volley, only managing to hit a single marauder in the leg, but their job was done. As they sprinted through the dark woods, they each switched magazines, certain they had not yet finished using their guns.

"What the hell was that gunfire earlier?" Emma said as shouts of *go after them* could be heard rising from the car park.

"I don't know, but let's hope Shaw achieved his mission, otherwise this is going to be the shortest escape ever," Barnes replied.

They carried on running for a few more seconds, and then they heard it. The grim and yet on this occasion beautiful sound of a high-pitched scream. Not just any high-pitched scream, however. They had become experts after all this time, and when someone had the flesh ripped from their neck by a blood-craving monster, there was a certain timbre to the voice. This was the first. It was the first of many as a chorus quickly began to accompany it.

Shots began to sound behind them once more, but they were landing wide. Mike, Lucy, Emma and Barnes were on home turf, and they could weave and wane through these woods better than most. They emerged out onto the road by the village hall and checked both ways, but their shortcut ensured they had beaten everyone else there. They proceeded across to the hall's car park, around the back of the building and through the other small wooded area separating it and the street where the librarians lived.

Shots were echoing all around now as the battle with the undead had begun well and truly. Automatic rifle as well as pistol fire boomed and cracked, shaking the once quiet village to its foundations. The four of them came to a stop before the wall and crouched down. Mike carefully raised his head. "There are bodies on the pavement and five people standing at the bottom of the street, looking towards the village."

"Ours or theirs?" Barnes asked.

"Can't tell, but the campervan's gone."

"That's got to be good … hasn't it?" Lucy asked.

"Well, we can't stay behind this wall forever," Mike replied, reloading the shotgun. "How do you want to play this, Barney?"

"Quickly."

"Fair enough." Mike stood, pulled the fore-end of the shotgun and jumped over the wall.

"Mike! Mike!" Lucy called after him.

Mike started walking down the middle of the street towards the figures. Even in the darkness, he could see one and then the others turn towards him. "Identify yourself," one of them called as they all raised their weapons.

"It's me," Mike called back, veering across the street and onto the pavement past the bodies that Wren had brought down.

"That's fucking useful, isn't it? Me who? And don't take another step."

"It's me, Mike." He could see the heads turn to each other in the darkness, he could almost hear the question clattering around their brains, *Who the fuck is Mike?* Then it happened ... what he was hoping would happen, Barnes took his cue. There was the familiar pfft sound, and a millisecond later the one shadow that had been asking the questions fell to the ground. Mike dived over the nearest garden wall as pistol and rifle fire filled the street. A bullet pinged off the wrought iron a few feet from his head; then another turned brick to powder. He kept his head down for a few more seconds until there was a short pause and then he sprinted, bounding over the fence of the neighbouring property then over the next before diving onto the lawn. Had they seen him? He'd find out soon enough. He waited a few more seconds and when no more shots came in his direction jumped to his feet.

There were three bodies lying in the middle of the road, but he didn't have sight of the other two. He turned the other way. Lucy, Emma and Barnes had not broken cover, and if the other two soldiers were in hiding, there was no way Barnes was going to get a clear shot. The screams continued to multiply and amplify as the infection spread. It would not be long before the whole village was a death zone, and they'd be just as screwed as everyone else. *Fuck it.*

Mike vaulted another fence, hoping he was shielded from sight by the overgrown hedges. He paused, one, two, three, then leapt over the gate back onto the street. He nearly landed on the female guard. Both of them were as taken aback as the other. She swung the rifle around, but Mike kicked out hard, knocking her from the crouching position she was in and into the door of the Land Rover they had procured from the village.

"Steve!" she cried as her head banged against the body of the vehicle. Another black figure appeared from around the back of the car and started to raise his weapon, but Mike was already waiting. He squeezed the trigger of the shotgun, and the giant Steve flew back a metre, crashing onto the concrete pavement. "No!" she screamed, gathering herself and bringing her own rifle up once more. Mike turned sharply, pumping the fore-end again, and before the woman could take aim, he fired. At that moment, he was more grateful for the darkness than he had ever been in his life.

"Clear!" he shouted. "Barney! Luce! Em! It's clear!" He ran around to the driver's side of the Land Rover. The light went on as he opened the door, and his face lit up as he saw the keys in the ignition. He jumped in and started the engine, pulling away from the kerb and heading down the street to meet the others as they climbed over the wall.

"Let's get the hell out of here," Lucy screamed as the sound of panicked shouts and running feet got nearer.

Mike did a three-point turn and put his foot down. He pulled to the end of the road and turned right. They only travelled a few metres before he applied the handbrake.

"Mike! What are you doing? Move for fuck's sake," Emma cried.

Barnes was about to echo the statement then he saw it too. This wasn't over.

27

Vicky, Prisha and Saanvi stayed up front with Talikha, Ryan and April as the people of Safe Haven resumed their march. Humphrey and Meg walked on either side of Talikha, the clear alpha leader of this giant pack. They had done their duty; they had warned their family then attacked and pinned down two of the wild things that came out of the dark until their humans finished them off with their sharp sticks.

"How much farther?" Vicky asked.

The half-moon had made an appearance in the sky and cast a generous light over the tree-lined road.

"Maybe another mile and a half," Talikha replied.

"I would kill for a hot bath and a glass of red wine."

"It may be some time before we are able to enjoy any luxuries," Talikha replied.

She felt Sammy's hand slip into her own once more, and she held it tight. "Things will get better," Sammy said. "Things always get better."

Vicky, Saanvi and Prisha all slowed down. "What is it?" Talikha and Ryan asked at precisely the same time.

"I saw something," Vicky replied.

Talikha clenched her fist around the spear. "What?

What did you see?"

"It looked like a light ... up ahead. A torch or something."

They all peered through the darkness. "Oh, shit!" cried April as a pair of car headlights flicked on about three hundred metres ahead. They all froze in stunned silence then became perplexed as they watched the vehicle do a clumsy three-point turn and disappear in the other direction.

"Who the hell was that?" Vicky asked.

"I don't know," Ryan replied, "but something tells me that, before tonight's over, we're going to find out."

*

Mercer and Jacobs figured out what was happening long before anyone else. Somehow the prisoners had got the drop on Troy and the others. Somehow, they'd escaped and beaten them at their own game by unleashing the zombie virus. Troy's army had entered Safe Haven as one well-equipped unit, but now it was every man and woman for themselves.

The car they had dived into would not win any drag races, but it was infinitely preferable than trying to escape on foot. Others had the same idea, and as the entire village descended into hellish chaos, the convoy of four vehicles sped out of the campground and onto the main road. They had tried to turn onto the quickest exit route, up and over the steep hill to the east, but a horde of beasts attacked the vehicles. They managed to change direction before being completely surrounded, and now they were heading the other way.

"We should have got onto one of the fishing boats," Mercer said.

"We wouldn't have stood a chance. Most of our crews are chowing down on each other right this minute, and did you see the dock as we went by? These fucking things are everywhere."

"So where will we go?"

"One thing at a time. Let's just get the hell out of here first."

Jacobs put his foot down on the accelerator then eased off for a second as a Land Rover tore out of a side street a hundred metres ahead of them. "Who the hell's that?" Mercer asked.

"I don't know, but I wish we had their wheels."

The Land Rover came to a sudden stop, and Jacobs's heart began to pound faster. He jammed on the brakes, and the small car skidded to a diagonal standstill, causing a mini-pileup as the three vehicles following all smashed into it, albeit lightly, causing Jacobs's car to shunt horizontally, blocking the way completely. *Had the creatures already managed to get this far? Were they blocking the route ahead?*

The doors of the Land Rover swung open. Two men climbed out, one with a shotgun, one with a handgun. They opened fire at the same time. Before Jacobs or Mercer could even duck, bullets and shot had entered their bodies.

Barnes took aim at the petrol tank of the lead vehicle. Round after round punctured it until a pool formed. "Mike, shotgun," he shouted, holding out his hand.

Mike threw Barnes the weapon. The headlights of the piled-up vehicles provided enough illumination for him to see what he was doing. He aimed at the rear wheel. The hubcaps had disappeared long ago, and the metal had rusted in places thanks to the harsh salty winds, but he achieved the desired effect. More than a dozen tiny sparks spat to the ground, igniting the fuel with a whoosh.

Mike looked on with admiration, and Barnes handed the shotgun back to him. "Nice work, Barney."

"Come on. Let's get the hell out of here."

They climbed back into the car and accelerated up the hill, watching the flames rise higher in the wing mirrors. They had not travelled more than a few seconds when they slowed down and turned into the designated meeting place. Before they brought the car to a halt, they could tell something was wrong. The light was on in the back of the campervan and Wren, Jenny, and George were standing outside with worried looks on their faces.

"What's wrong?" Lucy asked, climbing out of the Land Rover before it had come to a complete stop.

"Thank God you're here," Jenny cried.

"It's Jules, she's been shot," Ruth said.

Lucy immediately climbed into the VW. Raj and Shaw were doing the best they could to stop the bleeding. "We don't have any equipment. No bandages, no alcohol," Shaw said.

Lucy looked at Jules, who was still conscious but very pale. "Okay, let's get to our house, pronto. I've got materials there."

Shaw climbed out of the camper and explained to the others what was happening. In less than thirty seconds, the two vehicles were underway again.

"Find my brothers and tell them I love them." Jules's voice was frightened, like that of a small child.

"You're going to tell them yourself in no time at all. We'll all be together soon," Lucy replied, holding a torn piece of shirt against her wound. The others, on the opposite seat, looked on sadly. They had lost so much tonight, and now they were about to lose one of the bravest, most caring people in the community. Nobody ever had a bad word to say about Jules. She brought calm to even the most tumultuous days with her down-to-earth wit and humanity.

"No. They were at the East Ridge. It will take them forever to get to the North Ridge on foot, and that's if the daft bastards even figure out that's the way they should head." Lucy smiled and squeezed Jules's hand tighter. Even with a bullet wound, she was still funny.

"Sweetie, can you lift yourself up a tiny bit?" Jules winced as she angled her body. Lucy peeled back her bloody T-shirt. "Okay, this is good. You've got an exit wound. When we're back home, I'll make sure there are no bullet fragments in it, but that's a good sign." She turned to Jenny.

"Tear me another piece of shirt."

"I appreciate the effort, but we both know that I'm not going to make it," Jules said weakly, and her eyes began to flutter.

"Hey! Don't talk like that. You're going to be just fine. I'm not going to let you go anywhere. I need you around to help me keep Mike in line. You're the only one around here he's scared of."

Jules smiled, but it was fast becoming too much effort. "He's a good man. Look after him."

"Hey, stay with me, Jules. Hey! Hey!"

Jules's eyes flickered open again. "Sorry ... tired."

"What blood type are you?"

"Huh?"

"Blood type. What blood type are you, Jules?"

"O."

"O? O what? Positive or negative?" Jules closed her eyes. "Jules! Jules!"

A few seconds passed. "Is she dead?" Wren asked.

"No. But I need to get her seen to fast. She's going to need a blood transfusion. She's lost too much."

"But ... you don't know what type she is."

"No, but I know two people who can help."

"Who?" Wren asked.

"Mike and Emma."

"How can they help you if you don't know the blood type?"

"They're O negative."

"I don't understand. Jules only said, 'O.' We don't know if she's positive or negative."

Lucy turned towards Wren. "O negatives are universal donors. They're the only hope she's got."

*

"Stop right there!" shouted the woman's voice.

Talikha's heart sank to the floor. They were so close to Torridon, spitting distance almost. The way ahead was clear. Whoever had spoken was in the trees. "Please! We mean you no harm. We just want to pass through."

"You need to turn around," the woman shouted.

"We can't."

"You can, and you will."

"If we turn around, we will all die."

"If you take another step forward, you'll all die. It's your choice."

"Please let us talk about this. I'm sure we can come to an understanding. We only want to get to Torridon," Talikha said, looking towards the trees in the direction the voice had come from.

"Torridon is exactly where I don't need you to be. This is your final warning."

"They could be bluffing. We could rush them," Ryan said.

"I say we take the risk," Vicky added. "They might take some of us; they can't take all of us."

"What have we got to lose?" said Saanvi.

Talikha let out a deflated breath. The last thing any of them needed was a moonlit battle. She looked down towards Sammy, but Sammy wasn't there. "Sammy? Where's Sammy?" she asked Jake, who pointed. Talikha looked through the shadows to see Sammy's diminutive figure walking up the side of the road until it was more or less opposite where she believed the woman's voice to have come from. "Sammy, come back!"

"Please," Sammy shouted. "We've been thrown out of our homes. A lot of our friends have died. We've had to leave all our possessions. We have no food or water, and if we go back … if we go back…" She started to cry. For the first time in her life, she began to believe she would not see Mike or Emma again. "They've killed my sister and my brother, and they'll kill us."

There was a long silence. Then hushed conversations flitted between the trees.

"Is it true what she said? Were you forced out of your homes?" the woman shouted.

"Yes," Talikha replied.

"How?"

"First, they came from the sea with infected and tried to kill us all. When that didn't work, they invaded."

A figure emerged from the trees; then another and another. The woman slowly crossed towards Sammy then on to where Talikha was standing. Even in the dim light of the moon, Talikha could see that the group was made up of children and teenagers, and even the woman herself was not that old. "That happened to Sally and Max. We found them a few days back, just wandering. Sounds like their pirates paid you a visit. Look, I don't know how this will work, but we're stopping at this hotel."

"Ah! That is where we were heading. How many of you are there?"

"Twelve."

Ryan laughed. "And you were going to kill us all."

"It was worth a punt. How many of you are there?"

"About five hundred."

"Yeah, we might have struggled with that many." Sammy returned to join them, still wiping her eyes. "Brave little girl you've got there," she said to Ryan.

"She's not mine. Her brother and sister are back there," he said, pointing his thumb over his shoulder.

"Oh."

"What are you doing out here?" Talikha asked as the procession began to move forward once more and the remaining youngsters hiding in the trees came out to join their leader.

"We're looking for somewhere."

"What kind of somewhere?"

"A place that we'd heard about on the road, a place called Safe Haven."

"I am sorry to tell you that Safe Haven is what we have left behind. It has fallen," Talikha replied.

"No!" the woman said, stopping again. "It can't have done. We came all this way. We were told they'd take us in, that they'd help us."

"We are not really in any position to help anyone at the moment, but we will be again, soon enough."

"No offence, but if you've got no home, no food, no water and just sticks and rocks to fight with, you're not really going to be able to help anyone," the woman said.

"That is not all we have."

"Oh. What else have you got?"

"We've got each other."

*

The Land Rover skidded to a halt on the track, and Mike dived out, closely followed by Emma and Barnes, leaving Jenny and Ruth almost like statues. They ran the few metres to Mike and Lucy's cottage and burst through the door.

"I'll get the range heated up and put some water on," Barnes said.

"I'll get all the lanterns on," Emma said.

"I'll go get the weapons cache," Mike added, immediately bounding up the stairs, two at a time.

Less than a minute later, they heard the VW camper coming to a stop. Mike jumped down the last few steps with the holdall full of weapons and ammunition. He pushed it up against the wall to make sure no one would trip over it and ran out to the vehicles carrying the single quilt that he had ripped from Jake's bed. He climbed into the camper, and with Lucy, Raj, and Wren, they slowly lifted Jules onto the quilt and, taking a corner each, stretchered her into the kitchen, by which time the lanterns were all on. Jenny and Ruth had now joined Emma and the three of them were lighting candles and placing them in strategic positions to cast as much light around the room as possible.

The stretcher-bearers carefully placed Jules down on the solid oak table. "I'm going to need you and Emma to give blood. She needs a transfusion, and you're the only possible donors," Lucy said, looking towards Mike.

"Whatever she needs."

"Goes without saying," Emma added, lighting the final candle.

Shaw and George walked in, and both of them looked physically shaken at how pale Jules had turned.

"Shaw … Shaw! The weapons are by the door. Me and Em have got to stay here with Lucy," Mike said, rolling his sleeves up. Lucy disappeared out of the room to grab whatever medical supplies she could find.

"I know, Lucy mentioned it on the drive over here," Shaw replied. "I'm wondering if we should all stay here until morning. There'll be a few of them at that barricade and to be four troops down we'll be struggling."

"If we don't do this now, we'll completely lose the element of surprise. They'll know something's wrong if they don't know already," Barnes said.

Mike unclipped the enemy radio from his belt. "There haven't been any broadcasts from them. Hopefully, our luck's holding for the time being."

Shaw picked up the radio and stared at it long and hard. "Looks like it's just you and me, Barney."

"I'll go," Wren said.

Shaw looked uneasy. "I don't doubt your credentials as a markswoman with those crossbows, but it's going to be dark, and these guys are going to have guns."

"No, really? I thought they'd all be armed with peashooters."

Mike smiled. "You should take her. Wren's faced down people like this before. I'd feel just as confident having her by my side as one of you two."

"I can handle a gun too," George said. "Not a rifle but a pistol. I've had some practice."

"Okay, that's four of us," Shaw said.

"To be honest, the only people I need are Mike and Emma. Raj is pretty handy in a tight spot," Lucy said.

"Okay, Ruth and I might not be able to shoot, but we've been in the trenches plenty of times before, I'm sure there's something we can help with," Jenny said.

George walked over to the kitchen table and placed his hand on Jules's pale cheek. "Hang in there, poppet," he said before swallowing hard, wiping a tear from his eye, and heading out of the door.

The others filed out too, leaving Shaw with Lucy, Mike and Emma. "I'm sorry I can't go with you," Mike said.

"I won't lie. I'd feel a lot better about our chances if you four were with us."

"Wait a minute," Mike said. "How long does it take to give blood?"

"A pint will take about ten minutes," Lucy replied.

"Leave the Land Rover," he said, turning to Shaw.

"Mike, you'll be weak and a little dizzy after giving blood. You'll need time to rest," Lucy said.

"I'll be fine. I've lost plenty of blood before, I've always been okay," he replied.

"No, you won't be fine. Jesus, Mike, I do know what I'm talking about."

"Look, nothing about this is ideal." He rolled up his sleeve. "Get the needle in. Shaw, leave the Land Rover; I'll be with you as soon as I can."

Lucy glared at Mike and then realised there was no point in arguing, the decision had already been made.

28

George pumped the gas pedal three times and turned the key in the ignition. The old engine slowly spluttered to life, and he reversed down the track. Everyone remained silent; there was lots of blood inside the campervan, reminding them of how severe Jules's situation was.

"What do you have in mind exactly?" Raj asked nervously as the camper came to the end of the track and joined the side road. It slowly steered up the narrow lane until it joined the main carriageway. George negotiated the sharp left turn, and they were on their way to death or glory.

"I'm still working on all the details," Shaw said.

"That's reassuring," Wren replied, stroking Wolf's head.

"On the upside, Barney's got a night scope for his sniper rifle, and I've got one for the SA80."

"And what if they've got night vision too?" Wren asked.

"Even if they have, they won't have a sniper like him."

"Okay, but once he's taken a couple of them out, aren't they all going to go diving for cover so we won't be able to see them?"

"It's not like we've got a lot of choices, Wren. We can't drive straight up to them and let rip."

"Wren, Shaw's been doing this for a long time. If it wasn't for him, Safe Haven would have fallen long before now," George said.

"No, she's right, it's a shitty plan," Shaw admitted.

"So what's a good plan?" Raj asked.

"Making sure we outnumber them about five to one."

"Ah," replied Raj.

"Exactly, ah!"

"Hang on," Wren said.

"What?" Shaw asked.

"Okay, we can't outnumber them five to one, but we can make them think they're outnumbered five to one."

Suddenly everybody's ears pricked up. "How would we do that, Wren?" Barnes asked.

"Well, if we could split up and have Barney on this side of the checkpoint with his sniper rifle and a few of us in the trees on the other side, I bet it would be pretty easy to convince them there are more of us than them."

"How?" Barnes asked.

"Shaw would need to be in the trees. He shouts out something clichéd like, 'Put down your weapons, you're surrounded.' They probably won't believe us at first, but at that point they'll be looking towards the woods. That's when Barney takes a shot or two from the other side. Maybe you could wound a couple of them or something. They'll realise they're out in the open and covered on at least two sides. The only logical thing to do would be for them to put their weapons down."

"And if they don't?" Shaw asked.

"Well, if they don't, we're back to plan A."

"And forgive me for being dumb, but how do we

get to the other side of the checkpoint?"

"Err…"

"Hang on, I know," Barney said. "Stan Collinshaw's motorboat. You could take it up and around the cove. That would give you access to the woods. You'd be able to get bang opposite them without them even having a clue."

"That … might work. That's pretty impressive, Wren. How did you come up with that?" Shaw asked.

"I was out on the road a long time before I met you lot, remember. My sister and I did all sorts together."

"Well, I'm just glad you're on our side. I'd hate to go up against somebody as smart as you."

"Considering most of the bad guys out there are men, there's not much chance of that, is there?" she replied with a smile.

*

"I really don't like this, Mike," Lucy said, placing a plaster over the needle puncture.

"I'll be fine, trust me. Keep an eye on the road. I doubt if you'll see anything coming from the direction of the village, but if something goes wrong at the North Ridge…" He saw the look of worry intensify on Lucy's face. "Just keep a lookout, okay?"

Emma walked up to her brother and put her arms around him, giving him a big hug and kissing him on the cheek. "Don't say I never do anything for you," she said, handing him a pecan granola bar.

"You're my absolute favourite sibling over the age of twenty, do you know that?"

Emma smiled. "Funny fucker, aren't you?"

"Keep an eye out. I'll be back as soon as I can. Love you." He turned towards Lucy, who was already preparing the needle for Emma's arm. "Love you." She didn't say anything, maybe because if she did she would begin to cry. Mike walked out of the kitchen and headed straight out of the house towards the waiting Land Rover. The night air hit him, and he immediately felt woozy and disoriented.

"How is she doing?" Emma asked as Lucy slid the needle into her arm.

"Well, I've cleaned up the entry and exit wounds and stopped the bleeding. There aren't any fragments in there, which is great. The bullet didn't penetrate any major organs, and once we've given her this transfusion, I'm going to pump her with antibiotics and a little morphine for the pain. All we can do is keep a close eye on her and hope."

"What do you think her chances are?"

Lucy looked at Jules's pale face then turned to Emma. "She's as tough as they come, she's a fighter, and she's not got any other medical issues. She stands as good a chance as anyone."

Emma watched as her blood began to flow down the clear tube. There was a feeling deep inside her that said all this was for nothing.

*

Richard didn't know what he was going to do when he reached the North Ridge checkpoint. The guards would be heavily armed, and all he would have was a handgun of some description that he had no idea how to use. He rounded the bend to the final mile stretch of road then he heard a familiar sound carrying on the breeze. It was quiet at first, but gradually it grew in volume. He turned and saw in the distance a set of headlights. These headlights were distinctive though. They weren't the bright LEDs of modern vehicles that nearly blinded you as they approached. They were the round, not so bright little owl eyes of a VW campervan.

"It can't be," he said out loud. His heart began to race. There were only three people who knew how to start Sue's temperamental old hippy mobile now that it had been reconditioned. One of them was already dead, he was the other one, meaning… "George."

He watched as the lights disappeared and reappeared around bends and up inclines. For the first time in a long time, a small smile started on his face. If it was George that meant Ruth might be alive too. It meant all the council may have survived. Suddenly he had a purpose once more. He remained in the middle of the road watching the lights as they gradually got bigger and bigger. *What if it wasn't George? What if some amateur grease-monkey had figured out how to get it going?* If that was the case, so be it. He was tired and getting mowed down by the project that he and David had worked on like brothers would be a poetic way to go.

It was several minutes before the campervan finally chugged around the bend and came to a stop, by which time another vehicle's headlights could be seen in the distance. Despite the lights not being particularly strong, he still had to shield his eyes a little. The side door of the VW opened, and a figure climbed out. To Richard, it was just a silhouette, it could have been anyone. He held his breath as they slowly and silently advanced towards him. Then he saw it, the figure was carrying a pistol by their side. *Oh God. This is it!*

"Richard?"

For a moment he couldn't answer; then, as the figure ran towards him, he held out his arms. "Ruth? Ruth, is that you?" He began to cry.

"Oh, Richard, I didn't think I would ever see you again." The pair embraced, and even when other figures climbed out of the vehicle and began to crowd around them like spectators around the chimp enclosure at Edinburgh Zoo, they did not stop.

Tears combined as their cheeks met then, finally, they pulled apart. Richard took hold of Ruth's hand and turned towards the semi-circle that had formed between them and the campervan. "They murdered David."

Ruth's hand went limp in his. "What? Why?" Shaw asked.

"He stayed with them. He stayed with Angus and Maureen and the others while the rest of us carried on. Then there were shots. I ran back as fast as I could, but it was all over. There was blood everywhere. They'd tipped the bodies over the cliff. It was..." He started to cry again, and Ruth pulled him into her.

"There was nothing you could have done, Richie," she said softly in his ear.

He lifted his head. "There was, and I did."

"What do you mean?" Shaw asked.

"They were using the school minibus. I made them crash. They hit the rocks, and I heard them all screaming as they went down. I heard them screaming, and the sound lifted my heart. I'd got revenge. I'd got revenge for David and the others." He wiped the tears from his eyes and saw the headlights of the other vehicle much closer now. "There's somebody coming."

They all turned. Shaw and Barnes ran back to the campervan and retrieved their rifles, aiming them down the road. The tyres screeched as they followed the tarmac around and Barnes lowered his weapon as it continued to hurtle towards them. "What are you doing?" Shaw asked, keeping his SA80 on the speeding car.

"There's only one bastard mad enough to drive like that on these roads."

The car came to a skidding stop twenty feet away, and the driver side opened. "Okay, what's the plan?" Mike asked, walking towards them.

"See what I mean?" said Barney.

*

"So, what's your name?" the young woman asked.

"I am Talikha."

"Talikha? I like that. They call me Sam."

"Sam? I'm Sammy."

"Well, Sam's not my real name. This lot decided to start calling me it on account of my swords. Short for Samurai. They got tired of saying that though, so they shortened it to Sam."

"Oh," Sammy replied, disappointed.

"Is it much further, Sam?" April asked.

"Not much. We'll get water and rest and then

tomorrow we might come up with a fresh plan." A girl walking by the side of Sam began to cry. Sam placed an arm around her shoulder. "It's okay, Tess. We'll figure something out."

Talikha wondered how Sam had come to be in charge of all these youngsters, but there had been enough questions for one day. All she wanted now was to sleep and find a quiet corner with Humphrey to think about Raj. They made the rest of the short journey in silence and as they reached the entrance to the car park of the monumental hotel, Sam stopped.

"What is it?" Ryan asked.

She put her thumb and middle finger in her mouth and whistled loudly. There was a short pause, and then a young boy shouted, "Sam, is that you?"

"Yep, it's me. We've got some guests."

A car engine started, and a Vauxhall Corsa appeared out of the entrance to a farmer's field twenty metres ahead. It clumsily negotiated the turn, headed towards them and then steered left into the car park. The overhead light was on in the car, and Talikha could see the boy driving it was just a teenager. The children in the passenger seat and rear seats looked much younger. "The rest of your army?"

"Yeah. Aiden's thirteen. He's second in command and the one who spotted you. We headed out to try and change your mind about coming this way, and if we didn't come back within an hour, he was going to take the youngest ones and try to find somewhere else."

"You look after them all by yourself?" Talikha asked.

"There were more of us. I had a friend… She—" Sam broke off. She'd shared enough for one day.

Talikha knew not to press any harder. The horde followed the car into the hotel grounds. The half-moon cast a spotlight on the Highlands' stage and the hotel was the star attraction, once the venue for the upper classes, dignitaries and royalty, now a doss house for five hundred plus refugees.

"You said you had water?" April said. "None of us have had a drink in hours."

"Aiden!" Sam called the young boy over as the rest of them climbed out of the vehicle. "Show this lady where the stream is."

"Stream?" April said. "Isn't that a little risky?"

Sam pointed to the silhouette of a foreboding black mountain. "It flows from there. We've been drinking it, and it tastes good. Nobody's had the runs or anything."

"It's still a little dangerous to drink it without boiling."

"I checked it out this afternoon. I went halfway up. There wasn't a sign of anything to worry about, and it's not really like we've got a lot of choices. Every pot and pan in the place has been taken. Virtually everything's gone."

"Regrettably, that will have been our people," Talikha said.

"And now the ones who have taken over your town are reaping all the benefits while we sleep on hard floors and drink stream water."

"So it would seem."

"I'm hungry," Tess said.

"I know, I'm hungry too. We can't do anything about it right now, but first thing tomorrow we'll try to catch some fish or something. How does that sound?" Sam asked.

"Like I'll be hungry again tomorrow."

Tess didn't mean it to sound funny, but the adults couldn't help but laugh.

Sam stopped at the door as others began to file into the magnificent building. "I'm going to take the first watch," she said. "I'll make sure that if we get any visitors, at least there'll be some advanced warning."

Talikha was tired and hurting physically and emotionally, but everybody was looking to her now. "Humphrey and I will keep you company."

"Well, if you two have got the first watch, April and me will take the second," Ryan said.

"Okay," Sam said. "My spidey sense is telling me this night's still got more surprises in store for us."

*

"You okay, Jen?" Mike asked as Stan's motorboat bounced over the black water.

"I will be when tonight's over."

"You'll be fine. It will be like when we were back in Morecambe, remember?" he said with a smile.

"If you're trying to make me feel better, it's not working, darling."

"Hey, you've got a short memory. You dug in and did what was necessary. We're not going to be getting into a gunfight with these people. We're going to take them by surprise, they'll do the sensible thing and lay down their weapons, and Bob's your uncle."

"Don't take this the wrong way, Mike, but how much blood did Lucy take?" Shaw asked.

"Hardly any. I feel as fit as a fiddle."

"Uh-huh."

They continued in silence around the cove and Raj steered the boat towards the white sands. He cut the engine a few metres before dry land, and he, Shaw and Mike jumped out, pulling the boat clear of the water and allowing Jenny to climb out without getting her feet wet.

"You're such a gentleman," she said as Shaw took her hand.

"Jen," he replied, taking her a little to the side, "you understand why I brought you, don't you?"

She smiled and touched Shaw's cheek gently, a gesture unseen by Mike and Raj as they secured the boat and gathered the weapons.

"You really are very, very sweet sometimes, do you know that? Of course I realise. Barnes has to be where he is. There's no way we could put Wren in the line of fire if things went wrong, or George for that matter, and as much as I love Ruth and Richard, they're not really in the best place at the moment."

"Mike's right, they're not going to put up a fight after Barney's wounded a couple of them."

"If you say so."

"Trust me, I've got a feeling in my bones." He smiled in the moonlight, and his teeth almost seemed fluorescent, then he kissed her hand. "I won't let anything happen to you, Jen."

"Tell me something, are you sure you're gay? I mean maybe you just need an older woman to show you the ropes."

Shaw burst out laughing. He couldn't remember the last time he had laughed, but it felt good. It rose from within him and seemed to rattle his ribcage.

"What's so funny?" Mike asked as he and Raj came to join them.

"I'll tell you when you're older, sweetheart," Jenny replied as she took one of the rifles from Raj. "Come on then, let's get this over with." She slung the rifle over her shoulder, and the four of them marched off the beach and into the woodland.

"Okay," Shaw said, flicking on his torch, "we head south for a couple of hundred metres then we'll be next to the road. There'll be enough light for us to see then if we stay parallel to it."

"I do not wish to be the harbinger of doom, but doesn't that also mean that there will be enough light for them to see us as we approach?" Raj asked.

Shaw didn't answer. He widened the beam of his torch and started walking. Mike followed him, leaving Raj and Jenny standing there alone.

"Do you think he heard you?" Raj could not see Jenny's face, but he could tell she was smiling. "Come on, love, where's your sense of humour? We've all got to die sometime."

29

Emma stood at the landing window for the best part of five minutes before returning to the kitchen. "No lights, no movement, nothing," she said, looking at Jules's face as Lucy took her blood pressure.

"Well, that's healthier than it was. Her colour's a little better after the transfusion too. How strong are you feeling?"

"Huh?"

Lucy removed the stethoscope from around her neck and placed the blood pressure machine on the kitchen counter. "We should move her onto the sofa in the living room so that she's more comfortable. She's not going to be up and about for a while, and a kitchen table isn't ideal."

"Okay. Let me get a few lights in the hallway so we can see what we're doing." Emma collected some candles and lanterns and left the kitchen.

Lucy placed her hand on Jules's forehead. "Come on, sweetie. You keep fighting."

A minute later, Emma was back in the kitchen and

on the other side of the table. She grasped two corners of the quilt and Lucy did the same at the other end. "One, two, three." They slowly lifted Jules and even more slowly negotiated their way through the kitchen door, down the hall, and into the living room. They tenderly lowered the quilt and its cargo onto the soft sofa.

"Okay, you keep an eye on her, I'll go tidy up," Lucy said, starting to head out of the room once more.

"Jesus, Lucy, you've never stopped. The cleaning up can wait a while. Why don't you sit a minute?"

"I can't. While Mike and Sammy and Jake are still out there, I can't. If I don't stay busy, my mind starts playing tricks on me."

"They're all going to be okay. We know Talikha led everybody out, we heard that for ourselves. She would guard Sammy and Jake with her life. And Mike? Lucy, it's Mike."

"That's what worries me."

*

"I'm telling you something's wrong, they should have been here by now," the Hispanic female guard said, peering through the darkness, hoping to see a vehicle trundling around the corner to bring their replacements.

"And I told you, Rosa, there's nothing in the world of fuck I can do about it," Blaze growled. "The battery's gone dead on the radio, not that the worthless piece of shit was much good before that, but we're here until we're here so keep a watch on the road and stop pissing me off."

"Puto pendejo," Rosa mumbled, walking away once again.

"Watch yourself, girl. I know what that means."

"I bet you do, I'm sure you hear it a lot," she called behind her.

"Jesus Christ, the mouth on her," Blaze said as his best friend walked towards him holding out a packet of cigarettes. Blaze took one and placed it between his lips. His friend did the same; they lit them and stood in silence for a moment, savouring the taste.

"She makes a good point, y'know," he said in his cockney accent.

"What point's that, Bill? That I'm an asshole?"

"Well, two good points then." Blaze chuckled but Bill continued. "They should have been here long before now."

"You don't think I realise that?"

"Blaze, you and I have known each other a hell of a long time. Of course I know you realise that. Question is what are we going to do about it?"

"Look, by my reckoning, they're maybe an hour overdue. Could be anything. Could be vehicle trouble, could be that those folks Troy was holding managed to escape, could be all sorts. They've probably been trying to reach us, but since our piece of shit radio's given up the goddamn ghost, we're in the dark here. We'll wait for another half hour and then I'll send a team out. One of the properties on this end of the track must still have a functioning vehicle."

"You're right. It's probably a flat or something. These roads are a bitch. My guess is they weren't that great before everything turned to shit."

"I don't know why in hell Troy thought this was somewhere we'd want to live out our days."

"Hey, don't knock it. I'd live in a tent in the middle of Hyde Park if it meant I didn't have to spend another minute in that tin can."

"I suppose you're—"

"You're surrounded. Drop your weapons and put your hands up!" shouted the voice from the darkness of the woodland.

Despite the instruction, all sixteen men and women raised their rifles and aimed towards the tree line. "Steady, nothing rash," Blaze said to them before turning towards where the voice had come from. "How about you come out of there and show your face so we can discuss this man to man?"

A radio hissed in the trees, and within a couple of seconds one of the soldiers screamed and fell to the ground. "My leg. They got me in the fucking leg."

"Aaarrrggghhh!" One of the female soldiers howled this time as she fell face down, dropping her rifle as she went.

"They're firing from behind," another voice called.

"This don't feel right. I think this is smoke 'n' mirrors, Billy boy. If you had a greater force and surrounded people who'd killed a shit load of your friends and taken over your town, would you be asking them to put down their weapons or would you be blasting them all the way to Hell?"

"So what do we do?"

"Charge!" Blaze began firing and started running towards the trees where the voice had come from. Bill was right beside him for a second or two before the front of his head imploded. "Holy shit!" Blaze muttered. Bloody chunks of brain glistened in the moonlight as they flew through the air. Another figure, a woman this time, cried out but only briefly as her chest exploded outwards like a scene from a horror movie. Once they were in the woodland, they would be protected from the sniper at least.

A volley of automatic rifle fire from behind a tree thirty metres or so along the forest edge chopped down another three guards. Then, from the other direction, a more sustained attack took out another five. His squad returned fire, but the assassins had the trees to shield them. Another sniper bullet took out Rosa. She went down silently. *That was a first*, Blaze thought as he finally reached the tree line. There were only five of them left, and two of those were lying injured on the road. *How did they get the drop on us like this? Damn it, I screwed this up well and truly.*

He pulled a small flashlight from his belt and placed it between his teeth. The gunfire had stopped for the moment. Now they were playing hide and seek. "Payton, Carlos, stay with me, and if you've got flashlights, turn them on. I think we're looking for four perpetrators here—the sniper, the shouter, and the two sons o' bitches with the automatics."

"I don't like this. I don't like this one bit," Payton said.

"Keep it together."

A twig snapped to the left and Blaze shot around. His torch lit up the trees, and he shot a few rounds in the general direction of the sound but to no avail.

"I say we should switch the flashlights off. We're advertising where we are," said Payton.

"And I say you should shut your goddamn mouth and keep your eyes open. We ain't going to see shit if we don't have light, dumbass."

"Over there, what was that?" Carlos yelled. Blaze looked to where he was pointing. The branch of a shrub was flapping wildly as if someone had just brushed by it. The three of them raised their weapons and fired into the darkness.

"Keep it tight," Blaze said, taking the lead and heading towards the shrub. The other two followed as they went further and further into the woods like Hansel, Gretel and guest following a trail of breadcrumbs.

*

"Where's Mike?" Shaw asked as Jenny arrived back at the rendezvous point.

She let out a deflated breath. "When they started firing, he told me to run, so that's what I did."

The bushes rustled again, and Shaw brought his rifle up, night scope and all. "Raj, thank God. Have you seen Mike?"

"No. I came straight back here as you said."

"Shit!"

"It's my fault, I should have stayed with him,"

Jenny said. "I'm useless, absolutely useless. I didn't even get a shot off, I just ran."

"You can't blame yourself, Jen. The last thing we expected was for them to open fire. By my count, you got three, Raj. I got five and Barney killed three with two still down injured on the road."

"What should we do?" Raj asked.

"There's not much we can do. I'm going to head back to the tree line and keep my eyes peeled. The last thing we want to be doing is going on a bloody duck hunt in the woods at night. You two stay here and stay low." Shaw vanished into the trees while Jenny and Raj sat down on the wide, flat rock that they had all been told to meet back at.

"Oh God, I hope he's okay. I feel so guilty," Jenny said.

Raj took hold of her hand. "Mike told you to run and that is what you did. There is nothing to feel guilty about."

"I suppose you're right. I mean what bloody good would I be anyway?"

"Jenny," he began, placing his other hand on top of hers. "If it wasn't for you, there would be no Safe Haven. You helped build it from the ground up. Because you don't use a gun that does not mean you aren't a fighter. We are a whole. Alone there are things we cannot do; as a family there is nothing we can't do. Mike is a different kind of fighter but no more fierce than you."

"You're a sweetheart. You always know what to say, but I think you're wrong about me being fiercer than Mike. When someone tries to hurt his family, I don't think I've ever met anyone who is more frightening. My only hope is that out there, right now, he's the hunter and not the hunted."

*

"Barney, it's Shaw. Over," he whispered into the radio.

The volume was turned all the way down, so Shaw held the speaker to his ear. "Shaw, this is Barney. Go ahead. Over."

"Two injured on the road. Three loose in the forest. Myself, Jenny and Raj are all okay and accounted for. Mike's whereabouts and status unknown. Over."

The radio fell silent for a moment, and Shaw briefly wondered if Barnes had received the message. He wasn't left wondering long, however, as first one then the other injured soldier stopped moving. Barnes had finished them off. Nothing dramatic, no final cries or pleas, just expert marksmanship and a steely determination to get the job done. The radio hissed. "This is Barnes, we're on our way. Over and out."

*

Talikha and Sam sat on the wall next to one another. Humphrey and Meg continued sniffing at the air, listening, watching for anything that signalled danger.

"So are both of these yours?" Sam asked.

"No, just this one," Talikha replied, stroking Humphrey's head. "Meg's owner is ... with my husband, back there."

"Shit! I'm sorry. Look, who knows, they might be okay."

"You are right. Of course, you are right." She said the words but neither woman believed them.

"For what it's worth, I got separated from my family too, so I know how it feels."

Talikha looked across at her. "It's funny. I thought I wanted to be alone tonight, but sitting here with you is making me feel a little better."

"Not me," Sam said, standing up. "I swear I'm getting piles plonked on that bloody wall."

Talikha laughed and stood up too. "Actually, now that you mention it."

They continued their vigil standing, staring down

the road into the never-ending night. "Have you thought about tomorrow?"

"I don't understand."

"Well, y'know, we've got no food. I'm so hungry I could eat a scabby horse. We can't stay here with nothing to chew on but fresh air."

Talikha thought for a moment. "We have a number of people among us who can fish and forage. We can go out in groups for safety and collect as much food as we can."

"You really think you can gather enough oyster mushrooms and berries and catch enough fish to feed five hundred people?"

"We won't know until we try, will we?"

Sam laughed. "I suppose."

"What is funny?"

"Sorry … nothing. You remind me of someone, that's all."

Talikha shrugged. "I would like to stay here a little while longer. This is where I was told to come."

"You still think they're alive."

"Thinking and hoping are two different things, but I don't want to give up on hope just yet."

30

Blaze, Carlos and Peyton carried on through the woods. They had not seen or heard anything suspicious in the last few minutes, but their senses were still on high alert.

A loud clacking sound tore through the silent darkness. They all turned to the direction it had come from and started firing and running towards it. They continued past where the sound had come from, racing through the trees, eventually bursting through an overgrown fan of bushes and into a small opening. They shone their torch beams around, and as the rays intersected, they realised something was amiss.

"Where the fuck is Peyton?" Blaze said.

"He was right behind me." Carlos looked towards the direction they had travelled from and then shouted, "Hey! Peyton!"

"Keep your mouth shut, you dumb son of a bitch," Blaze ordered. There was no reply to Carlos's call, and the two of them began to retrace their steps, moving much more slowly now, scouring every inch of their surroundings as they walked.

Carlos came to a juddering stop, pointing his torch

towards his feet. Blaze pointed the beam of his own flashlight towards him and saw Carlos cross himself. "Santa Madre de Dios."

Blaze went across and shone his torch down too. Peyton was lying dead, a gruesome mess, his torso full of machete-sized stab wounds.

"What the fuck?" Blaze's voice tailed off.

They continued to stare down at the defiled corpse of their compatriot until something whooshed through the air. By the time Blaze looked up, it was too late to avoid the peach-sized stone. It smashed into his nose, cracking cartilage in a bloody, gory burst. "Fucking mother fucker," he yelled, staggering backwards and bringing his hand up to his face.

Carlos began to fire in the direction the stone had emerged from. Chunks of wood splintered from trees, and branches fell as the spray of bullets chopped through them like a giant scythe, but the attacker had fled.

"Where did he go?" Carlos asked.

"I am going to tear this piece of shit a new asshole when we find him," Blaze said, looking down at his blood-covered hand. "Come on."

*

Raj jumped to his feet and brought his rifle up as he heard movement in the bushes. He could see very little, but just pointing the rifle somehow made him feel safer.

"Raj, Jenny, it's Shaw!"

Raj lowered his weapon. "From the gunfire, I am guessing they have found Mike's trail."

"Or he's found theirs," Shaw replied. "Come with me out to the road, they're bringing the camper up."

Jenny climbed to her feet, and the three of them walked back out into the moonlight as the VW and Land Rover came to a halt. George and the others climbed out.

"Do we go in looking for them?" Barney asked.

"While ever they're still firing, it means Mike's still

alive. It would be really easy to have a friendly fire incident in the woods at night," Shaw replied.

"So … what? We're just going to leave him in there by himself?" Wren asked, horrified.

"I don't like it any more than you do, Wren. But the fact is we could do more harm than good." Right on cue, more gunfire sounded from deep in the woods.

"That's bullshit!" Wren said.

"Wren!" George hissed.

"It is, Grandad. If that was any one of us in there, Mike would be after us in a heartbeat."

George sighed, he couldn't disagree with her.

"Look! I'll go in alone," Shaw said.

"No!" Barney replied. "I'll go in. Let's face it, your leg's not great, and I'm a better shot."

"Cheers Barney, but please stop before my head gets too big."

"Come on, you know this is the smart move."

"Okay, but don't take any risks."

Barnes placed his sniper rifle back in the campervan and pulled his Glock 17 out. "Wish me luck," he said, but before anyone got the chance to say anything, he was sprinting towards the sound of gunfire.

*

"How much ammo have you got left?" Blaze asked.

"This is my last mag," Carlos replied.

"Son of a bitch! This is what he's wanting. He's wanting us to use up all our bullets."

"Who is this guy? I mean what he did to Peyton; that was some fucked-up shit."

"Don't think about that. This is just some pissed-off local yokel who's handy with a knife. I don't care who the fuck you are; you get into an argument with a bullet you're always going to come out the losing end. Now come on, soldier. Let's put this motherfucker to bed."

The two men continued in the direction they

thought the assassin had gone, but they knew they were on a bug hunt and it was going to be harder than Blaze's bravado suggested. They went deeper and deeper into the woodland. The vegetation became thicker, and every step they took made the whole expedition seem more hopeless.

"This guy hasn't shown himself in a while. Maybe we got him and we just didn't see the body."

Blaze shone his flashlight in a full circle. Nothing looked out of place, but that didn't make him feel any easier. "Maybe. Maybe not. I know this is getting us nowhere. Let's start heading back towards the road, see if we can try to pick up a trail again. I've got bupkis here."

"The road. Yeah, that makes sense."

They turned and started to head back. "Whoa!" Blaze got his foot tangled up in a root and stumbled.

"Shit! You okay, boss?"

Blaze shuffled onto his side and laughed. He still had his weapon, but his torch had fallen out of his hand and rolled a couple of feet. "Yeah. Must be getting flat feet," he replied, chuckling again. "Give me a hand up, compadre." He extended his hand.

Carlos stood there looking at him then collapsed to his knees, wide-eyed and gasping. "Boss!" He fell face down, on top of his torch.

Blaze scrambled towards his own flashlight and shot the beam around. There was a spreading patch of red on the back of Carlos's shirt. Not pausing for a second, Blaze started firing. *Jesus, this motherfucker had murdered Carlos in front of him ... literally.* "Oh, you wanna play?" he said, jamming his last magazine in. "Let's fucking play!" He fired in a wide arc; the bullets decimated the surrounding trees and bushes. When he stopped, he was panting and sweating. He started forward again. *If it's the last thing I ever do, and it may well be, I'm going to gut this bastard.*

*

Emma and Lucy each sat in an armchair watching

Jules and hoping. They had turned all the lights and lanterns out so as not to attract attention in case any unwanted visitors passed by. Moonlight illuminated the room in a blue-white glow, and, while their friend was unconscious, that was enough.

"What do you think happens from here?" Emma asked.

"Well, let's pray she wakes up. Then it's—"

"That's not what I meant. I meant with Safe Haven. What happens to Safe Haven?"

"I don't know, sweetie. That's a problem for another day. I suppose we have a lot of decisions ahead of us."

"I suppose. Do you think they took out the soldiers at the North Ridge?"

Lucy didn't answer. She stood up, walked to the window and looked out across the rippling bay. "So much beauty in the world, so much horror."

"That's always been the case."

Lucy let out a long breath. "I suppose, but this place was always more beauty than horror … until today. We've had our ups and downs in the past, we've had casualties of war, but today we had real evil in town, the kind of evil from history books."

"Lucy." It was barely more than a whisper.

Both Lucy and Emma ran to the sofa and knelt down. Emma took Jules's hand while Lucy touched her soft cheek. "I'm here, sweetie."

"Em?"

"I'm here too, Jules."

"How are you feeling?" Lucy asked.

"Like I've been shot."

"Good. That's how you should be feeling."

"Where am I?"

"I'll go get a couple of lanterns," Emma said, rushing out of the door.

"You're at our house. We managed to stop the bleeding and give you a blood transfusion. You've had antibiotics, and I gave you something for the pain too."

"It's not fuckin' working."

Lucy smiled. "I can give you some more soon."

"You gave me Emma's blood?"

"And Mike's."

"Oh fuck! I'm never going to hear the last of that, am I?"

Lucy giggled. "No, you're probably not. Look, why don't you just rest and not think about anything but feeling better right now?"

Emma returned with a pair of lanterns, a couple of candles and a bottle of water. She handed the water to Lucy, who angled Jules's head up enough to give her a few sips.

"Where's everybody else?"

"They'll be back soon enough," Lucy replied.

"Did you find my brothers?"

"Not yet, Jules. You weren't out that long, but we will."

"Mike's not going to let me… I … tired."

"Just rest." Lucy stroked her friend's head until she went back to sleep.

*

Blaze regretted spraying bullets everywhere in anger. Not only had he wasted ammo, but there were so many broken branches and ruffled leaves that there was no hope of picking up a trail. He headed back to where he had left Carlos, to scavenge whatever he could use. There might still be a few rounds left in the magazine, and having a spare torch was never a bad thing.

He reached Carlos's corpse and went cold. His jaw dropped open as he saw his friend's face and body slashed and stabbed almost beyond recognition.

"What in God's name?"

The shotgun blast took out Blaze's right knee, and

he crumpled like a matchstick tower. He wanted to fire back, but the pain coursing through him shattered any possibility of that. Before he had even come to rest on the ground, another shot blew his hand off, rifle and all. He didn't realise he was screaming, everything seemed like a dream now. He lay on the ground with the torch by his head pointing straight towards his hand and rifle almost as if it was taunting him, laughing at him.

It was only as the blurred figure came out of the darkness that the last vestiges of self-preservation kicked in, and he reached for his sidearm. Another shot boomed, and he brought his arm up to see his other hand had been reduced to muscle, bare bone and bloody gristle. He looked down to see no sign of his gun, and a gory mess where the holster had been.

The figure flicked on his torch and pointed it in Blaze's face. "Stop screaming!" he ordered, slapping Blaze hard. "You're losing a lot of blood, and if we don't act quickly, you're going to die."

"Fuck you," Blaze said, trying to sound tough but, as tears of agony rolled down his face, not pulling it off.

"Your people killed an awful lot of my people, and, unfortunately, as you're the only one left, you're going to pay the highest price." A feeling of calm came over Blaze as the blood flowed out of his body. He would be at rest soon, and then this nightmare would be over. Let this vengeful psychopath have his moment of glory. Nothing mattered now.

"Sure, whatever," he said. The figure grabbed hold of him and dragged him towards a tree, propping him against it. He could feel his eyes drifting, but he looked down and saw that he was being tied to the tree. "What the hell?" His words were clumsy, his tongue tasted blood, and it felt twice the normal size. The psycho crouched in front of him and pulled something from his rucksack. It looked like a syringe. "What the fuck's that?"

"Good question. We're about to find out because I'm quite curious myself. My best friend was injected with just a little bit of this stuff, and he's not around for me to ask anymore."

The figure stabbed the syringe into Blaze's neck and pushed the plunger until it was empty. For a few seconds, Blaze felt nothing; then he realised that he would never experience that warm, inviting eternal rest he craved so much. "What have you done to me?" More tears began to flood down his face, his physical pain forgotten. "What have you done to me?" he screamed. His attacker stepped back, flicked the rucksack back onto his shoulders and pointed the torch directly at Blaze.

"I don't know how long the infected can live without food, but with no hands, no knees, and no way to untie yourself from that tree, I'm going to be able to find out. I'll be sure to keep coming back to check on you from time to time."

"No! No! Nooo!" He was freezing cold, a cold like he'd never experienced before ... a fear like he'd never felt before. "Please. No. Kill me!"

"You want mercy? Like all your victims up and down this coast? Like all those people from Kyle? Like my friends? Mercy like that?" He crouched down again. "You can feel it, can't you? You can feel it taking over you, taking over who you were." The figure's eyes reflected the fires of hell as he stared at him. "I am so hoping the answer is that you can live forever in this state. I mean I doubt it, but that would be really poetic, wouldn't it?"

He was smiling ... enjoying every second. *What kind of monster was this?* Blaze opened his mouth to ask, but nothing came out. This was it. His body was not his own anymore. That dark thing, the freezing cold entity rising up inside, it was taking over. He tried to plead one last time, but it was too late. It was here. The darkness clutched him like a giant's hand, suffocating out the last of who he was and squeezing in the foul, rotting scent of death. No, not death, something more than that ... darkness, sadness, anger, hate, evil—hunger.

Mike stood up and took a breath as the creature began to struggle and strain against the rope. "Fucker!" he said and turned around to leave. He looked up, and a small break in the canopy gave him all the information he needed to figure out where the road was. His heart was still beating fast as he walked back through the woods. The adrenaline was shooting through his body. He stopped and shone the torch around. He listened to the sounds of the forest. There were none of Fry's taunts. Had he gone too far? No. He only wished he could have done the same thing to every last one of the marauders. Beth, Annie, John, Bruiser, David. They were his family, and when anybody hurt his family, there would never be mercy.

Mike froze as he saw a man with a torch and pistol spin around towards him. He remained glued to the spot for a second. "Thanks, Mike. Thank you for getting a little justice at least."

Mike raised his own torch to see Barnes. He walked over to where he was standing and cast the beam down to the ground. It was the first soldier he had killed ... more than killed, butchered. "They had it coming."

"You get them all?"

"Yeah."

"You've got blood on your face." Mike lifted his T-shirt and wiped his face clean. Barnes could see the look in his eyes. He could see the fire still burning. "Whatever you did, it was the right thing to do. C'mon, let's go find the others." Barnes placed a brotherly hand on Mike's back, and the pair of them headed towards the road.

"I wish I could do it again," Mike whispered. They continued in silence before reaching familiar looking ground.

"It's Mike and me," Barnes shouted as they stepped

out from the trees.

Shaw appeared from behind the VW closely followed by the rest of the group. The bodies of the other soldiers still littered the road as a reminder of the day's events, but that didn't matter. It was all over.

"Oh man! Are we glad to see you." Shaw's limp was barely noticeable as he rushed to meet them. He shouldered his rifle and gave them both bear hugs.

"They're all dead," Barnes said.

The others greeted and hugged Mike and Barnes, and their collective relief was palpable. Conscious of the fact that their night was not yet over, they cut the mini celebration short and headed back to the vehicles.

Shaw hung behind with Barnes while the others boarded. "Was everything … y'know, was it…"

"Mike took care of it," Barnes replied.

"What does that mean?"

Barnes turned to look at Shaw. "He did what had to be done."

31

"Another hour and we can grab a kip ourselves," Sam said.

"I might stay up. I don't know if I can sleep tonight," Talikha replied.

"I know what you mean, but if I don't get my beauty sleep, I'm not nice to be around."

Talikha giggled, and Humphrey licked Sam's hand. "I don't believe that for a second. Humphrey is an excellent judge of character; he would not slobber over anybody's hand."

Sam looked at the saliva casting a sheen over her fingers. "Yeah, thanks for that, Humphrey, I feel really honoured," she said, wiping it off on her jeans.

Talikha laughed again. "You'll get used to that."

"That's something to look forward to."

Both dogs suddenly sat bolt upright. Their eyes fixed on something beyond the night, and their ears stood to attention. Talikha picked up her makeshift spear and Sam reached over her shoulder to place her fingers on the grip of one of her swords. They both peered down the road but didn't see or hear anything for some time, until...

"It's a car," Talikha said.

"It's two cars," Sam replied.

"This is either going to be very good or very bad."

"Come on, let's head to the entrance, we can see if they drive by, and if they don't, we can wake the others."

The two women and two dogs ran over to the grand entrance of the hotel and crouched down taking watch at a porch window. The vehicle lights got brighter until, finally, they turned into the car park.

Sam jumped to her feet, starting to head into the hotel to wake the others.

"Wait!" Talikha said, grabbing her arm.

Sam crouched back down, a little irritated. "We should be waking people. If we need to put up a fight—"

The vehicles, one Land Rover, one vintage VW campervan, came to a halt in the sprawling car park. Two figures immediately climbed out of the smaller vehicle.

Sam turned to Talikha, and the younger woman could see tears of joy were running down her face. "It is him. It is my Raj." She stood up and sprinted out of the building; Humphrey ran by her side, let out two joyous yelps, and Raj knew there and then that his family was safe. He ran to meet them, and they fell into a tight embrace in the beam of the headlights. They kissed and touched faces and whispered, "I love you," over and over, and then they both crouched and Humphrey knocked Raj to the ground. Each time he tried to get up, the ecstatic Labrador Retriever would push him back down and lick his face again, causing both Raj and Talikha to laugh uncontrollably.

Meg burst from the doorway next, more than likely catching a whiff of Jenny's expensive perfume on the breeze she moved across the car park like a puppy. Jenny burst out crying. Earlier on that day she had been convinced she would never see her beautiful dog again. Meg stood on her hind legs, extending her paws onto Jenny's shoulders. It was their greeting, their hug. "I missed you, little girl," Jenny said as tears ran from her face onto Meg's fur.

The others slowly emerged from the vehicles and into the headlights to greet their friends. It had been the longest day, and, finally, they were on the home straight. Wolf jumped down from the campervan to go say hello to his pals, and Mike, Barnes and Shaw stood back watching everything with sad smiles on their faces. They had lost so much that day, but seeing this gave them some small amount of happiness.

Suddenly, two little figures came dashing out of the hotel towards the vehicles while another taller one followed them out more sedately. Their silhouettes immediately brought a bigger smile to Mike's face as he dropped to his knees and opened his arms wide. Sammy almost knocked him over as she flew at him.

"I was so scared," she cried. "I tried to be brave like you taught me to be, but I was so scared." Mike squeezed the pair of them tight, the warmth from their happiness radiating through him.

"You've no idea how good it is to see you two." Eventually, they pulled back, and Mike stood up, taking their hands in his and walking them over to Shaw and Barnes. The two children wriggled loose at the sight of Ruth and Jenny and both ran across to hug them too. The taller figure that had appeared from the hotel walked up to greet him, it was Tabby.

"Emma … is she…?"

"She's fine. She's back at the house with Luce and Jules."

"Oh, thank God. That's all I needed to know."

"So, what now?" Wren asked, walking up to them.

Mike wiped the tears of happiness from his eyes. "I'm going to go find Andy, Jon and Rob."

"Need some company?"

"I think you've done enough for today, Wren. I'll

go with Mike," Barnes said.

"Honestly," Wren replied, "it's not a big deal, there's no way I'll sleep anyw—" Suddenly she sensed something. She didn't know or understand what, but she stopped talking and looked towards the entrance of the hotel.

"Wren? Wren, are you okay?" Mike asked.

Sam slowly appeared from the entrance porch, slowing even more as she reached the edge of the headlights' beams. She stopped completely and just looked. Wren took a few paces forward then stopped too.

Sam and Wren burst out crying, and for a few seconds everyone fell quiet, not understanding what was going on.

"Wren?"

"Bobbi?"

They ran towards each other like children in a playground; whatever was going on around them, whatever had happened that day didn't matter anymore. This was everything. The two sisters locked in an embrace, making it impossible to see where one ended and the other began. Their cold cheeks pressed against each other, immediately creating warmth that neither had felt in the longest time.

They could have stayed like that forever, but Sam – Robyn – opened her eyes and saw an old man just a few feet away from them. Tears were running down his face too as he shared the moment.

"Robyn?" It was a desperate, disbelieving question. The silent salty streams became torrents as he walked towards the two girls, understanding for the first time that his eyes were not deceiving him.

"Grandad?" Robyn reluctantly broke her embrace with her sister and ran towards George. "Grandad!"

The tears were infectious as they spread around the assembled group like whooping cough. It was several minutes before George and Wren pulled themselves together enough to walk hand in hand with Robyn back to the others.

"Friends, this is my other granddaughter, Robyn."

*

Mike drove the Land Rover while Barnes rode shotgun. They snaked along the country roads, high hedgerows making every turn and bend a surprise. "I'm not an idiot, y'know, Mike."

"Eh?"

"You think I believe that you and Wren happened to stumble across a RAM that had become caught up in some barbed wire?"

Oh shit! "I thought Wren was pretty convincing. Hell, I believed it, and I was there."

This was no time for humour. There was an icy silence in the car as it took another bend. "I was going to wait until it was all over today and then knock seven bells out of you."

"So is this it? We're going to pull up in a layby and hammer it out?"

"No ... no."

"I thought it was all over, Barney. I thought it was me against them and it was a last-ditch attempt to try to save Lucy, Em, Raj, Shaw and the rest of them. And..."

"And what?"

"It doesn't matter."

"Tell me."

"And it wasn't John," Mike whispered, on the verge of being overcome with emotion.

"I don't follow you."

"John was a sweet little boy. He was the rosy-cheeked kid I found curled up next to his mother in the pantry back in Leeds. He was the friend who always made Jake laugh, no matter what. He wasn't that grey, ghoulish monster. That thing I cut up was just dead flesh."

"I miss them so much."

Mike did not look across towards Barnes, but he could tell the soldier was trying his hardest not to cry. "I'm not a religious man, Barney. I don't believe we all go to some wonderful place when we die, but I do believe that we live on forever."

"I don't understand what you mean."

"Every conversation, every interaction, every kindness, every time we laugh, everything. Whether it's John, Beth, Annie, Bruiser, David, Samantha, my gran, my mum, Alex … whoever it is. All that stuff lives on inside our heads. It shapes us, so, in a way, they live on through us and the interactions we have with other people. I don't know … maybe it's because my gran was an old hippy, but that's what I believe. None of us ever really die. Our bodies might, but we don't."

Barnes didn't answer for a long time. He sat there, digesting what Mike had said. "You're right; it probably was because your gran was an old hippy." They both laughed. "Actually, that does make me feel a little better. It's a nice way to think. I do really, really miss them though."

"I know exactly how you feel, Barney, and I'm always here for you, mate."

"Holy shit!"

"What?" Mike said, braking.

"I saw lights in the distance."

"You sure?"

"There, look!" he said, pointing. "They look like torch lights. They're too dim to be headlights. Three of them."

"It can't be Andy, Rob and Jon. No way could they have made it this far on foot."

The car set off once more, and Barnes reached for his Glock. He checked the magazine and placed it in his lap. "No point in taking any risks."

"I don't see the lights anymore."

"Whoever it is they're obviously as suspicious of us

as we are of them."

They carried on for a while longer but then slowed down. "I'm pretty certain it was around here somewhere," Mike said, pulling on the handbrake and climbing out of the car. He reached into the back and grabbed his rucksack then killed the lights. Barnes got out as well, and they both stood in the darkness, listening ... waiting.

"If you can hear me, we're not looking for trouble. We're out here trying to find our friends," Mike shouted.

He pulled the shotgun from his backpack and both he and Barney walked around to the back of the Land Rover to give themselves cover in case of a fire fight. A few seconds passed, and then a familiar voice called out, "Mike?"

"Rob, is that you?" Mike opened the driver door and flicked the lights on. Rob, Andy and Jon emerged from a hedgerow wheeling small bicycles. The smallest one had a little woven basket attached to the front.

"Oh, I would have paid good money to see them riding those," Barnes said under his breath.

"That makes two of us," Mike replied.

"Where's Jules?" Andy asked.

"She's at our place. She took a bullet."

"No! Is she okay?" The three brothers looked towards each other with panic-strewn faces.

"Lucy's looking after her. She's had a blood transfusion. The last thing she asked me to do before I left was to find you three, so I know if there is anything that's going to help her, it's hearing your voices."

Mike put his foot down on the return trip to the hotel. He dropped off Barnes and collected Sammy, Jake and Tabby. The car was cramped, but twenty-odd minutes later he was bringing the Land Rover to a stop on the track outside the gate to the cottage. Andy, Rob and Jon piled out of the car, hurdling the gate and sprinting to the door. They charged through, nearly giving Lucy and Emma a heart attack.

"Jesus, guys," Lucy said, placing her hand over her chest.

"Where is she? Is she still alive?" Andy was almost crying as he asked.

"Calm down. She's okay. I'll take you through to see her."

Lucy led them down the hallway to the dimly lit living room. All three brothers walked over to the sofa and knelt down. None of them spoke as Jules opened her eyes and smiled. "Took you fuckin' long enough to get here, didn't it?" she said quietly before a contented smile washed the pain and drowsiness from her face.

"We were so worried," Rob said.

"I don't know what we'd do if anything happened to you," Jon added.

"Andy's the eldest, he'd look after you."

"Exactly," Andy said, "we wouldn't last five minutes."

Jules smiled again and put her hand out. Rob took it; then, feeling the need to touch her, to make sure she was real, Andy grabbed her wrist, and Jon clutched her forearm. "It's good to see you boys. I was so worried about you."

"We found bikes. We knew our people would be heading north, so that's where we headed," Rob said.

"Bikes? Cool."

"Yeah," Mike said from the doorway. "There was a Barbie one, a My Little Pony one and I think the other was Pokémon. They were awesome."

Andy looked irritated for a moment, but then he laughed. "Yeah, they were pretty lame, but they got us here quicker than if we'd been walking."

"You leave my brothers alone, you little gobshite, or you'll have me to deal with," Jules said in little more than a whisper.

Mike walked over to the sofa, leaned down and

kissed her on the cheek. "Good to see you're getting back to your old self. Hell, now that you've got a pint of my blood inside you, you'll probably turn into some kind of superwoman."

"Oh, Jesus. Not in the door two minutes and he's already mentioned it."

"Don't worry. That was the first and last time. It's not like I'm going to mention that my blood saved your life at every available opportunity, is it? I mean it's only blood."

"Please. Get him out of here," she said, smiling.

"Did I mention I saved your life?"

"Somebody kill me. Kill me, please."

Mike started to walk to the door but then looked back. "Love you, Jules."

"I love you too. Now fuck off and let me be with my brothers."

Mike entered the kitchen to see Jake glued to Emma and Sammy squeezing the life out of Lucy. Tabby was leaning against a counter, her arms folded, a relieved smile decorating her face. It was several minutes before the joy and excitement waned.

"Is it true what Sammy said, that Wren found her sister?" Lucy asked.

"Yeah. It was pretty surreal." Mike flopped down into a chair and reached for the hot mug of chicory that was sitting on the table in front of Emma. He took two gulps then placed it down again. "Don't mind, do you?"

"Like I've got a choice." She turned to Sammy and Jake to see they were struggling to keep their eyes open. "I think you two have had way too much excitement for one day. Go on, bed, I'll be up in a minute." The two children reluctantly said their good nights, first hugging their family then going in to do the same with the visitors before finally climbing the stairs.

"We should set up a lookout shift," Emma said.

"We're seven miles out of the village, and I don't

think they'll stray far from the hunting ground for the time being," Lucy said.

"Nevertheless, Em's right. We can't be complacent. There's no way we can risk moving Jules at the moment, so we need to make this place as secure as possible."

Lucy let out a sigh. "So, what comes after this?"

"Well, tomorrow, you, Em, Shaw, Jen, Ruth and Raj are going to sit down and figure it all out," Mike said.

"Err... Mike, I don't think it's going to be that easy."

Mike took hold of Lucy's hand. "You're our council. A place doesn't make a town, the people do. Whatever we end up deciding, wherever we end up going, there will always be Safe Haven."

The End

A NOTE FROM THE AUTHOR

I really hope you enjoyed this book and would be very grateful if you took a minute to leave a review on Amazon and Goodreads.

If you would like to stay informed about what I'm doing, including current writing projects, and all the latest news and release information; these are the places to go:

Join the fan club on Facebook
https://www.facebook.com/groups/127693634504226

Like the Christopher Artinian author page
https://www.facebook.com/safehaventrilogy/

Buy exclusive and signed books and merchandise, subscribe to the newsletter and follow the blog:
https://www.christopherartinian.com/

Follow me on Twitter
https://twitter.com/Christo71635959

Follow me on Youtube:
https://www.youtube.com/channel/UCfJymx31Vvztt B_Q-x5otYg

Follow me on Amazon
https://amzn.to/2I1llU6

Follow me on Goodreads
https://bit.ly/2P7iDzX

Other books by Christopher Artinian:

Safe Haven: Rise of the RAMs
Safe Haven: Realm of the Raiders
Safe Haven: Reap of the Righteous
Safe Haven: Ice
Safe Haven: Vengeance
Before Safe Haven: Lucy
Before Safe Haven: Alex
Before Safe Haven: Mike
Before Safe Haven: Jules
The End of Everything: Book 1
The End of Everything: Book 2
The End of Everything: Book 3
The End of Everything: Book 4

The End of Everything: Book 5
The End of Everything: Book 6

Anthologies featuring short stories by Christopher Artinian

Undead Worlds: A Reanimated Writers Anthology
Featuring: Before Safe Haven: Losing the Battle by Christopher Artinian
Tales from Zombie Road: The Long-Haul Anthology
Featuring: Condemned by Christopher Artinian
Treasured Chests: A Zombie Anthology for Breast Cancer Care
Featuring: Last Light by Christopher Artinian
Trick or Treat Thrillers (Best Paranormal 2018) Featuring: The Akkadian Vessel.

CHRISTOPHER ARTINIAN

Christopher Artinian was born and raised in Leeds, West Yorkshire. Wanting to escape life in a big city and concentrate more on working to live than living to work, he and his family moved to the Outer Hebrides in the northwest of Scotland in 2004, where he now works as a full-time author.

Chris is a huge music fan, a cinephile, an avid reader and a supporter of Yorkshire county cricket club. When he's not sat in front of his laptop living out his next post-apocalyptic/dystopian/horror adventure, he will be passionately immersed in one of his other interests.

Printed in Great Britain
by Amazon